BLOOD
&
BREATH

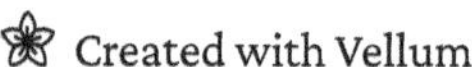 Created with Vellum

BLOOD & BREATH

JILL RAMSOWER

PROLOGUE

FENODREE

I stood perfectly still in the vacuum of sound of the Shadow Lands. My senses were trained intently on the thicket of shrubs some distance ahead.

I heard what made no sound.

Saw what could not be seen.

Hunted what was not there.

That was the only way to survive in these desolate lands where nothing came easy. After spending centuries in this ungodly wasteland, survival techniques were among the few things I had in abundance.

The other was time.

For nearly a millennium, I had called these grassy plains my home.

At first look, a newcomer might have believed the land to be barren. Those of us who were unfortunate residents of the Shadow Lands knew it was teeming with life—look hard enough, and you could find every twisted, vile creature imaginable.

Granted, not every soul in that dark place sought to destroy. On occasion, I came across a wayward creature equally as out of place as I. In the early years, I would use those rare instances to indulge in the illusion of companionship. As time went on, I shed the weakness of my need for intimacy and personal connection like a snake emerging from its outgrown skin.

I found strength in solitude.

I treated the few natives with whom I could converse as a necessary evil. Trading wares with the Shadow Fae was one of the only reasons I managed to survive as long as I did.

That was what I had done—survive. That might not be enough for some, but for me, there was satisfaction in survival. It was a feat few could boast. I had no doubt that had any of the people I had known in my prior life been in my place, they would have lost the fight long ago.

A life without sun—days in the Shadow Lands were what a moonlit night would have been back home. Nights were shrouded in an inky darkness that hid every type of evil in its velvet curtains. The silence alone was enough to drive any man mad, but together, with the darkness and solitude, it had been a miracle I had not devolved into a complete savage. Although, I had my moments through the years.

The challenges I faced had molded me into the man I was—every brush with death was a sculptor's tool, trimming and refining until I became a deadly part of the land.

It took me weeks to achieve my first kill when I arrived

even though I had been an accomplished hunter back home. Despite the seemingly impossible nature of the task, I never gave up. Hunger was a constant motivator to master each skill—the construction of my weaponry, the stealth of my attack, the precision of my aim. Foraging could hardly sustain me, and when I finally witnessed the shaft of my arrow pierce flesh, I experienced a euphoric elation unlike any I had known.

Nearly feral with hunger, I dove upon the creature. There would be no roasted meat or stewed bones until after I had quenched my hunger—a naïve mistake only one new to starvation would make. I had hardly made a dent in the small carcass before my distended belly rejected the lumps of raw flesh. Yet another lesson filed away in what would eventually become an extensive archive.

The wealth of knowledge I had gathered over the years had honed my instincts until I was a force to be feared in my own right. Those acquired skills and knowledge led me to a thicket of dense shrubs in the hunt of a small wollyhog soundlessly hidden in its depths.

I inhaled an inaudible breath as I raised my bow and took aim. The slightest wisp of sound was enough to seal the creature's fate. I released the taut bow and was rewarded with a death squeal from my prey.

My aim had been true, and the arrow a direct hit through its heart. It was an ideal kill, large enough to feed me for the better part of a week but not too large to carry. Butchering a kill away from home where I was unprotected was not an option. I lowered my pack to the ground and lay out a leather skin in which to roll the carcass and transport it back to my camp.

Blood dripped from the animal's rounded snout, and I took care to avoid the sharp spines protruding from its coarse gray fur. The creature was not large but well-armed with spines and tusks to defend itself when needed. I secured it in the leather and strapped it to my pack.

As I turned for home, the skin on the soft underside of my forearm began to tingle and burn. A warning—my protection runes back at camp had been triggered.

Someone, or something, had encroached upon my home.

One of my first missions when I arrived in the Shadow Lands, aside from mastering my ability to acquire food, had been to seek out methods to protect myself and my home. I traveled far and wide, encountering a vast diversity of beings, and assembled an arsenal of spells. With the knowledge I had gathered, I created a home for myself—a shack that might have been unseemly to the eye but was sturdy and well protected. I had outlined the perimeter of my camp with a warding spell that alerted me to the presence of outsiders. Within that line, a secondary spell repelled any creature who would do me harm.

That spell had required dark magic acquired at a great price.

It had not been an easy choice, but I decided the risk of losing my soul to the lures of blood magic was worth the protection the magic provided. I was lucky the risk had paid off. With blood magic, you could only call upon the dark power so many times before you became bound to the need for blood.

I hurried soundlessly back toward my home on the other side of a cluster of small trees. While I wanted to see what had approached, I had no desire for it to see me. The Shadow Fae were primarily nocturnal, so the daytime alarm was an unusual event, and I had no idea what I might be facing.

Reaching a small cluster of trees not far from my home, I paused to scan the area for intruders. My muscles coiled at the ready in preparation for either fight or retreat.

"Fenodree?" a familiar voice called out. "It's me, Rebecca. I'm here to get you out of here."

Standing not far away was a young woman I had never expected to see again. But there she stood, and her words had shocked me to the point of immobility.

For centuries, I had been alone. Then some months ago, I had been sought out by the members of the Wild Hunt to help Rebecca understand her magic. She possessed the unlikely combination of both Seelie magic and the dark magic of the Shadow Fae, previously thought to be an impossible combination. After hearing rumors of my long years navigating the Shadow Lands, the Hunt had tracked me down, hoping that I knew enough about Shadow magic to teach Rebecca. Neither the cultured Seelie nor the barbaric Unseelie ventured into the Shadow Lands of their own volition. Because of that, little was known about their dark form of magic. I was one of the few to survive an extended stay in the hellish landscape.

At first, I had refused my assistance—a lifetime of solitude and distrust made me wary of any newcomers. However, Rebecca had found a way to appeal to a softer side I had thought long dead. We worked for weeks honing her abilities to prepare her to fight against a formidable enemy threatening Earth.

When they could not delay her fight a day longer, she and her escort, Lochlan, had returned to Earth. I was alone yet again but now changed. Before their appearance, I had believed myself to be immune to the longings for the life I had led before my exile. Weeks of companionship had proven me wrong. The reminder of what I no longer had became my new constant companion, one I could not seem to shake.

"What you offer is a dangerous prospect," I replied gruffly. I stepped forward out of the shadows, and a warm expression lit her face as she hurried in my direction.

She had a compassionate soul that found purpose in aiding others. Perhaps admirable, but also a quality that would likely get her killed.

I was not interested in carrying the guilt of her death.

"Dangerous for whom?" she jested at my comment, but only because she had not lived a lifetime of punishment over defying Queen Guin.

The Seelie monarch could be ruthless.

The risks involved in opposing the Fae queen could not be taken lightly. "Dangerous for you. Helping me would be directly disobeying the queen. You cannot understand what you are offering."

"I'm not her subject. As of today, I am officially an autonomous nation of my own. I am the Queen of the Twilight Realm. I'm also my only subject," she said with a wry grin. "Her mandates don't apply to me, so if you're willing to risk fleeing to Earth, I'm willing to take you there." She looked at me in challenge, but I was too experienced to jump at an offer.

Instead, I mulled over the implications of her words. *Rebecca was not subject to Guin's rule?* Regardless, the queen would not look kindly upon her participation in my escape. Rebecca had to know this, yet she was willing to risk herself for me. Willing? Perhaps just naïve or ignorant even. It had been so long since anyone had acted on my behalf at their own risk that the concept was foreign. Selflessness was not a trait fostered by the Shadow Lands.

Rebecca and Lochlan's stay with me reminded me of what life had to offer. After weeks of unsuccessfully repressing that seed of longing, I could no longer avoid the fact that I craved more from my life. I was hesitant to involve Rebecca, but I knew no other way to get my freedom. I had not survived so long because of the goodness of my heart. If she was willing to risk herself for me, that was her choice. I was certainly not fool enough to stop her.

"When do we leave?"

"Now! Gather what you want to take with you, and we'll go." She smiled broadly, but I did not reciprocate. I had been in that life too long to give in to the premature excitement, but I did feel a sense of anticipation similar to the moment just before a kill.

Would I walk away a champion? Or would this be the challenge that finally ended me?

There was only one way to find out.

I had few possessions but grabbed the things that might serve me well. As I did so, Rebecca attempted to explain her plans and the extent of the changes I would experience back on Earth. She used unfamiliar words that left me more confused than enlightened. The Earth I had last visited a thousand years earlier would be a far cry from the modern day, but I doubted the transition would be anything like the difficulties I experienced adjusting to the Shadow Lands. Thoughts of Earth brought to mind a lush and prosperous landscape that would easily provide for my basic requirements.

We walked to a small clearing, and Rebecca raised her hands to open a shimmering portal to the Twilight Realm —a place between worlds where stars glittered above and below as far as the eye could see. From there, she opened another portal, this time to Earth. She and her mentor, Merlin, were the only two who could open portals to the Twilight Realm, which could be used to circumvent the magical walls the Seelie Queen had erected to prevent travel between worlds.

Breath frozen in my lungs, I stepped through onto soft green grass.

Rebecca closed the portal behind us. The sky was dark, but not in the same ominous way as the Shadow Lands. The brilliant moon, so much brighter than any on the other side, shone on nearby stones and illuminated the land around us. We stood in the center of a large stone circle, collapsed and eroded into ruins.

I looked around in awe at the buzzing activity around me. All manner of insect and night creatures chirped and busied themselves openly, without fear of imminent death.

The chorus of sounds around me was overwhelming.

A breeze rustled the leaves on nearby bushes, and tall grass swayed to the gentle rhythm. The moving air engulfed my senses in the musky scent from the moisture in the soil and sent a shiver down my spine at the stimulation of all the fine hairs on my exposed skin.

My heart pounded frightfully fast in my chest as I attempted to adapt to my new surroundings.

Rebecca's voice drew my attention back to her worried face. "I hate to leave you so unprepared, but I have no choice if we're going to keep your escape a secret."

"I survived in the harshest landscape imaginable. I'm certain I will manage," I offered distractedly.

She looked up at me with a slight smirk that did not reach her dark eyes. "Welcome to Ireland, Fen. There's a town not far from here called Strabane—you can stay there for a while until you adjust. When the sun rises, head in its direction—that will take you east. You'll come across several small roads. Just keep going east until you hit a large road. You should be able to tell the difference; this road will be much wider than the others. Follow that road south, and you'll pass a small river before you get to the town. Your leathers will stand out too much here, so you'll need to change. Hopefully, you can find some modern clothes to ... borrow along the way. Just before you reach the center of town, a red-roofed building provides lodging—we call them hotels." She held out a fist wrapped around a wad of papers. "This is our money—it should be enough to get you started, and I'll bring more when I come back in a few days. Tell the clerk inside the hotel that you would like a room for the week. He should take the money and give you a key to a room. I've also included a bunch of information in a letter to help you get adjusted.

"I'm so sorry I can't take you somewhere myself. On Earth, I can only open portals within stone circles, so I couldn't bring you directly into town. I probably should have done this when I was away from Lochlan, but I hated the thought of you being stuck in that place any longer than necessary. He's waiting for me back in Faery, and if I don't go back now, he'll find out what I've done and end up involved. This has to stay between you and me. If he helps in any way, and Queen Guin finds out, it could mean war between the Hunt and the Seelie Court."

I knew she felt the need to explain herself, but she could have dropped me naked into the thorny branches of the tallest tree, and I would not have balked. I was grateful for any help I received.

I fingered the odd form of currency, wondering how the papers could be of any value rather than coin. It was doubtless one of a myriad of changes to which I would need to assimilate.

"Be safe, Fen. I'll see you again soon." Rebecca flung her arms around me, and after a stunned moment, I embraced her in the first hug I had been offered in centuries.

"Thank you, Rebecca. This favor you have done for me will not be forgotten." I pulled back and bowed my head deeply in respect.

She was evidence of the good still left in the world. I only hoped my hardened soul was worthy of such kindness.

~

IN LESS THAN A MINUTE, Rebecca had opened a portal back to the Twilight Realm, and I was alone again. Yet, the word 'alone' did not carry the same connotation as it had just hours earlier. Solitude was something I had resigned myself to accept. It had even become a part of who I was. I might always live a solitary life now that it had become my custom, but there was freedom in knowing it was my choice to make.

This new world presented an overabundance of choices. The prospect was almost daunting but also filled me with some semblance of optimism. It was a trait I had possessed before, but it had been squashed in the name of self-preservation. Acceptance of dire circumstances was crucial if one was to persevere through the roughest times. I found that holding on to scraps of deluded hope merely led to disappointment and heartache, making life that much harder.

I was aware that I had hardened over time; however, I had not realized the extent of my change until repressed memories began to bubble to the surface. The tickle of the breeze against my skin, the hoot of an owl calling out across the open sky, and the freedom to wander as my spirit desired. All the experiences that had been out of my reach had been packaged up and stored in the recesses of my mind.

In an attempt to align myself with the horrors of my life, I had forgotten the wonders that existed in the world outside my prison.

Even at night, the deep green of the grass could be seen as I made my way toward a cluster of trees gently swaying in the wind. I was stunned to discover what an enormous difference a simple breeze could make—the smells it carried, the cool touch along my skin, the sounds it made as it forced its way across the landscape, and the sense of exhilaration that came from a deep breath of that fresh air.

Never would I allow someone to take that from me again.

Attempting to shake the ominous thought, I found a hollow in the ground that was well-padded with fallen leaves and butted up against the trunk of a broad tree. The night was brisk, but I was no stranger to discomfort and was able to burrow into the leaves for warmth. The decaying mass had been there for some time, which hinted at the fact that I had returned during the spring months.

Seasons. Yet another part of life the Shadow Lands had denied me.

I lay for some time in my leafy cocoon, enveloped in the sounds around me. I had doubted my ability to sleep at all, but to my surprise, the next thing I knew, I was opening my eyes to the breathtaking sight of the sun cresting over the horizon.

What magnificence.

The sky lit in colors I had thought only existed in my imagination. How could I have not wept each and every day at the loss of such beauty? The rising sun was brilliant and inspiring—it was life itself.

I will die fighting rather than return to the Shadow Lands.

Once the golden orb had fully ascended over the horizon, I set off in its direction. The blinding light was painful to my sensitive eyes, but in a good way. Growing pains were the best sort of discomfort. Soon, my eyes would adjust to the light of day, and I would emerge from the darkness in which I had been shrouded for so long.

I crossed several small roads, as Rebecca had described. Instead of dirt or cobbled pavers, the roads I encountered were constructed of an unfamiliar solid material. The journey took me through open fields and was easy to traverse, but there was little in the way of trees or brush to keep me hidden. I was not in the habit of walking in the open. The Shadow Lands had little variety in the way of vegetation, but the tall grasses and clusters of scrub trees had provided ample cover. Being exposed kept me on edge, repeatedly looking over my shoulder to scan my surroundings.

My vigilance alerted me to the growing hum of something approaching extremely quickly. I ducked into a cluster of taller grass, peeking toward the source of the roaring noise. As it grew closer, a heavy unease settled in the pit of my stomach. A shining metal carriage flew past me at a dizzying speed.

Did they now use magic on Earth? How had the thing been propelled without horses? How woefully behind was I to find myself?

I had expected changes, but for the first time since Rebecca offered me an escape, a new kind of apprehension set in. Not that I would have refused the chance to flee the Shadow Lands, but I realized that my adjustment to the modern day might be more problematic than I had anticipated. Unfortunately, nothing can be done about my ignorance but to continue and adapt as quickly as possible.

I had been concerned that I would not know which

road was the 'larger' one she had mentioned, but there was no mistaking the thoroughfare when I came to it. Carriages flew along the roadway in a steady stream, and I kept far from their sight.

In her rambled warning about modern Earth, Rebecca had insisted the most danger I might face would result from misunderstandings. I would take her at her word that there were no physical threats, but my instincts had me highly guarded. I had little in the way of weaponry, and my knowledge of spells would do me no good in the heat of a battle. My survival techniques in Faery had hinged around remaining a step ahead of my adversaries. Here in this strange new land, that simply was not an option.

I continued south, keeping the road in my sights until I came upon a cottage nestled in the gently rolling hills. Brightly colored garments hung from a line in the garden, and I gazed down at my worn leathers. There was no question that I would be noticeably out of place unless I changed clothing.

With practiced stealth, I approached the house unseen and rummaged through the basket of clothes set below the drying line. I located a tunic that stretched in a similar fashion to my leathers, and pants that were coarse but would hopefully be protective against any scrub. Some of the pants were cut unusually short such that only half of the leg would be covered. I could not imagine a reason for such an odd garment. I left those articles in the basket.

I had not worn shoes for so long that I did not bother locating a pair. Instead, I took the items that looked my size and hurried from the property. When I found a safe place to dress, I was pleased with the comfort of the tunic but disappointed at the restrictive, angry blue fabric used to make the pants. They impeded my movements, and I could only say to their benefit that they contained several well-designed pockets that would be handy in my travels.

Once I had changed, I added my leathers to my pack. They symbolized all I had accomplished in Faery, and I was not yet ready to discard them. I walked for the better part of the morning, wary of each metal carriage and structure I passed. For so long, I had been forced to fear the unknown—in the Shadow Lands, an encounter with something new was rarely a good thing. Reminding myself that this place was not the same, I acknowledged my apprehension but did not let it rule over me.

I found the river that signaled my approach to the town. Not far from it was a cluster of buildings where a gathering of children carried on boisterously. Their care-free nature was reassuring, but it was also somewhat unsettling. I rarely witnessed any creature openly draw such attention to itself. While Rebecca had assured me these lands were safe, her words did not dissipate years of ingrained caution. I would never be as openly gregarious as the children. Still, I hoped that I would be able to live without the constant anticipation of danger one day.

A few young people gazed in my direction out of apparent curiosity. Despite my updated wardrobe, my differences were still noticeable—whether it was my lack of shoes, long-grown hair, or merely the way I carried myself. I would need to accept that I might stand out for some time until I acclimated to the modern culture.

The red-roofed inn was easy to spot, and relief eased

the tension in my shoulders. I would feel better knowing I had somewhere safe to retreat, notwithstanding the apparent lack of threats. I cautiously made my way past the slumbering carriages lined in rows in front of the establishment. Just inside the front door, an older man stood behind a counter and greeted me with a wary look.

"Good morning, sir. Checkin' in?" He spoke with a heavily slurred Irish accent that was hard to decipher. Not only had it been ages since I had been on Earth, but my time spent there previously had been primarily in the Nordic region.

I gave him a respectful bow before approaching. "Yes, I am in need of a room."

"You're in luck. It just so happens I have one available. I'll just need your license and a card for incidentals, and you can shore up at check out." He looked at me expectantly, but I had no idea what he had said. Even if I could decipher his words, their meaning was lost on me.

Reaching into my pack, I pulled out the stash of papers given to me by Rebecca and handed the pile over to the man. "I need a room, please," I repeated, keeping my voice from showing my growing frustration.

The man's eyes rounded as he gingerly accepted the currency. "A room it is. Let me get yer key." He pointed with one hand, and with the other, he handed over a thin rectangular object that looked nothing like any key I had ever seen. "That'll be for room fifteen, just down the hall," he said warmly, pointing at a hallway behind the front counter.

Not wanting to draw further attention to myself, I accepted with a tight smile and walked in the direction he had indicated. I found a door labeled with a fifteen and stared at the black box beneath the handle. There was a small slit just the size of the rectangular object, so I inserted it into the hole, and a small light briefly shone green. I heard a lock unfasten and then, a moment later, re-latch. Again, I inserted the key, but this time I turned the handle when the light went green, and I was rewarded as the heavy door pushed open.

CAT

I KNEW WHAT MY MOTHER WOULD HAVE SAID.

You're no daughter of mine with your fierce notions that you know better than the hundreds who came before ya. Scarlet for your mother for havin' ya. She would think I was too stupid to breathe.

A small part of me wondered if she wouldn't be right.

After all, the Druids had successfully hidden from the Fae for hundreds of years. Here I was, about to spend a weekend in their stronghold, making friends with them and ignoring everything I'd ever been taught. My mother would shit herself if she knew. But she didn't, and I planned to keep it that way.

"We really do have the building to ourselves, don't we?" I asked Rebecca as she led me into the locked Huntsman building. All of the warriors who comprised the Wild Hunt had left for Faery to induct her boyfriend,

Lochlan, as the new Erlking. Rebecca and her best friend Ashley had decided to use the opportunity to have a girls' weekend, and I was thrilled to have been included. I adored both of them. Mom constantly warned me to keep away because they were Fae, but I didn't see the danger. Becca had become the closest friend I'd ever had.

Now, the men were another story.

They were born hunters. My logical mind told me they weren't a danger to me, but my gut churned every time I was near them. Years of my mother's warnings weren't so easily overcome where they were concerned.

But tonight, the men were gone, and it was just us girls. I couldn't wait.

"Yes, and as you know, we are locking ourselves in while the guys are gone. We don't want to face any catastrophes without the guys here. I'm decently capable of defending us, but that's not how I want to spend my night."

"I suppose fighting for your life probably isn't a typical girls' night," I teased as the elevator lifted us toward the third floor.

"Actually," Becca mused thoughtfully, "that's not all that uncommon for Ash and me lately. But tonight, we're aiming for the traditional spa treatments and girl talk—more like what you're used to."

"I know what a girl's night is in theory, but I've never actually been to one."

Becca's mouth fell open as she turned to me in shock. "You can't be serious."

"I am. My mom's always been so overprotective that I haven't had much opportunity. I've never had many close friends, and by many, I mean any. I certainly wasn't allowed to do sleepovers or go to parties like other kids my age."

"No kidding! Some of my best memories are times with Ash in college and sleepovers with my friends back home in Texas."

"Once, years ago. I snuck out to go to a party that a girl from school was throwing. Her parents were super cool, and loads of people were going to be there. After the party, when I snuck back into the house, my mom was sitting in the dark waiting for me. I'll never forget the fear I felt when I saw her sitting on the sofa, still as a statue."

"What happened?" Becca asked with wide eyes.

The memory still stung, literally. "I got lashings, couldn't sit for a week. After that, nothing ever seemed worth the risk."

"She *lashed* you? I don't even know what that is, but it sounds barbaric."

"Be glad you don't know," I muttered.

We walked the rest of the way to the apartment she shared with Ashley in a weighty silence.

None of the doors were numbered, which was somewhat odd. Since they all knew each other, I supposed there wasn't any confusion or need to label the apartments. Becca hadn't even taken out her keys when the door flew open, and a grinning Ashley ushered us inside.

"Come on in, ladies! Let's get this party started—I've got margarita mix in the fridge, salt on the glasses, and limes already wedged."

Rebecca dropped her work tote by the door and returned Ashley's warm enthusiasm. "That sounds ah-

maze-ing. Let me get changed, though. I'll just be a minute."

"You're welcome to use my bathroom if you want to get more comfy," Ashley offered me.

"I'm fine. I don't have to get dressed up like Becca." I felt a bit self-conscious around the two older girls. They were crazy gorgeous without even trying.

"Either way, you're welcome to make yourself at home since you're stuck here for the next thirty-six hours or so. I got a new deep conditioner and face masks we can try out."

"So that's why your hair is always so gorgeous. I should really spend more time with mine, but it's such a hassle." My red curls had a mind of their own. I wouldn't have said I hated them, but I was unquestionably jealous of Becca and Ashley's silky locks. Even when I straightened my hair, it never had the glossy shine they could accomplish.

"What?" Ashley gaped at me. "Your curls are adorable, and that color?" She kissed her fingers as if denoting perfection.

I rolled my eyes. "It's my burden in life. Never sexy or seductive, but I nail adorable every time." When I lifted a brow in mock exasperation of my third-world trials, we burst into a fit of giggles.

"What's so funny?" Becca bound back into the room in pajamas and fuzzy slippers.

"I was just telling Cat how *gorgeous* she is," Ashley said.

Becca's eyes widened. "Don't tell me you're unaware

of how stunning you are. I bet you've had boys lined up since you were little."

"That shows how little you know. Not only were they not lined up but I've also had exactly two boyfriends if you could call them that. I've hardly even fooled around—I'm twenty and still a virgin!" I couldn't believe I'd admitted such a scandalous fact. Maybe not scandalous, but a twenty-year-old virgin seemed like an urban legend in this day and age. What normal girl hadn't fooled around at least a little?

Me. That's who.

"Nothing? Even with the boyfriends?" Ashley stared at me like I'd confessed to having a secret love child with Justin Beiber.

"It's not *that* hard to believe, especially considering the circumstances of my family. I wasn't allowed to socialize with just anyone, and the Druid boys were all ... *eww*." I sought an escape from their scrutiny off in the living room, sinking into the cushy sofa next to Knight, the giant white wolf who had sort of adopted the girls. He'd been sent by the Fae sorcerer Merlin to protect them, but I'd only seen him act like a big softie.

Becca sat across from me. "Lochlan said he met with some of your elders yesterday to strengthen trust between the two groups. Well, mostly for the Druids. The Fae didn't even know they existed until recently."

"I think my mom was there. She was in a right awful mood at supper." That was being generous. She'd raged for nearly an hour about not only the Fae but the Druids who had agreed to the meeting and were entertaining open relations with the Hunt. Mom had been irate.

"Yeah, he said she wasn't impressed. Hopefully, they'll come to accept that the Hunt isn't the enemy."

"Some already have, but there's a group of holdouts like my mom who are always fearing the worst."

Becca grimaced, turning to Ashley. "Cat's mom is massively overprotective. She's like the exact opposite of your mom."

Ashley grimaced. "I'm not sure which is worse."

I shrugged. "Well, it just means I'm that much more grateful for you two. You've already made my life infinitely better just knowing we're friends." I wasn't sure if I was being presumptive to tell them how much they meant to me, but the words just came out. I couldn't hide my fondness for them. I certainly couldn't sever ties just because they'd been turned Fae. As far as I was concerned, they were just Becca and Ash. My friends.

"Oh, my God, you can't say stuff like that!" Ashley cried. "There's no crying on girls' night! I'm going to make the margaritas, and then no more sappy stuff, capisce?" She rushed back to the kitchen, leaving Becca and me alone on the sofa.

When I looked back at Becca, I was surprised to find her sobered, eyes fixed on me intently.

"Cat, I've debated about asking you something. As much as I don't want to draw you in, I don't think I have any other choice." She chewed on her bottom lip and mulled over her next words, which were a complete mystery to me. "I have an errand I need to run out of town in a week or so. It might be an overnight trip, and I'd like you to come with me—specifically, I need you to drive. I'll explain on our way if you're willing to join me. If Ashley or any of the Huntsmen discovered the reason for my trip ... it could mean trouble for them, so I'd like to keep them out of it, but I need someone's help."

I was incredibly curious about what she could possibly need my help with, but she didn't have to explain. I was more than happy to help her in any way I could. "Of course, just tell me when, and I'll be ready."

The rest of our night was utter perfection.

We drank. We laughed. We watched a movie and played cards. I had more fun with my friends than I could recall having in the whole year before these two American girls showed up in Belfast.

The following night was less ideal. Ashley had some sort of premonition that the guys were in trouble. She and Rebecca took Knight with them to make sure everything was okay. I stayed behind. Worrying about them was maddening, but I wasn't going to complicate matters by insisting I join them. In the end, everyone came home safely.

There was never a dull minute with those two around.

In fact, I was only home a few hours on Sunday before I got a call from Rebecca.

"Hey, Becca, is everything all right?"

"There's been a change of plans," she whispered into the phone. "I just got word that Queen Guin has sent over one of her Valkyrie guards to watch things. I had hoped to run our errand this weekend, but it can't wait. Can you get away tomorrow afternoon? It would mean missing Tuesday morning as well." The museum was closed on Mondays. Sometimes Rebecca went in to handle administrative tasks, but my job manning the visitor's desk was never required on Mondays.

"Yes, of course. Tell me where, and I'll meet you."

"I'll ask for Tuesday morning off, and you can call in sick—that way, no one will suspect we were together. I know your family is strict, and I don't want you in any trouble."

"Don't worry about me. I'll be fine. I can tell this is important, and I'm happy to help."

"I'll tell you more on the way there, but the main gist is I freed a man who had been exiled to the Shadow Lands of Faery. He's a good man, wrongfully punished, and now I need to make sure he stays safe. With everything going on, it's hard for me to check on him as often as I'd like. I need someone the queen isn't watching who can help me."

My heart raced with excitement and trepidation. I had been so sheltered all my life that a part of me craved adventure, even though I wasn't innately much of a thrill-seeker. It was amazing what a little repression would do to a girl. "Sounds like a plan. I'll have a bag packed in my car and be ready to leave after work."

My enthusiasm must have sounded in my voice because Rebecca chuckled. "You really do need to get out more."

"I'm working on it."

"I know you are. Just don't work too hard. I don't want to be the reason you get in trouble with your mom."

"You leave her to me. She'll never know I was gone."

God, I hoped so.

CAT

"Jesus, I feel like a getaway driver. You sure you didn't just rob a bank?" I teased as I pulled my old beater car into traffic.

I'd arrived at the coffee shop around the corner from the Huntsman as I'd been instructed to pick up Becca. She stood waiting when I pulled up to the curb, and as soon as I stopped, she tossed a large suitcase into the back and jumped in the passenger seat.

"Hey, that's not a bad idea!" she said with a laugh. "You're pretty good at this driver business, and you are still looking into careers."

"I think my mom would prefer armed robbery than to know I was off consorting with a Fae."

"Did you tell her you were coming with me?"

"Absolutely not! Aileen, the girl I'm supposed to room

with soon—she's a weird one, but not a bad sort—she agreed to give me an alibi."

"That doesn't sound so weird. She sounds cool."

There was a time I would have agreed with Becca, but things had changed over the years. Aileen and I didn't go to the same school but had always hung in the same crowd at Druid family gatherings. She was loud and hilariously funny. My quieter personality was easily drawn in by her boisterous nature. We grew apart around the time I was graduating from school, and ever since, our conversations had been awkward. Even my phone chat with her the night before about giving me an alibi had been odd.

"Aileen, I need a favor from you. I'd like to spend the night with a ... special friend, but my mom wouldn't be thrilled, you know how overprotective she can be. Is there any way I can tell her I'm staying with you?" I infused my voice with pleading, knowing I had few other options if Aileen wouldn't help me.

"You're always welcome with me," she said in a sing-song voice.

"I appreciate that, but I'm not actually going to stay with you. I just need to tell my mom I'll be at your place."

There was silence on the line for a moment, and I wondered if the line had gone dead.

"Cat, it's not a good idea to lie to your mother." Her tone had changed, dropping with a hint of warning.

"I know, but this is really important to me, and I don't have any other friends or family to go to. I need your help."

"We're family," she asserted firmly.

I paused for a breath, surprised at her conviction. "Yeah, I suppose we are. So can I tell my mom I'll be with you?"

"I'm happy to help; family is everything." Her voice became

whimsical again, and I shook my head, wondering if she was hitting the sauce a little too heavily.

"Right ... thanks, Aileen. Talk to you soon."

Our conversation had gone as most any of our exchanges—sort of like seeing your gynecologist outside of the clinic. You want to be pleasant but can hardly get past the awkward tension of knowing they've had their face in your girl bits. Aileen wasn't who I would pick to live with. Still, I was easygoing enough that I didn't think it would be a problem, assuming her odd behavior wasn't drug-related.

I snapped back to the present, responding to Becca's comment that Aileen sounded cool.

"One time, she collected a jar of butterflies and glued them each to a string attached to a small cutout of Peter Pan. She said she was helping Peter fly like Tinker Bell."

"Holy crap! That's not weird. It's *insane*."

"Tom-a-to, tom-*ah*-to."

"Well, I'm glad you got an alibi, and I'm sorry to drag you into this. I told Lochlan I was staying with Ashley tonight, so my car needed to be parked back home."

"Don't you always stay with Ashley, you know, since you live together?" I asked with confusion.

Becca gave a shy smirk, and her hands fiddled with her sleeve. "Lochlan asked me to move in with him a while back, so I've been staying with him as I move my stuff."

"Rebecca Peterson!" I said in a chastising gasp. "How is it you haven't told me this already?"

She shrugged sheepishly. "It all happened kind of fast, and it just didn't come up. I'm still adjusting to the idea myself."

"That's so exciting! I'm really happy for you."

"I am too, and I feel bad not telling Lochlan what I'm doing, but I don't want to put him in the middle. As the Erlking, he and Queen Guin have a tenuous relationship at best. If she finds out he was a part of Fenodree's escape, it could lead to war. Hopefully, she'll never know Fen got away, but if she figures it out, I want Lochlan to be able to honestly say he wasn't involved. Ashley is in the same boat, except she's even more vulnerable—it wouldn't take much for the queen to revoke her free pass to live here on Earth."

"I wonder what it is about Merlin's relationship with the queen that she grants him the freedom to roam?" I mused, knowing none of us had a concrete answer.

"Lochlan says Merlin uses his power to help both the queen and the Hunt, so I can only assume she needs to stay in his good graces. I'm just glad he claimed Ashley as his apprentice so that the queen would grant Ashley the same privileges as Merlin, but that all hinges on the queen not changing her mind. Should the queen decide to push the issue, Ashley would have to go. I was the reason Ashley got dragged into this life, and I'd never forgive myself if she was forced to live in Faery."

I didn't fully understand why the Faery queen had erected her magical wards a thousand years ago to keep our races separate, but I knew it was definitely for the best. There were too many nasty creatures in Faery to allow free travel between the worlds. The Huntsmen were the only group of Fae who were exempted from her wards. The group had long ago established their autonomy from the queen bet maintained a long-standing truce with the Seelie monarch.

"At least you're in the clear," I offered hopefully. "With your power to use the Twilight Realm, it's not like the queen could stop you from going where you pleased."

"I'm not so sure about that. I'd be more worried that if Guin wanted to stop me, she'd simply send someone after my head. I try not to think about those possibilities. The man we're helping, Fenodree, he taught me what no one else could, and he was under no obligation to do so. Had he not helped me, I would never have survived my clash with Morgan. I owe my life to Fen, and the least I can do is try to return the favor," she said grimly.

I admired her courage. Just going behind my mother's back made me nervous. I couldn't imagine defying a queen.

"I think what you're doing for this man is inspiring. I want to hear more about him, but first, where exactly am I going?"

"Sorry! To Strabane, he's staying at a hotel there. We could have made a day trip if we could have gone on a weekend. I want to be able to run to any stores or help him tomorrow morning if there is anything he needs."

I flicked on my blinker before making the nearest turn in the proper direction. "What else can you tell me about Fenodree?"

"Be prepared. He comes off as a little brusque and uptight. He's lived alone for a long time, and before that, he lived in a very different time than us. The poor man had been exiled to the Shadow Lands for hundreds of years—"

"*Hundreds?*" I cut in, too shocked to stop myself from interrupting.

"Yeah," she confirmed sadly. "I'm not sure what you know about the Shadow Lands, but it's a savage, desolate place, and he lived a life of total solitude."

I had whined about being sheltered, but this man had his entire life stripped from him. I sat quietly as I contemplated how someone could survive such a loss. Would he be jaded and bitter? Surely not if Rebecca was willing to risk so much to save him. What had his life been like? How would I have handled being exiled to another land where I had to live entirely alone? I wasn't exactly a social butterfly, but being alone for hundreds of years was enough to make even a hermit crazy.

"How long has he been here?" I asked.

"About a week and a half. I've stopped in a few times, but now that Lochlan and I are living together, it's hard to disappear without an explanation." Guilt tugged at her voice.

"How has he adjusted so far?"

She pulled her lips into her mouth, biting down on a smile. "I think as well as can be expected, considering the circumstances."

"He hasn't been living off neighborhood cats or something, has he?"

She lifted her shoulders in a shrug. "I couldn't say for sure, but I wouldn't put it past him. I've tried to show him the basics and provide for him the best I can, but there's no telling what that man does when I'm not around."

"Good Lord, that's a little terrifying."

Becca had brought this man to Earth for a second

chance—would he be able to reintegrate into society after such an experience? How had he managed on his own since Becca brought him over?

Even more intriguing, what had he done to be punished so severely?

For the remainder of the trip, we chatted about random bits of gossip as the passing landscape fell into twilight. The drive wasn't long, just enough time for my stomach to knot and my palms to line with moisture before we arrived.

What was I worried about?

If Rebecca trusted him, then I should do the same.

I looked up at the chipped siding of the ordinary hotel where we'd parked and thought about how odd it was that an ancient Fae man was staying in a room inside those walls. Everything about the place looked ordinary, yet this man was anything but. We strolled past the reception desk, and I took a deep breath as Becca led me to a room, knocking softly at the door. The light through the peephole darkened as someone approached on the other side.

I took a shaky breath before the door clicked open.

My thoughts stuttered to a stop. I'd known the Fae were beautiful creatures, but somehow, I failed to anticipate the image that would stand before me.

He was a living, breathing dichotomy, and my mind struggled to reconcile my varying impressions.

Despite being well-dressed and clean-shaven, he broadcasted an air of savagery. He was young in appearance, but his fathomless eyes spoke of a vast agelessness. His movements were controlled and precise as he gave us a bow, yet his presence filled the small hallway to a stifling degree. His skin was a warm copper, and silky black hair fell down the length of his back. He was around six feet tall, and though he was solid with muscle, it was the lean type that came from an active lifestyle. No smile, no words of greeting, only a simple nod to convey our welcome.

He was beautiful and damaged and totally captivating.

"Hey, Fen!" Becca greeted him. "I hope you don't mind that I brought a friend with me. This is Cat. Cat, this is Fen."

I could feel her gaze dance between us, but my eyes were locked on Fenodree. Common decency told me not to stare, but I couldn't have broken our contact had the building begun to crumble around me. I was totally entranced.

I couldn't speak.

I couldn't breathe.

My entire world tilted on its axis until nothing made any sense. Until I no longer recognized myself.

And Fenodree's fathomless stare held mine unflinchingly, his dark gaze just as guarded and unknown as the ocean's deepest depths.

"Uhhh," Becca said awkwardly.

Only then did his eyes ever so slowly turn from mine.

What had he been thinking during those countless seconds? Did he think my staring was rude? Had I offended him?

I sucked in a much-needed lungful of air and steadied myself against a wave of dizziness.

Oh, shite. Please tell me I didn't just feck up everything.

I took one step to follow Becca inside the room before

a hand clamped tight around my throat, and I was thrust up against the wall. I was too shocked to make a sound. My lips parted, but only a gasp slipped past my constricted throat.

Ruthless black eyes bore into mine.

"What are you?" Fenodree hissed, his face inches from mine.

"Fen!" Becca cried, pulling at his arm. "I told you, she's a friend. Let her go!"

"She has triggered my wards. That would only happen if she possessed magic." He made no move to release me.

"I can explain, Fen," she whisper-yelled, glancing up and down the empty hallway. "Let her go, and we can talk inside."

The tiniest twitch tugged at the corners of his eyes before the hand on my throat loosened, and he backed away, his eyes still tracking my every movement.

My heart hammered a punishing rhythm against my rib cage as my hand lifted to where his had been. His sudden assault had been frightening, but I couldn't totally blame him. After what Becca had told me about the harsh realities of his life, I could hardly expect him to trust easily.

"I'm sorry," I said hoarsely. "I didn't mean to alarm you."

He glanced at Rebecca, then stepped aside to allow us both inside. "Years of wariness are not easy to discard. I hope you understand." His accent was unlike anything I had heard, only adding to his intrigue. It reminded me of Shakespearean movies when the actors spoke in formal Old English, which was yet another contradiction, considering his modern appearance in a black cotton T-shirt and jeans.

"It's my fault," Becca interjected. "I should have warned you last time I saw you that I might bring someone. Cat is part of a long line of humans who know about the Fae and have some experience with their magic. Since she isn't ruled by Guin, though, she should be safe to help us. Visiting you unnoticed won't be easy, so I'm hoping she might visit when I can't make it." Rebecca grimaced in what must have been a silent apology for not mentioning her expectations earlier.

She may have believed her request was an imposition, but I didn't see it that way. I had been happy to help before we'd even left. Now that I'd laid eyes on the mysterious man she'd rescued from Faery, I was even more compelled to lend a hand if it meant learning more about Fenodree.

I squeezed Becca's hand reassuringly, and the worried creases in her forehead visibly relaxed.

We helped ourselves to the chairs at a small dinette situated beside a picture window. Fen remained standing, leaning stiffly against the nearby wall. The room was unnervingly quiet. It also looked unlived in except for a leather pack on the dresser and a glass of water set on the nightstand.

"How have you been since I last saw you?" asked Becca, finally breaking the silence.

"I have not had any problems," he said tightly, but his head tilted just a fraction and his brow furrowed. "Although, I find that I cannot sleep on the bed. I sink into its cushion, and it feels as though I am being swallowed by the webs of Black Annis."

I bit down on my lips and tried with everything I had not to laugh, but the image had been too much. Fenodree's eyes fell on me, and to my astonishment, he lifted a single brow. *Was he being playful?* A full-blown grin blossomed on my face.

This man was a total enigma, and I was fascinated.

Rebecca asked a question during our exchanged glances, and I had to rack my brain to recall what she'd said. Seeing even a tiny hint of humor on Fen's stoic face had stolen my attention. I ran through her words and surprisingly found that her question had been something I could answer. "Black Annis, she's a hag that steals away small children ... or at least that's what the legends say."

"Delightful," mused Becca sarcastically. "I'm sorry the bed isn't comfortable, but not much can be done about that. Have there been any other issues?"

"The bed is not a problem, merely a surprise. I had assumed I would appreciate returning to the comforts of civilization. Still, I have slept on the ground for so long that I find the firm footing more comfortable than any bed. I don't understand most of what I see when I go out, but otherwise, there have been no issues. Please, stop worrying."

"I'll try, but it's not easy. I brought a few things for you." She stood and hurried over to the loaded suitcase we had brought with us and lifted it easily onto the bed. Even though Becca was now Fae, she seemed like any other human such that I forgot our differences until she exhibited her superior strength or magical abilities.

The stuffed luggage popped open the moment it was unzipped, and Fen's face looked stricken at the mountain of items packed inside. "What in the seven hells is all of that?"

"I brought some clothes and supplies for you, including a phone. We don't have to go over it yet, but eventually, you need to be able to work one." She set an old smartphone on the bed and turned back to Fen. "I'll let you go through this stuff later. I thought we could do breakfast in the morning and then shop for anything else you might still need and get some more groceries. Cat and I haven't checked in yet, and it's getting late. Are you ready to settle in, Cat?" Rebecca asked with her attention now directed at me.

I swiftly rose to my feet, despite my urgent desire to stay right where I was. "Of course." My eyes returned to where Fen still stood, staring at the luggage. "It's been a pleasure meeting you." Heat rose in my cheeks, and I was sure they had flooded with color.

Fen turned back to look at me, his eyes tightened almost imperceptibly, but his features were otherwise unreadable.

I had no clue what he was thinking, which made me even more self-conscious.

Fortunately, Becca came to my rescue when she grabbed my hand to pull me toward the door. "Okay, we'll see you in the morning, Fen."

I glanced behind me to where he stood, and again, my eyes became ensnared in his gaze. When he opened his mouth to speak, I nearly lost my footing as his words sent me reeling.

"I regret my actions, Cat. I hope I have not harmed you." His softly spoken words feathered over my skin, enveloping me in warmth.

"I'm fine," I said in a rush, hurrying after Becca to escape the suddenly stifling tension building in the air.

Becca tugged me behind her, waiting until we were at the front desk to speak. "I'm so sorry, Cat. I had no idea that would happen."

"It's okay, really. I'm sure it's not easy adapting like he's had to do." Outwardly, the man was contradictory in every way. I could only imagine what a mix of emotions he was on the inside.

"That's why I've been so worried about him. I'm glad I was able to bring him here, but it's a big change. Between him and everything going on at home, my nerves are shot."

"I can only imagine. Let's get checked in, then we can find something mindless on the television to watch." I smiled to reassure her.

"*God*, that sounds divine."

We got settled in our room and watched a couple of programs before turning out the lights, both of us quieter than usual. Becca had any number of reasons to be distracted, but my attention was singularly focused on one thing. One man.

Was Fen asleep on the floor in his room? Did he at least use the pillows and blankets? How harsh had his living conditions been that he hadn't had any sort of bed?

Questions drifted across my mind like minnows flitting across the surface of a pond. All the while, a penetrating set of obsidian eyes had been imprinted in my mind's eye as though he were still there watching me. Assessing me.

It took ages to go to sleep. When Becca's alarm went off the following morning, I audibly groaned. The memories from the night before filtered back to me, injecting me with adrenaline. I was dressed in record time at the prospect of seeing Fenodree again. I wasn't sure why. He hadn't seemed overly fond of me. He could have killed me, to be sure, but my fascination overrode all logic. I was endlessly curious how a second encounter might go.

What I received wasn't as satisfying as I'd expected. I hadn't even been sure what I expected, but it wasn't to be almost ignored. All through breakfast, it was like I wasn't there. I never caught him looking at me once, though I stared unabashedly. Soaking up his every response to the new world around him. His grimace after his first sip of coffee, or the way his eyes widened when we walked into a shoe store. Seeing things through his eyes gave me a fresh appreciation of all the little splendors around us.

Rebecca, on the other hand, checked her phone religiously. She was clearly distracted, and her unease was infectious.

"Bec, we can head back anytime. I know you're anxious to check on Ashley and everything going on back home," I offered as time drew on.

"I didn't mean to rush us. I'm just so worried about her. And I don't want to leave too quickly because I don't know when I'll be able to get back here."

"You know I'm happy to return to Strabane for you." As I said the words, I could finally feel the heavy weight of Fenodree's stare prickling the back of my neck.

Her eyes glanced over my shoulder at Fen before settling back on me. "That would be a huge help." She stepped back to include Fen in our conversation. "I know you can take care of yourself, Fen, but I refuse to drop you here and abandon you."

"How would I survive in this treacherous landscape without you?" he quipped wryly.

I fought a smile at his jab of dry humor.

"Yeah, yeah. I get that you're Mr. Survival Man, but that won't stop me from worrying or coming out here to check on you. One of these days, you'll need to leave Ireland, but I don't think that's a good idea until you're more adjusted to human culture, and we figure out a way for you to make a living."

A hint of panic stirred in my belly. *Leave Ireland?* It made sense if he needed to stay hidden, so why did my gut churn at the thought? Surely, I was just uneasy about sending someone so green off into the world. There was no question he needed more time to learn and adapt. That was it, I told myself as I struggled to swallow the lump in my throat.

Becca began to riffle through the contents of her purse before pulling out a card. "Fen, this is my business card—it has the museum's name with my phone number and address on it. If you need to find me, use this, but only if it's an emergency. Guin has her people watching us, and I don't want them spotting you and asking questions. We didn't get to go over how to use the phone yet, but one of us will do that on our next visit." She handed over the card, and he slipped it into his back jeans' pocket.

"Believe me, I have no desire to draw Guin's attention," he offered coolly.

She gave him a tight smile and waved. "I'm so glad you're away from that awful place. Please be safe while we're gone. One of us will be back soon."

His deep brown eyes caught mine, narrowing a fraction.

What could he have been thinking? Did he want me to stay away? Or was he merely curious about whether I'd come in her place? His ability to guard his thoughts was impressive. The Irish weren't exactly known for being levelheaded. I was used to everyone wearing their emotions on their sleeves. If we felt angry or happy or the littlest bit miffed, you'd better believe we'd let everyone know. But Fenodree? He existed behind a thick wall of one-way mirror, allowing him to see out and block the world's view.

The only way to get a glimpse behind the curtain would be to spend time with him. To observe him and get to know the little pieces he allowed to be seen.

I wanted to collect them all, and maybe then, the puzzle would take shape.

I couldn't wait to come back to Strabane.

CHAPTER

THREE

FENODREE

Considering the recent unexpected turn of events my life had taken, I wondered if the gods were toying with me when I opened the door, and my eyes landed on a ginger-haired woman. Rebecca introduced her companion as Cat, but all I could see was Hilde.

Red coiling curls piled on top of each other in a battle for dominance framed her delicate features. Her creamy skin was dotted with freckles, and her eyes were the vibrant green of freshly sprouted spring leaves.

Much greener than Hilde's had been.

Cat was petite and familiar in so many physical respects, but it quickly became evident that the similarities between the two women were purely superficial. Cat's eyes had a haunting innocence that my Viking warrior had never possessed. Cat was demure where Hilde was brash

43

and bold, but the visual reminder of my prior life was still unsettling.

When she set off my wards, my first thought was that she had been sent by the queen to torment me. What were the chances someone bearing such a striking resemblance to my past would wander to my doorstep? Someone touched by magic, no less. My reaction had been involuntary. I sensed a threat and had to subdue it.

What I did not expect was the undisguised vulnerability shining in her eyes despite my attack. I was not in the habit of seeing emotion or any sign of weakness in those around me, but hers was on full display. No anger or revulsion. Every vibrant expression on her face was painted in shades of purity and innocence.

I could not recall ever meeting anyone like the young woman, even before my exile.

The first time I laid eyes on Hilde, she was clad in leathers, alone on a rocky shoreline on the Nordic coast. She would have preferred death over being forced to wear a frilly dress, nor would she have kept to feminine chores like cooking or stitching. In the crisp morning hours, I found my Hilde masterfully wielding an axe to chop a mountain of piled wood. Her red curls, as disobedient as she, sprang free from the simple braid she had plaited to contain the unruly locks. I approached from behind, and though I could not see her face, that first sight of her was a vision I would never forget.

She reminded me of the Valkyrie soldiers Queen Guin had amassed as her personal guard. The all-female Fae warriors were impressively fierce, and this human woman would have easily been their equal as she chopped at a stack of wood with single-minded ferocity.

She never turned in my direction nor hinted at her awareness of my presence. Captivated, I watched for some time before her sultry voice called out to me.

"You watch me with the eyes of a hawk. Am I to be your prey?" Her steady voice was calm but firm, and only after she finished did she slowly swivel her head to where I stood in the tree line some distance behind her. She kept the axe clasped in her deceptively strong hands and stared at me with challenge in her eyes. As if she wasn't already beguiling enough, the sight of her face solidified my fate. High cheekbones and full lips were the perfect feminine complement to her rugged apparel and fearless demeanor.

I was hopelessly ensnared in her thrall.

"The hawk does not eat the fox. It is his worthy adversary, as they are both hunters after the same prey." I had spent some time in the Nordic lands and quickly picked up the language. I might even have passed for a local had my dark coloring not marked me undoubtedly as a foreigner.

"Equals?" she asked with cautious curiosity, turning the rest of her body to face me. She was not particularly curvy, but something about seeing her in men's leather trousers made my own pants suddenly too tight for comfort.

I simply nodded, not trusting my voice to keep from going guttural with want.

Her chin lifted a fraction, and the corners of her mouth curved up. "If they are equals, they should work together, and they could catch twice the prey in half the time."

I could not help responding with a grin as I retrieved

my own axe from where it hung off my pack. She did not flinch as I approached, placed a log on the stump she was using, and sliced my axe down with resounding force. We worked together in companionable silence, just our grunts and the thwack of our axes filling the crisp air.

Once each log in her pile had been reduced to the appropriate size, she tossed her axe to the ground and walked to the rocky shoreline where she sat facing the sea. I followed her lead, sitting at an appropriate distance so as not to alarm her.

"You are not from these parts. That much is clear," she mused, turning her eyes from the dark waters. The day had been pleasantly mild. Even the sea was placid and as still as deep waters could be.

"Yes, I've traveled a great distance over land and sea," I admitted. I could not tell her that my journey had been far more complex than that. These people would not understand or accept that I had come from another world entirely.

"Why have you left your people to come here?" Her hands absently removed her hair from its plait as she waited for my answer.

"I suppose my spirit was made to wander. Adventure calls to me, and I follow its lead."

Rumors of the conquering customs of the Norsemen were widespread. Her people were known for their travels and exploration, and as I expected, she nodded in understanding of my plight.

"How is it you speak my language? Have you been in these parts for long?"

"I spent some time in a southern village where I

learned the language, but I speak many languages. I am a fast learner." I gave her a roguish smirk, and she raised an appraising brow in response. She attempted to run her hands through her wild curls, but her fingers got caught repeatedly on tangles. "I think I can help with that." I stood to retrieve my pack that I had left by the wood pile and returned to sit by her as I dug through my leather bag. "Here it is, try this." I handed over a whale-tooth comb I had acquired recently in another village.

She stared at the object with confusion, so I took her hand in mine and guided the instrument through her waving locks. As soon as she realized how well the comb sifted through her hair, her eyes lit with excitement. "Did you make this?"

"No, I purchased it from an elderly woman in another village. I am happy for you to keep it—you clearly need it more than I," I offered playfully.

She smacked my arm with a laugh. "Well then, foreigner, perhaps you should come with me. You can show my village what all you have to teach us." She rose to her feet and held out a small hand lined with calluses and marked with dirt.

I took her hand and stood, towering over her petite frame without releasing her warm fingers from my grip. "If I am to come with you, should I not know your name?" Up close, I saw that her mossy-green eyes were flecked with gold, hinting at her fiery spirit.

"Hilde," she offered proudly.

I pulled my eyes from her rosy lips and returned her amused gaze. "I am Fenodree, but you may call me Fen."

"Very well, Fen. This way."

Grabbing her axe and a small pack, she led me inland through a dense forest of trees up and over a hillside. We did not appear to follow any particular path, yet she clearly knew where she was going. Once we had descended on the other side of the large hill, the trees thinned into an open valley. Nestled at the base of the hill was a small village teeming with activity.

There was no protective wall, but anyone who approached would be easily seen from a good distance in all directions. The establishment was situated on a swiftly moving stream that wound its way through the hills toward the coast. Each of the dozen buildings was constructed to resemble miniature mountains bursting from the Earth. Two leaning walls met at a high peak in the middle, serving as walls and roofs. Soil and grass covered the surfaces to make the buildings almost disappear into the grassy valley if one were to look from the proper angle.

One large building near the center stood out from all the others. As Hilde led me in its direction, the village inhabitants stared curiously. Still, I did not receive an overall threatening vibe. The sun had fallen behind the hills, casting long shadows in the dimming light. I had spent many nights out in frigid temperatures, so I was hopeful that I would spend that night warm under furs by the heat of a fire.

Just as we neared the door to the main hall, a large man lumbered over to stand between us and the entrance. His blond beard was divided into two braids, and a fur pelt hung over his barrel chest. "Hilde, who is this outsider?" he grumbled with a glare in my direction.

"He's a traveler. I found him near the shore," she spoke defiantly, arms crossing over her chest.

The man's icy glare narrowed further. "And you led him here to our camp? What were you thinking?" he spat at her face.

Not only did she not cower but a fire lit in her eyes as her hands went to her hips and she leaned forward. "This man knows things he can teach us. I, for one, am open to learning ways that will make our lives better," she growled up at him fiercely. "If you have a problem with that, get your sword and *fight* me like a *man*."

I had no doubt the young man could have taken her on easily in a fight, but he simply snarled with a glance in my direction before stomping away.

Hilde grabbed my hand and pulled me away from the door and around to the side of the building. "I was going to announce your presence to the Earl, but now everyone will already know of your arrival," she explained while dragging me behind her. Not far from the main hall, she tugged me inside one of the other buildings. She slammed the door shut and shoved me back against the solid wood. Her small hands pressed at my shoulders, and her eyes casually swept their way up my chest to my face. "You have acquired great knowledge in your travels, yes?" she whispered seductively before reaching to nibble softly on my bottom lip. "Show me, Fenodree. Teach me what you know."

On her exhaled words, I lifted her into my arms, and her legs wrapped firmly around my waist. That night, I claimed her body as her soul had already claimed mine.

Our fates had been inextricably intertwined from the moment I chanced upon her on that rocky shore.

Cat was a wisp of a woman compared to the force of nature that was Hilde, but the two looked strikingly alike. The most noticeable difference would have been their eyes if they had been standing side by side. The color and the personalities they conveyed.

Where Hilde's green irises were dotted with gold, Cat's eyes were the purest green I had ever seen. A purity that mirrored the gentle innocence of her expression. Where Hilde's eyes lit with a keen understanding of the battles required in life, Cat was all childlike naïvete.

She was dripping with guileless innocence.

I was torn between wanting to claim that purity for my own and a dark desire to sully her until she was unrecognizable.

No doubt the pull I felt toward her was owed to her familiar appearance, but there was a chasm of life experiences between us.

She was practically a child.

Moreover, I did not care to dwell on the memories her sight brought to mind. There was only one purpose Cat might serve, and even that was unlikely.

CHAPTER
FOUR

CAT

MY MOTHER AND I HAD A LOT OF GREAT TIMES TOGETHER, BUT her overbearing tendencies suffocated me. It had always been just the two of us, so I had grown up trying my best to keep her happy. Maybe I had finally matured past the need to please her, or maybe my friendship with Rebecca had changed me. Either way, I found it harder and harder to tolerate my mother's paranoia each day.

She kept tabs on my every movement, and there would be no avoiding the subject that I stayed away for three nights in a row. I had intentionally texted her my plans the past few days rather than tell her in person to delay the argument that would result. Now that I was back from Strabane, it was only a matter of time.

When I first informed my mother that Becca had the sight and was linked to the Fae, it took her days before she allowed me to return to work. She reluctantly agreed to send me back to the museum because my boss was one of our fellow Druids and could "look out for me."

The Druids had descended from the humans who had been taught magic by the Fae. A large number of those had been a group of women who had served as the handmaids to the Seelie Queen. The group became close with the queen, and in return, she taught them all about magic and the Fae world. When the queen closed the portals between our worlds, she sent the human women back to their homes on Earth. The Wild Hunt came in search of the women not long after, claiming the queen had sentenced them to death.

The Fae warriors killed many of the queen's handmaids, causing the rest to go into hiding. The surviving women remained close and passed on their knowledge and fears to each subsequent generation. For centuries, the Druid people lived in hiding, unsure if or when the Wild Hunt might come after them again.

When Rebecca showed up in Belfast, everything changed.

We learned that the Seelie Queen had not ordered the murder of our ancestors as we'd believed. Morgan Le Fay had been the culprit behind the killings. She despised Queen Guin and had fooled the Erlking Odin into thinking the order had come from the queen. Morgan's actions had caused a war between the Hunt and the Seelie Court, only settled after the queen had killed the Erlking. The truth surfaced that the Fae cared little about the existence of the Druid people, and we no longer had reason to hide.

However, my mother still had not backed down from her staunch belief that the Fae would kill us on sight if given the opportunity. She had no idea that I'd been spending time at the Huntsman, let alone that I'd found several of the guys were a lot of fun to be around. It was easier to leave her in the dark. Maybe someday, her prejudices wouldn't taint her perceptions, but I wasn't about to hold my breath.

Our relationship was already strained, and I didn't want to make things worse.

Mom was the only family I had in the world, aside from an aunt I rarely saw.

"What can I do to help?" I asked my mom as I entered the kitchen.

"The potatoes are ready to be mashed. If you'll do that, I'll start cleaning up while the sausage cooks." She handed me the masher and made her way to the sink. "You goin' to be around this weekend?"

"I should be. Why?"

"Just wondering. Three nights in a row, you have been gone. Anything I need to know about?" Her words were spoken casually, but I knew better.

Here we go.

I took a fortifying breath and kept my eyes glued to the chunks of potatoes steaming in a pot. "I told you, spending some time with Aileen. Figure it's good to get better acquainted since we'll be living together soon."

My mother made a snorting sound as she swept vegetable remnants into the sink. "You sure it has nothing to do with that Rebecca girl?" She spat the name as though it tasted bitter on her tongue.

"You don't have to say it like that," I murmured under my breath.

"What's that, girl? You defending her?" She swung around, wielding a wooden spoon in her hand. "You been off sneaking around with that lot?"

My mother had me at a young age and was still an attractive woman. Her hair was a deep red like mine, although not quite as curly, and she had hazel eyes that creased in the corners when she laughed. It wasn't a common occurrence, but I understood that she had a world of worries on her shoulders as a single mom.

"No, Mom. I only see her at work," I hurried to explain, then paused, chewing my lip. "But ... I wish you'd give her a chance. I know you just want me to be safe, but Rebecca really is a sweet girl."

Her eyes narrowed to frightening slits.

"Well, look at you, all cozied up with the filth," she sneered as she glanced at my body disapproving. "You think I don't know that you've been sneaking around with them? Those vile creatures murdered our ancestors. They rape and destroy at every opportunity, feeding off humans like we were lambs at the slaughter. And there goes my own flesh and blood, offering herself up as the next victim. I raised you better—raised you smart enough not to hand yourself over to the devil."

Her hate-filled description of the people I knew to be kind and generous made my heart ache with disappointment. It's a terrible thing to be let down by a parent—not only is there anger, but the guilt is overwhelming.

Guilt that I couldn't love her like I should.

Every time we argued over the subject, I struggled to see goodness in my own mother. Knowing her prejudices damaged my love for her weighed on my heart.

How do you love a bigot? Do you look past the hatred that seeps from their pores? Are you then condoning their behavior?

I didn't want to put more distance between my mom and me, but I also wasn't going to walk away from the best friend I'd ever had just because my mom was incurably prejudiced. I wouldn't live my life burdened with the bitterness she carried daily. I didn't know how to reconcile the two parts of my life, and my helplessness sapped the energy from my fight.

"I don't know how to talk to you when you get this way. Rebecca and Ashley aren't going to hurt me, but nothing I say will convince you."

"You don't have to convince me of anything." She lifted her chin and steeled herself. "But if you don't stay away from them, I'll be forced to take you before the elders."

The air in my lungs burst from my lips as if I'd been punched in the gut. "You're threatening me?"

"I'll do what it takes to protect you, no matter how ungrateful you are." She looked down her nose at me.

"Protect me? You mean to punish me!" I spat back in uncharacteristic defiance.

"I've been talking with Deaglan, and he agrees that you can't keep carrying on the way you've been. You're heading down a dark road, and something must be done."

"Deaglan O'Connor? Mom, he's a lunatic. You can't listen to him—"

The slap came out of nowhere.

I hadn't seen her raised hand, which was best—I

didn't want to carry with me the image of my mother at the moment she had broken my heart.

The burning pain from her blow had run more than skin deep, and my despair was crippling. We were both aware of our difference of opinion concerning the Fae, but it had never escalated to such a heated extent.

With my hand protectively covering my aching jaw, I met my mother's livid eyes with pleading in my own. I showed her my heartbreak and shock, only to be met with cold indifference.

It was clear on my mother's stony face that she felt equally as wronged as I had.

My chest hollowed with the realization that she had zero remorse for her actions despite her malicious behavior. She felt she was in the right, and until she made room for an alternate perspective, nothing would change.

Tears filled my eyes.

With a defeated shake of my head, I walked away from my mother, knowing our relationship would never be the same.

CHAPTER
FIVE

CAT

The following morning, I had an unexpected visitor waiting for me outside the museum. Daeglan O'Connor sat on the stone steps, his legs crossed as if he was simply out enjoying the weather. He may have been my mother's friend, but I had never liked the man. That certainly didn't change when he recently tried to harm Rebecca when they tried to retrieve the Sword of Light from the British Museum.

I had made the mistake of telling my mother that Rebecca and Lochlan had located the long-lost artifact and were going to retrieve it in London. Mom passed the information to Daeglan, who raced to London and tried to steal the sword out from under Rebecca. It was a powerful Fae weapon, but the most notorious of its powers was the ability to force the truth from anyone at its blade.

Daeglan wanted the Druids to have it and didn't care if anyone died in the process.

I hated that his ruthless influence held sway over my mother. Daeglan wasn't a good man, and no good could come of his appearance outside the museum.

"Good morning, Daeglan," I offered warily.

He stood as I approached, a smarmy grin on his thin lips. "Mornin', Cat. I know you have work now, but I was hoping we could talk for a minute. Your mother's been awfully worried about you lately."

"I'm aware, but I'm not sure what business it is of yours."

"She's my friend, and I don't like to see her upset. She loves you. Don't begrudge her for wanting to protect her only child. Family is everything, Cat." His words were valid, but his condescending tone counteracted their effectiveness.

Daeglan was about five-ten with dark hair combed neatly back and a closely trimmed salt-and-pepper beard. His eyes were a dusky gray beneath a prominent brow, and his tanned skin covered pronounced cheekbones. He would have been attractive had it not been for the malignant aura surrounding him. The essence may not have been visible, but I could feel its snaking tendrils trying to coat me in his malevolence whenever I was near him.

I shifted myself to put more space between us. "There's a difference between protecting someone and indulging in irrational fears."

"What's more irrational—guarding against a magical race of beings who feed off humans or pretending those beings are harmless?" he asked with a lifted brow. "You know our history with the Fae. You know how important it is to keep our people safe, yet you continue to make poor decisions. If you insist on associating with the wrong *individuals,* it may be necessary to re-educate you on the fundamental principles of our society."

"Are you saying the council would make me *repeat* my lessons?" I asked with astonishment. When Druid children were old enough to be told about the Fae, they attended two years of weekly lessons on our history and rune training, not unlike Catholic children taking confirmation classes. There was no way I was sitting through that crap again. "I'm an adult. They can't send me back to training."

"The council can do whatever they wish. For the moment, we are somewhat crippled while Paedar still presides as chief, but his days are numbered. Change is upon us, and in the months ahead, I see a new council with a clear understanding of the importance of a united Druid people. I'm just here to look out for you. I don't want you getting hurt."

I didn't know what Daeglan was hinting at, but it wasn't good.

Paedar O'Shea was known by all Druids because of his role as leader of our people. He was a levelheaded man, good at keeping the peace and diplomatic when spats arose. I couldn't imagine him punishing me for having Fae friends now that our secret was out, but Daeglan's warning sounded ominous.

His eyes slid to the side, bringing my attention to where my boss, Fergus, stood at the museum's front entrance. Fergus was a fellow Druid and one of the only reasons my mother had allowed me to keep working at the museum despite Rebecca's presence.

"Good day, Daeglan. Cat, I'm in need of your assistance if you're ready to clock in." Fergus addressed us in an abnormally chilly tone with his eyes set harshly on Daeglan.

Daeglan gave a cagey smile. "No problem at all. Cat and I were done talking. You two enjoy your day." He gave us a nod and strolled casually away from the building.

I hurried up the steps to where Fergus held the door open for me, already returning to his jovial self.

The tough-guy persona Fergus had just displayed in sending Daeglan away had been a far cry from his normal warm personality. One of the few Druids born outside of Ireland, Fergus was originally from Scotland and had moved to Belfast later in life. He had red hair like me, but where I tended to be more reserved, he was outgoing and vivacious in a way that captivated everyone's attention.

"Ach, that man. I hope he wasn't bothering you, lass," grumbled Fergus in his heavy Scottish brogue as he closed the door behind me.

"Not exactly. I got into an argument with my mom, and Daeglan took it upon himself to smooth things over," I explained as we walked toward my workstation at the visitor's desk.

"That sounds about right—he's always thinking he knows best."

I gave him a tight smile and set down my bag, unable to shake the sense of unease that had settled over me from Daeglan's words. "Fergus? Could the council force me to retake my lessons if they thought I was behaving out of line?"

He cocked his head to the side and looked at me as if I had told him it was perfectly acceptable to wear white shoes all winter. "Don't be daft! If the likes of you is a problem for the council, then we're all in trouble. Besides, now that the Fae know about us, what is there to enforce? Our secrecy? It would be a little late for that. You just ignore whatever it was Daeglan said, you understand?"

I smiled at the amazing man I was lucky enough to call my boss. "Thank you, Fergus. You're pretty awesome, you know that?"

"It's all a part of being fabulous—a burden I proudly bear." He accented his point with an exaggerated bow before scurrying off toward his office.

CHAPTER

SIX

CAT

More than happy to latch onto Fergus's advice, I decided to plan my next outing to Strabane. Rebecca and the others had their hands full tracking down an Unseelie creature that had been killing young women in the city. I was little help in their investigation, but I could at least ease her burden by visiting Fenodree.

In all honesty, I didn't need a reason beyond my own burning curiosity.

Questions about him had consumed my thoughts in the days since I'd met Fen. He had been relatively quiet and stoic, but all things considered, he had also been surprisingly normal. How could someone who had been through such hardships still function as if none of it had ever happened? I wouldn't have been surprised had he been half feral after living alone for so long.

Everything about the man and his situation captivated me.

When my mom told me she would be visiting her sister all day Friday, I decided it was the perfect opportunity to see him again. Cara was Mom's only living relative. She lived some hours away near Clifden in County Galway, but we rarely saw her. The two didn't get on well.

Any curiosity I might have had about why Mom was going to see her sister was quashed by my relief at escaping her constant watchful eye. If she was going to be gone for the day, I wouldn't ask questions.

I arranged for another worker to fill in for me at the visitor's desk and let Becca know my plans. First thing Friday morning, I left for Strabane. By the time I arrived at his hotel, I had chewed my nails to the quick and started to second-guess my decision to come alone.

Chiding myself, I tried to remember that the visit was not about me. Fen needed our help, and I wouldn't abandon him just because the situation was intimidating.

I quietly knocked on the door, and before long, I was gazing again into his impenetrable dark eyes. "Hey, Fenodree. I've come by for a visit. I hope my timing isn't a problem."

His brows drew together as he peered around the hallway. "Has Rebecca come with you?"

Was he annoyed that I'd come alone?

"N-No," I stammered. "I had the chance to come out, and she was busy ... I hope you don't mind."

His lips thinned, but he shook his head and stepped aside to let me in. "Of course not, come in."

Not the most convincing denial.

I tried to keep the sting at bay. Fen was complicated, and I wouldn't do myself any favors reading into every word he uttered.

I walked to the chair I'd occupied at my last visit and set down my backpack before curling up in the chair, knees drawn up to my chest.

Fen stood stiffly at his post against the wall not far from me. In the silent room, it became painfully obvious that I had not considered how our interaction would go without Becca's outgoing personality to grease the wheels.

"How have you been?" I asked hesitantly.

"I have been well," he replied formally.

Well, fabulous. This was off to a delightful start.

Just as I started to contemplate grabbing my bag and running from the room, I recalled the items I'd brought with me. "I almost forgot! I brought you some things," I said as I lowered my feet to the ground and pulled my backpack onto my lap. "Becca said you could read—I hope it doesn't offend you that I asked. Anyway, she said you weren't big on television, so I brought a book you might like. I imagine sitting in this room gets pretty boring, although maybe you're used to boring." My spine stiffened, and I turned wide eyes to Fenodree. "I'm sorry, that's not what I meant. I just meant it must have been boring while you were in exile, being all alone. Not that you, yourself, were boring."

Spectacular, Cat. Could you make a bigger fool of yourself?

Not likely.

Fen's posture relaxed, and he released a sigh as if in

exasperation. "I am not offended, and I appreciate your concern."

My cheeks heated as I bit down on my lip. "Most of what I read is romance books, and I didn't figure that would interest you. In school, we read a book called, *The Hobbit*. It can be a little heavy at times, but it's about a group of people who go on a grand adventure. Since you seem to be the rugged, adventurous type, I thought you might like it." I handed the book to him and waited as he gave a cursory flip through the pages.

"Thank you." His intense eyes met mine, and I squirmed with embarrassment before turning back to my bag.

"I also made some muffins yesterday, so I brought a few. They're banana nut—hopefully, you don't have a nut allergy. But then, I guess the Fae don't have allergies, do they? Maybe you shouldn't eat them; I'd hate to be the reason you died when you only just got your freedom." I held the plastic container full of muffins to my chest and sucked my lips into my mouth. "I'm rambling, aren't I? When I get nervous, I tend to ramble. I'm sorry."

Fen pushed away from the wall and slowly prowled over to where I sat.

I watched wide-eyed, my head tilted back to hold his gaze as every thought evaporated from my mind in a puff of smoke.

He took one of my curls in his hand and gently drew away so the strands eased achingly slowly between his fingers.

"Stop apologizing," he warned in a silky voice. He lifted the container of muffins from my hands. "If I wish for you to stop talking, have no doubt that I will tell you. And I am not sure what an *allergy* is, but I see no reason I cannot eat what you have prepared. You would likely be horrified to know some of the things I was made to eat in order to survive. I dare say *these* will not harm me." His features remained impassive, but I detected a spark of emotion in his eyes.

What I would have given to know the substance of those hidden thoughts. To know him.

Maybe then I could find a way to breathe in his presence. To hold a single coherent thought when he was this close. Close enough to touch. To smell his musky scent unaltered by artificial lotions or cologne.

I got the sense that everything about Fenodree was pure and natural. No pretenses or airs. He was exactly who he was without apology. When he spoke, he was forthright and honest. When he acted, it was out of instinct.

He was sparing in offering those views of himself, but honesty lay beneath when he did give a glimpse below the surface. My gut told me Fen was a man who could be trusted.

The realization helped me to finally relax in his company.

I took a calming breath as he retreated back to his place against the wall. "Okay, no more apologizing." I pulled out an orange I had brought with me and dug my nails into the thick skin. A spray of tangy citrus juice shot out as I bent back the peel. "I was thinking that since we didn't get around to teaching you how to use the phone on our last visit, you and I could do that today."

He glared at the small black device lying on the

dresser. "Rebecca has already attempted to instruct me on its use, but I am not interested in learning. I have lived this long without the need to communicate with others instantly. I feel certain I will continue to survive in the same manner."

"Well, you should at least keep it charged in case you need it," I suggested, ignoring his rejection of the device.

His brow creased, and his head tilted to the side. "What do you mean *charged*?"

"I'm so—" I stopped myself from apologizing and grimaced. "There are so many things we take for granted, it's hard to know how much to explain. Did Becca bring a cord with it? Like a thin little rope?"

"I believe so." He opened a drawer and pulled out the charger.

"Perfect!" I plugged in the charger and connected it to the device. "The phone has to have energy to work. Our power sources are wired into the walls of our buildings. Connect the device to the power source, and let it absorb power until it's fully charged. Once you use up all the power, you'll have to charge it again."

"Not unlike magic, then." He looked thoughtfully at the phone and then toward the window. "Every time I explore the town, the people I see all carry this device. They either talk into it or stare at it endlessly as if bewitched by it."

"Phones can be pretty addictive," I agreed as I sat back down in my chair.

"I watched a man walk into a tree as he stared into the device and a woman transfixed while ignoring the cries of her young child. I understand the need to communicate with others, but I am not interested in losing sight of the world around me." He sat down, this time in the other dining chair, and scowled at the phone warily.

"You don't have to be like those other people. In fact, I doubt you could be if you tried." My gaze connected with his, summoning a flood of heat to my cheeks. "How about we let it charge for a bit, and I show you the basics on how to text, which is sending written messages back and forth to someone. You don't have to use it if you don't want to, but I think it's important for you to know how just in case of an emergency."

"You are more persistent than I would have thought." His eyes narrowed at me with playful scrutiny. "I suppose I could agree to a brief lesson."

I dropped my eyes to the orange as I finally separated the fleshy sections of fruit. "Growing up, it was just my mom and me, and she is super overprotective. If I wanted to do anything, I always had to argue and push."

"And your father?"

I bit into a section of orange, closing my eyes as I savored the delicious flavor. "Oh, my God, this orange is amazing. You have to taste it." I walked to where he stood and offered an orange wedge in my outstretched hand.

He stared blankly at the offering for a moment. "It smells bitter."

"That's just the peel. The fruit inside is delicious, and this one is particularly sweet—try it." I held my hand even closer to him until he relented and picked up the fruit.

He lifted it to his nose and sniffed, his eyes narrowing at me in suspicion.

"Go on, it's not a trick. I promise."

Fen bit into the fleshy fruit and licked the errant juice from his lips.

A relay of electricity ran down my spine and coiled deep in my belly. I stumbled back to the safety of my chair, overcome with sensation.

"You didn't answer my question." He popped the remainder of the orange slice into his mouth.

"About my father?" I asked dumbly, suddenly unable to hold a thought. "He didn't live with us—I never even knew who he was. It was just Mom and me. I always considered us alone in the world, but my alone was nothing like yours. I can't imagine surviving what you went through." As I finished, my eyes lifted back to his.

Beneath his prominent brow, his dark eyes swirled with what I could only guess were memories of the hard life he'd led. "There is much in life we cannot control. We simply do our best to adapt, but for some, it is harder than others."

My eyes danced between Fen and my hands as I debated asking the burning question in my mind.

"What is it you want to know?" he asked quietly.

My hands stilled, and I smiled over at him. "Was I that transparent?" I teased before sobering. "You don't have to tell me if you don't want to, but I was wondering why you were exiled."

"I don't mind. You must remember, Cat, that it has been a very long time." His tone was laden with a lifetime of struggle. "I was exiled because I took a human wife."

"*What?*" I gasped, sitting tall in my chair.

"The one caveat given when the Fae were allowed to

roam Earth was that there were no human-Fae relationships."

"So having a human wife was, what? *Illegal?*"

"Yes, the queen was adamant that there would be no intermingling of the races aside from feedings."

"So sex was allowed, but no meaningful relationships? It's not like the two races could bear children, so there would be no reason for such a law. That's just the most absurd thing I've ever heard," I scoffed indignantly. "And now, is that still the law?"

His eyes met mine briefly in a glance that stirred a swarm of butterflies in my chest. "The Fae are no longer allowed here, so the point is rather moot. However, I suppose the edict still stands. I cannot imagine the queen's staunch desire to protect the purity of our culture would have waned."

"I thought she called the Fae back to Faery because of the crusades and other human campaigns to conquer."

"That was the primary reason. The Fae did not want war with all of mankind, which likely would have happened had there been a widespread discovery of our existence. She also observed that humans grew more advanced each year at an alarming rate, and she feared the eventual mingling of our races. If the two peoples lived one among the other, eventually, their differences would blur and melt together. I believe she viewed the Fae race as superior—to her, it was vital that the Fae retain their own identity."

My next words were barely above a whisper. "What happened to your wife?"

His gaze stayed locked on the floor near the bed as he

spoke in a monotone voice. "She was killed as a part of my punishment. I'd known the risks, but her spirit had possessed me so completely that I ignored the potential consequences. Of course, I also believed no one would ever know. One chance encounter with a man loyal to the queen, and our fates were sealed. My wife's human lifespan would have been much shorter than mine, but I never expected our time together would be so brief."

It was no wonder Rebecca had wanted to help this man. His life had been destroyed because of his undying love for a woman—I could not think of anything more unjust. I imagined Fen carted off into exile after the love of his life had been murdered.

My heart cracked wide open for him.

Tears filled my eyes as I stared down at my hands. "I'm so sorry, Fen," I said in a shaky whisper. "I'll never understand why people have to hate one another." After a long moment of silence, I lifted my gaze to Fen and was surprised to find him glowering at me.

"What do you know of hate?" His words were clipped, raw emotion surfacing in his voice.

A part of me wanted to cower at his rising temper, while another side grew angry that this man clearly assumed me to be a naïve child. Compared to him, maybe I was, but that didn't negate my life experiences.

I wiped the moisture from my eyes and threw aside my ingrained teachings regarding the importance of secrecy about my people. "My family has centuries of experience with hate and fear," I asserted firmly. "My ancestors were the handmaids for Queen Guin, and when she closed off Faery from Earth, her human companions were sent home. Not long after their return, the Wild Hunt slaughtered them one by one. Few survived, but those who did passed on the knowledge of the Fae and their magic, along with a heavy dose of hate-filled propaganda. For centuries, my people have feared and resented the Fae."

Fen studied me clinically. He made no move to apologize for his assumption, but he also didn't belittle the history of my people. "I take it the secrecy is no longer an issue?"

"We recently discovered that the handmaids' murders were unsanctioned by the queen. She never wanted them killed, and we may never know what happened, but the result has meant freedom for my people. Unfortunately, not everyone has been willing to accept these recent developments. Secrecy and fear have been ingrained in us since birth. Some are apprehensive about letting go of those teachings."

"If you were indoctrinated with the same beliefs, how is it you are now friends with Rebecca?"

Squirming in my chair, I offered a sheepish smirk. "I wish I could say it was out of my deep love of all creatures, great and small, but that wouldn't be the truth. The fact of the matter is, when I met Rebecca, I thought she was entirely human. By the time I discovered she was becoming Fae, my impression of her had already been formed."

"The knowledge did not change the way you felt about her?"

"Quite the opposite. What I've learned has changed the way I see my people. Rebecca and the Hunt are nothing like what I'd been taught. Once the foundation of that wall began to crumble, the whole thing came down. I've been questioning everything I thought I knew."

His chin lifted slightly as he continued to assess me. "I believe many people would have turned their backs on the new friend rather than alienate themselves from their families."

"Yeah, that's what my mother's done. She's horrified that I remained friends with Becca and has threatened me to stay away from both Becca and Ashley. They're my closest friends, though, and as much as it hurts me to upset my mom, I refuse to walk away from my friends because of some stupid, small-minded prejudice." I held his eyes determinedly, hoping he would see that I was not like my family.

His gaze intensified until the air around me felt electric, and gooseflesh rose along my arms.

"Some things are worth the risk of defying authority, and others are not. If you take that risk, you must be prepared to accept the consequences. Because there are always consequences."

SEVEN

FENODREE

I had cursed my ever-putrid luck when I opened the door to reveal Cat standing alone. Judging by her timid nature, I had doubted she would have the confidence to visit without Rebecca present.

Not only had Cat come alone, but I had been surprised to find our conversation ... intriguing. I was not often wrong, but I begrudgingly admitted that there may have been more substance to the young woman than appearances would have suggested.

When I asked about what she knew of hate, I had not expected more than inconsequential musings. How was I to know there was a brotherhood of humans who not only knew about the Fae but were also united in their hatred of our kind? In my time, it was common for the Fae to view humans as inferior for their lack of magic, but the human race was ignorant of our existence and could not form a reciprocal opinion. A man may think flies are annoying, but the fly hardly has any opinion regarding the man.

Since my exile, so many things had changed, including human knowledge of the Fae. This sect of people had kept their knowledge to themselves. Would that always be the case? Was Guin truly ambivalent about this race of people? What kind of intolerance had Cat witnessed from her family that made her willing to walk away from them? Did she fully comprehend what she was risking? Could anyone truly grasp such concepts until after facing the consequences of such actions?

I did not get the impression that Cat was simply a rebelling child seeking to test her boundaries. She recognized a fundamental flaw in how she had been raised and had the fortitude to reject those teachings. That took uncommon strength and self-awareness. However, the true test of character would lie in how she handled her family's response to her rejection.

"Tell me, how is it you discovered that Rebecca was Fae?" Interested in learning more, I sat in the chair opposite her and continued our conversation.

"At first, I thought she was like me—human with the ability to see through a Fae glamour. Becca and I were at a pub when we witnessed a Leannan-sidhe luring a human man out to feed on him. When I looked at Rebecca's face, I could tell she had seen through the creature's glamour and was just as scared as I was. She explained that her necklace enabled her to see the Fae as they were, and I had no reason to doubt her statement. It wasn't until sometime later that my people discovered there was more to her power than a simple necklace."

"And your people—how can you see through a glamour?"

She chewed at her lower lip as she waged a silent internal debate. Her decision made, she slowly turned in her chair and lifted her long red curls to expose the back of her slender neck. On the delicate area just below her hairline was a small symbol inked into her ivory skin.

"Much of what my ancestors were taught was the use of rune magic. This symbol, the truth rune, gives us the sight and enables us to see through glamours. We certainly aren't immune to all magic, but this helps us at least know what we're dealing with. It's hard to protect yourself in a world of magic if you can't see the dangers around you."

I had unknowingly leaned toward her in my examination of the rune. When she dropped her hair and turned around, our faces were mere inches apart. Her eyes widened, and the movement of her lips parting drew my eyes down to her mouth.

A lick of lust trickled down my spine and caused the briefest skip in my nearly reptilian heartbeat.

It was a sensation I hadn't felt in a very, *very* long time. Something I hadn't thought to ever feel again. As much as I wanted to cling to the sensation and savor every invigorating drop, I worried if I relinquished myself to the need, I might lose all control. Cat was too innocent. Too pure to handle the kind of repressed desire I might unleash.

I quickly withdrew, pulling myself back into my chair and clearing my throat. "I had no idea such a pocket of people existed," I said, my voice now coarse and uneven.

"You are almost a hybrid—humanity and Fae magic combined."

She smiled shyly and pulled her knees back into her chest, hugging her legs. "I don't know about that. I've heard what the Fae can do; our powers don't compare."

"During my years in the Shadow Lands, I learned some rune magic; however, most of what I acquired was dark magic that is too dangerous to toy with when not absolutely necessary. You said the queen taught her handmaids their knowledge of magic. Have you any idea where the form of rune magic was originally derived?"

Again, she looked at me with uncertainty before her features set in determination. "I don't know where the magic comes from, just that it was taught to the Druids by the Fae."

"Druids? How is it that people in hiding were given a name?"

"The name was given before they went into hiding. Those who had learned magic used their knowledge to help their villages. If a well went dry, everyone knew that the local Druid would be able to find the best place to dig a new one. They became revered in their communities, often considered spiritual leaders, and the term 'Druid' evolved for such a person. For the most part, they were of benefit to the people they served and continued to help even after they went into hiding from the Hunt. A few of the power-hungry Druids fell into using blood magic, and rumors began to spread that the Druids condoned human sacri-fices. There are always troublemakers in every group, and that small sect's clamor for more power tainted our image. Because of that, the Druids, who had already been secretive, withdrew even further until it appeared that they had faded from existence entirely. Up until now, we've led private lives and regard secrecy above all else." She finished with a hint of a frown, uncertainty clouding her gaze.

"And now?"

Her piercing eyes lifted to mine. "Everything's changing. There's discord among the elders—some want things to stay as they have been, while others want us to remain a secret to the human population but ally with the Fae. Yet others want us to out our abilities completely. Those individuals see us as a chosen people, better than other humans."

"What about you? What do you see as the proper direction for your people?" I pushed softly, surprisingly curious about her stance.

The deep green of her eyes darkened as sadness ghosted over her features. "I don't have a particular need to remain secretive, but I think revealing ourselves to the human population would forever change life as we know it on Earth. I'm not sure there's any way to predict the myriad of ways life would be affected by the widespread knowledge of the existence of magic. Maybe I'm just a coward, afraid of what I don't know, but my gut tells me that a reveal like that would be catastrophic. I don't think we should hide from the Fae, but I'm not sure telling humanity about Fae magic would benefit anyone. Unfortunately, it doesn't matter what I think. I'm not an elder, and I doubt anything I say would have any impact, even if I did try to speak up."

This was not the first time she had considered the

subject. In fact, I would be willing to bet that a great deal of thought had gone into her situation.

How surreal it was to speak with a woman who looked so remarkably similar to Hilde but who was so starkly different at the same time. Hilde had been brash and bold. She had been confident and vivacious in a way that was infectious to all those around her.

I had not known Cat long, but from what I had learned, she possessed a rare degree of maturity for someone so young in years. She was methodical and observant, demonstrating an understated strength behind her words and actions.

What caught me off guard the most was how refreshing I found her perspective and demeanor. Perhaps the feeling was simply the product of the many lifetimes without companionship. Perhaps her physical resemblance to Hilde endeared her to me, and maybe the draw was just my practical nature seeing her as a means to an end.

I needed to try to recharge my magic so that I would know one way or another whether it was forever gone.

I was not sure where Cat fit into the picture, but the growing urge inside me insisted that our paths had crossed for a reason, and I did not like it.

"Why are you looking at me like that?" she asked hesitantly as she knotted her hair upon her head.

I would not tell her where my thoughts had taken me. "Your hair, what is it that you have used to tie it up?" I asked instead, hoping the question had explained my unintended staring.

"Oh! That's a hair tie or rubber band. They're specially

made to hold hair. Would you like some?" she asked, already beginning to dig through her bag.

"I would appreciate that. I did not bring any leather straps with me, and I do not have the proper tools to trim my hair."

She looked at me hesitantly from under her thick lashes. "Would you like your hair trimmed?"

I had not put much thought into my hair. It had been a trivial matter relative to all the other changes in my life. But once she had mentioned it, I realized that it was refreshing to get rid of my beard and might be equally as pleasant to shed the long layers of hair as well. "Actually, I think I would."

"I could take you to get it done, or if you prefer ... I can do it. My mom and I cut each other's hair—it saves a load of money. Next time I come, I could bring the scissors." Her eyes flitted around the room, and color flooded her freckled cheeks.

An errant thought had me wondering what other ways I might be able to induce that lovely flush. I forced the image from my mind, repositioning myself in my seat to relieve the unexpected pressure swelling in my pants. "If you are able, that should suffice."

I must have been harboring some self-hatred to punish myself in such a way. Those delicate fingers touching me freely, without having the right to touch back. It would be torture.

Looking at those full rosy lips and the trail of freckles disappearing beneath her blouse, I could not have said no had I wanted to.

CHAPTER

EIGHT

CAT

EXACTLY ONE WEEK AFTER MY FIRST SOLO VISIT TO SEE FEN, I found myself back in my brick-red 1995 Fiat on the road to Strabane. The trip was unplanned and far more spontaneous than normal for me. When I'd woken up that Friday morning, I discovered that my mom had already left the house for the day. The moment I realized she was gone, I sent a text to Fergus explaining that I wasn't feeling well. Twenty minutes later, I was on the road.

I'd spent every waking moment of the week thinking about Fen. It wasn't like me to obsess over a man, but Fen was different. He was fascinating and so totally alone in the world. I wanted to know his every thought and hear stories of his harrowing past. I wanted to feel the weight of his penetrating stare because when his eyes were on me, I felt seen like I'd never been seen or understood before. I couldn't fathom how a man from such a different world could possibly know anything about me. Yet I got the feeling he intuited more about me than even I knew. It was there in the questions he asked and subtle touch of his stare when he listened to my answers.

Fenodree made me feel special.

Was that all a product of Fae manipulation? Maybe I was just naïve, but my gut swore to me that Fen was as honest and transparent a man as I'd ever met.

I was so anxious to see him again that I had to force myself not to speed to Strabane. My mother was much more apt to find out about my excursion if I ended up with a citation for reckless driving. That simply wasn't an option.

When I finally arrived, Fen greeted me with amusement in his eyes. The softened expression contrasted starkly with the stern features he'd worn at our previous encounters, filling me with exhilaration.

"Cat, I was not expecting any visitors for at least another day. Is that not what you said at our last visit?" He held the door open, and I helped myself inside, hoping I could keep my fluttering heart rate from turning my cheeks bright pink.

"Yes, I didn't think I would be able to get away until tomorrow. Lucky for us, there was a change of plans, and I was able to sneak away sooner." *Lucky for us? Did I just make it sound like we were a couple on a secret rendezvous? Oh, hell. And there goes the pink cheeks. I probably look like I'm twelve.* "So how have you been?" I squeaked awkwardly.

His lips tipped up with the hint of a smirk as he joined me in our usual chairs at the small dinette. "I'm well, and yourself?"

"I'm good. What have you been up to this week?" I asked, trying to redirect the attention from myself.

"I read the book you left with me. It was … entertaining."

"Really?" I exclaimed in surprise. "I didn't expect you to have read it already. Otherwise, I would have brought you a new one. I'll bring more next time if you'd like."

He tilted his head in acknowledgment but said nothing. His formal speech and aloof manner would have been off-putting from anyone else. Knowing his behaviors resulted from a centuries-old upbringing followed by solitary exile helped me understand that his mannerisms were a testament to his background rather than his opinions. After only a couple of visits, his formal nature became an endearing part of his personality.

"After the time we spent last week going over how to use the phone, I thought maybe I'd hear from you. Did you try to call or text at all?" I hadn't been optimistic about his adoption of the phone for communication, but a part of me had hoped.

"I told you I had no interest in these twenty-first-century devices," he grumbled somewhat petulantly. "I have been thrown into this modern world like a dog thrown into the ocean and told to grow gills. I can only change so much. Once I go off on my own, it will be to live a simple life. I will not require such devices."

"I can understand that. My aunt has a large piece of land on the western coast. I love it out there. She's got horses, and there's no other houses or people, certainly no internet or television. It may seem boring to some, but I always feel so at peace out in the heather listening to the waves crash on nearby cliffs. My aunt's a drunken sod, but the scenery is amazing."

I fiddled with my sleeve as I spoke, smiling to myself at the comment about my aunt. When Fen didn't reply, I raised my eyes to find him watching me raptly. I couldn't fathom what he was thinking, and his attention made me agonizingly self-conscious.

"Oh! I nearly forgot. I brought my shears if you'd still like a haircut," I offered, glad for a reason to redirect his attention.

"Ah, yes." He shook off whatever he'd been thinking and glanced around the room. "Shall we go outside?"

I dug around in my bag for the shears and clippers. "No, the bathroom will work fine. Just pull one of the chairs in there and have a seat."

When I entered the small bathroom, he sat shirtless under the fluorescent lights. I had never seen a more perfectly sculpted physique outside of movies and magazines. My fingers itched with the need to touch his golden skin where it dipped and curved around solid muscle. He'd been spending plenty of time outdoors. From what I'd been told, the Shadow Lands existed in a perpetual state of night, and he'd clearly been soaking up every scrap of Belfast sun since arriving. The hint of a tan suited his naturally olive complexion, making him even more tantalizing.

The room was just large enough for me to maneuver around him, but his masculine presence made the space feel even smaller. My heart pounded against my ribs, and my hands shook with a slight tremor as I set my tools on the vanity.

What had I been thinking? This had to have been the worst idea I'd ever come up with. What if I completely botch his hair and leave him practically bald?

Breathing slowly in through my nose and discretely out through my mouth, I attempted to settle my racing heart.

This is just a haircut—something you've done a hundred times or more in your life.

That's all this was. A haircut.

Right. Like I can simply ignore the enigmatic, drop-dead-gorgeous man beneath the hair.

"How short would you like it?" My voice rang out high-pitched and strained in the small space. Inwardly, I crawled into a cave and swore I'd never attempt human communication again. Outwardly, I gathered a towel and draped it casually around his shoulders as if he was just one of a dozen gorgeous men I regularly treated to my hairstyling services. His black mane cascaded down nearly two feet in length. It was in surprisingly good condition, considering how he'd been living. I could only imagine what it had looked like when he'd first arrived here.

Fen examined himself in the mirror, seemingly unaware of the mental breakdown I was having behind him. "I suppose it would be best to have a modern style to help me blend in."

"That would be pretty short. Are you sure you're okay with that?"

His eyes met mine in the mirror, and I felt their hold like a physical touch. "Cat, it is only hair," he said in a deep rumble.

I nodded distractedly and whispered, "Okay."

I gathered the long strands and secured them with a rubber band, then held the scissors just above the hair tie near the base of his neck. "Last chance to change your mind."

He lifted a brow in response, telling me to get on with it.

One chunk at a time, I sliced through his thick black hair until the ponytail was no longer attached. I held it aloft with a delighted grin.

Fen—the stoic exile—smirked and rolled his eyes at me.

It was the most playful, lighthearted gesture I'd seen from him. I had to suppress a hysterical giggle that bubbled up from deep inside me. Biting back the outburst, I set his hair aside. When I turned back to continue, nerves seized me again.

I hesitantly lifted my trembling fingers and wove them through his remaining hair close to his scalp. The thick strands were silky and smooth, unlike my own coarse curls.

Wholly focused on my hands exploring, I almost missed Fen's molten stare in the mirror.

Almost, but not quite.

His eyes seized mine, and for several thudding heartbeats, I was lost. All that existed were those obsidian depths and the searing heat that ignited every inch of my skin.

Only after my head began to swim with dizziness did I force my gaze away.

Clearing my throat, I took out the clippers and began to trim the hair around the sides and back of his head.

Once I got working, my nerves eased, but I couldn't shake my constant awareness of him. How my chest was inches from his face when I trimmed the front of his hair. The way my thighs brushed against his as I repositioned myself.

I stood between his legs, eyeing either side of the cut to ensure it was even, when I felt his hands tentatively grip my hips. I stilled, soaking up the possessive feel of his fingers clutching me like the throaty pleas of a dying man's last wish.

I could hardly breathe through the overwhelming wave of arousal that engulfed me.

A shiver rippled through Fen's entire body. "If you were wise," he whispered coarsely. "You would not respond to me in this way."

My eyes closed in a long blink as I tried to think clearly. "I can only be who I am."

His fingers gripped tighter before swiftly retreating. I brought my eyes to his face, but he kept his gaze cast to the side and said nothing.

"I don't believe you'll hurt me, Fen." I got the sense he thought of himself as a threat to me, but I also felt down in my bones that he was wrong.

He finally brought his shuttered gaze to mine. "Danger comes in many forms."

"And I believe you're as lethal as they come, but that doesn't make you dangerous to me."

Fenodree grunted and looked away.

A grin teased the corners of my mouth as I finished the last touches of my work. I left a couple of finger lengths on top but kept the rest trimmed close to his head. His jaw and cheeks were lined with heavy stubble, the perfect complement to his new trendy haircut. He would look like a footballer or maybe even a model to anyone on the street. Only those who knew Fen would understand just how much more there was to the man.

"What do you think?" I asked nervously, lifting the towel from his shoulders and dusting off his neck.

He held my eyes, not once examining his new look. "I think you're good with your hands," he murmured.

Heat blazed across my cheeks. "Well, you may want to shower off the extra hair. I can just wait out there."

He stood from the chair and looked down at me, giving me a perfect view of his chest and delicious abs. "I think fresh air is a better idea. I can bathe later. The sun is shining today, and I have been trying to enjoy its warmth every chance I get. Are you interested in a walk?" Despite his casual words, his voice was thick and affected.

Relieved that he had provided a distraction from the mounting tension between us, I jumped on the suggestion. "That sounds perfect. I spotted a trail down by the river on my way into town that looked gorgeous."

"I am happy to follow your lead."

We gathered our things and walked to the front of the hotel. In the car park, I led us to my rusty old car, cringing inwardly that it was the best I had to offer. As I began to unlock the driver's side door, I realized that Fen had followed me to the driver's side and stood uneasily next to me.

"Has Becca given you a ride in a car yet?"

His jaw clenched as he eyed the vehicle warily. "I have not been inside one of these metal carriages, no."

"There's nothing to worry about, I promise. And you really have to get used to these. Unlike a phone, cars are an essential part of life these days." I took his hand and walked him around to the passenger side.

He followed reluctantly, but when I opened the door and motioned for him to get in, he became rooted to the ground.

Was he looking at the ripped upholstery?

A flood of embarrassment washed over me.

"I know, it's dirty and old, but it's all I've got. It gets me where I need to be, and that's all that matters." I bit my lip, wondering if it would have been better to simply walk.

"It's an iron cage," he mused softly.

Silly, Cat. His reluctance has nothing to do with you.

I was reminded of just how much change this man had been forced to overcome, and I hated myself for not being more considerate. "I'm sorry, Fen," I said more softly. "We don't have to ride in the car. We can just walk."

"No, this is simply a new experience like all the others. I only needed a moment." He gave an almost imperceptible nod before slowly lowering himself into the passenger seat.

Who would have thought I'd ever find such joy in seeing someone sit in a car? Pride swelled in my chest at the sight of Fen as he dubiously eyed the dashboard and interior. This man had more courage and fortitude than most anyone I knew, and I considered myself beyond lucky to have met him.

With one more glance to sear the moment into my memory, I offered a warning that I was going to close the door, then scurried around to the driver's side. As soon as we were both inside the vehicle with the doors shut, I looked at Fen with a smile so broad it made my cheeks hurt.

"Do what you must, woman. Let us get this over with," Fen grumbled with just a touch of humor.

Laughter bubbled up from my chest—a mixture of relief, joy, pride, and a hint of worry for this man, who was quickly becoming one of the few people I called a friend.

I started the car, noticing Fen's white-knuckle grip on the door handle. I didn't think introducing the seat belt was a good idea yet, so I let that one slide.

The day was shaping up to be absolutely gorgeous. The sky was a brilliant blue, not a cloud in sight, and the air was comfortably warm without being overly hot. The trees in late May had regrown the leaves they'd shed last fall, and their heavy branches swayed gently in a light breeze.

Fen relaxed noticeably on the short drive over to the canal waterway. We rode in comfortable silence, and I looked at the passing scenery through new eyes. I wondered at the questions he might have and what all he'd already learned in my absence. If I could, I'd have joined him every single day to share in his exploration. I didn't want to miss a moment.

Instead, I would have to settle for stolen moments and soak up each minute I could.

The pedestrian walking path along a canal system off the River Foyle looked to be a perfect location for an outing. The area was somewhat outside the city, and being a workday, the car park was empty upon our arrival. I sensed Fen preferred nature to an urban setting, and the waterway was lovely.

The moment I turned off the engine, Fen exhaled a lungful of air into the quiet car. I kept my chuckle to myself as we both exited the vehicle.

"I know it's man-made and not exactly nature at its finest, but it has a certain appeal," I offered as we walked toward the path. A simple wooden fence like the kind used to contain livestock had been erected along the path to keep the pedestrians away from the water. The scrub trees and tall, variegated grasses were not particularly elegant, but it was still beautiful, nonetheless.

"Should you ever have the misfortune of seeing the Shadow Lands, you would never again doubt the beauty of this world," he responded wistfully as his eyes roamed the vegetation around us.

"Becca told me a little about it—that the leaves on the trees all look withered and dead but never fall to the ground. She said the landscape exists entirely in shades of tan and brown, and there is no wind or sounds or sun, just perpetual twilight and darkness. I couldn't imagine living alone in a place like that."

"What seems strange to me now is how thoroughly I had adapted. I thought returning to Earth would have been second nature, despite my long years away. However, when Rebecca first brought me here, it took days for my head to stop aching from the constant sounds around me. I spend more time than I would like in my room to escape from the relentless activity I encounter when I go out."

"That makes sense. It's only been a couple of weeks compared to the centuries you spent there. You'll find your new normal. It just may take a while." I gave him a soft smile as our eyes met briefly.

The simmering heat in his dark eye sent a swirling warmth through my insides before I returned my gaze to the still waterway.

The length of the canal was not particularly long, and we walked the remainder quietly with only an occasional comment on the scenery. When we reached the end of the pavement, we both leaned against the wood fence and looked out at the River Foyle in the distance.

Fen cleared his throat somewhat hesitantly, an uncharacteristic gesture from the usually self-assured Fae man. "Cat, do you think it would be possible for you to teach me your rune magic?"

I looked over in surprise, but Fen kept his gaze locked on the view before him.

"Why would you want me to do that? Surely your magic far exceeds anything I could teach you."

He gave a fleeting glance in my direction. "Rebecca did not tell you?"

"Tell me what?"

"I assume you are aware that the Seelie use sexual energy to replenish their magic? Without the opportunity to charge my powers, they faded away within the first year of my exile." His voice was matter-of-fact, but the loss must have been profound.

A leaden weight pressed against my chest as I took a small step back from the fence.

As if the death of his wife and a lifetime in exile hadn't been enough, Fenodree had been forced to suffer the loss of his magic. How had I not connected the dots on my own? Had I been so caught up in my own fancies that I hadn't noticed this Fae man had not once used magic around me?

I couldn't imagine how hard those first years must have been. Yet he didn't even seem resentful or outwardly bitter about what he'd suffered.

The man was incredible.

"Of course, I'll teach you," I said in a hushed tone.

He glanced back to where I stood, and as our gazes locked, I felt my mind shift perspectives like some sort of out-of-body experience.

He was no longer Fae, and I was no longer Druid.

We were simply two people getting to know one another.

My lips spread into a wide grin, and my heart grew so full it could have burst. "Would you like to start now?" I asked, pulling a water bottle from my satchel and looking for a flat surface. "We can use these fence boards. They're worn decently smooth."

I opened the cap on the plastic bottle and poured some water into the palm of my left hand. With my right, I handed the bottle to Fen and then dipped my finger in the water like a quill in ink. "The first rune every young Druid learns is the truth rune for sight. Each rune has formal names and origins, but you don't need to know that stuff to be able to use them."

After a couple of dips back into the water, the symbol stood out on the light gray wood. Fen stared at the symbol for a moment, then took a small step back and slowly lifted the hair off the back of my neck.

My breath stuttered and then froze as his warm finger traced the lines of the tattoo on my neck.

"Are all the runes drawn onto your flesh?" His voice had gone guttural, its vibrating tenor resounding in the most delicious part of my belly.

I twisted to look back at him, and he slowly released my hair. "No, some runes can be used that way, but that is the only one I have. In a special ceremony, it was given to me using a spell to maximize the rune's potency. It's the most important because it helps protect us from Fae enchantment." My own voice had become shaky, and my head felt weightless as I turned back around.

"That sounds extremely helpful."

"It is," I breathed. "I'll have to do my best to learn about the spell so that maybe I could give it to you one day. You have just as much need of its protection as we do." I cleared my throat and attempted to continue with the lesson. "Next is the symbol for protection—and don't worry, I'll write these down for you once we get back to your room. This one can be used on a talisman that you wear or carved into the doorway of your home to ward off evil. Of course, you can't use it at the hotel, though. I doubt the management would appreciate you decorating their door."

He dipped his finger into the water with a coy smirk and outlined the symbol I had drawn. After that, I displayed the runes for strength and stealth, which he dutifully practiced and set to memory. I went to refill my hand with water and accidentally tipped the bottle more than was needed, splashing myself with the contents. I yipped and jerked back as if I could escape my own hands, and Fen barked out a laugh.

The sound was beyond incredible. A laugh from him felt like liquid sunshine raining down from the sky, warming every inch of me.

Wanting to keep the playful mood going, I grinned at him. "You thought that was funny, did you?" I raised a brow and pursed my lips together before sloshing the water bottle in his direction and sending a spray of water across his chest.

I was to a point where I was infinitely more comfortable around Fen, but we hadn't known each other all that long. For a split second, time came to a stop, and I questioned if I had overstepped my bounds. That was until he tucked his chin with a devious grin and sprang in my direction.

I dropped the bottle and bolted with a shriek.

"It was an accident! A hand spasm!" I hollered behind me as I tore back down the path.

"Cat, why do I not believe you?" Right on my tail, Fen grabbed for my hand. My momentum swung around to bring me flush against his chest, his hands binding mine snuggly at my back.

With heavy breaths, our gazes locked, and the world around us melted away.

His heated stare dropped down to my parted lips.

Desire like I've never experienced snaked and coiled its way from my center to every tiny nerve ending until my body was alight with sensation. Adjusting to this foreign ache inside me, my back arched, pressing me further against his hard chest.

Fen's every muscle was rigid with restraint, but when I arched and wriggled, the last thread of his control snapped. His hands clutched me tighter, one finding its way into my curls. He angled my head to give him access to my neck. Only the weakest puffs of air managed to pass through my constricted lungs as his lips lowered to the delicate skin of my throat.

"It has been … so long, Cat. So long since I have touched a woman." His words ghosted across my skin. "I only have so much restraint within me."

I licked my now parched lips, straining to think through my lusty haze. "Is there a reason to restrain yourself?"

He pulled back, his eyes tracking mine, almost pleadingly. "There is *every* reason, yet none seem sufficient."

I couldn't help myself.

I didn't care why he seemed to be begging me to stop him. I needed his lips on mine like I needed my next breath. I wanted Fen to be the very air I breathed.

Tossing aside his wordless plea, I lifted onto my toes and brought our lips together in a tentative kiss. Fenodree held perfectly still, chiseled in stone. I began to question if he'd respond to my advance until I made one last effort and trailed my tongue along his full bottom lip, desperate to taste him.

The contact drew forth a savage groan from deep in his chest before his lips crashed down on mine.

I'd never felt more desired in my entire life. Not just desired. *Owned.*

As though my body was his to command in a way I'd never known was possible. Invisible strings bound us together, tightly woven and impossible to ignore. Even our hearts pounded with the same punishing rhythm.

His tongue tunneled inside me with relentless possession, and I was his willing captive.

I'd never been certain of my purpose in life, but at that moment, I knew it was him. He was my purpose. My very reason for being.

I would have continued kissing him forever had he not reluctantly pulled away, resting his forehead against mine. Our shallow breaths shuddered and melded as we regained our bearings. If he was half as disoriented as I was, it would take weeks rather than days to come down from this high.

My kiss-swollen lips lifted in a small smile before I pulled back to peer up at him, but all my newly acquired joy froze over and crashed to the ground in an icy heap when I saw the look on his face.

Unadulterated disgust dripped from his snarled lip while his eyes sliced me wide open with cutting disappointment.

I stumbled back a step, unable to formulate a word through my shock.

"I'm sorry," Fen mumbled, running a hand through his newly trimmed hair. "I should not have done that."

"What? Why?" Had I done something wrong? How had I misread our kiss so drastically? I'd thought we were both equally as swept away by the current running between us, but now, I could only sense turmoil and regret.

Did he think he was taking advantage of me? Couldn't he tell I liked what we'd done?

"Fen, I—"

"Enough," he cut me off in a harsh tone. "It is time we get back. I am sure you will need to return home soon." He kept his gaze cast aside, erecting an impenetrable barrier between us.

I didn't feel comfortable arguing with him, though a voice inside me pleaded helplessly with him. I had no clue what had happened, but now wasn't the time to push for answers. He was clearly upset.

I nodded and followed in his wake as he led us back to the car. We made the entire trip to the hotel in awkward silence, and minutes later, I was on the road back to Belfast, completely at a loss.

CHAPTER

NINE

CAT

THE LINE BETWEEN WALLOWING AND RELAXING WAS AMBIGUOUS at best. I spent most of the following day in bed watching television, assuring myself that my debilitating lack of energy resulted from a busy week. I hated to think Fenodree's emotional slap could affect me so profoundly. We hardly knew one another, after all. I'd only met him weeks before. But after a full day of fighting off thoughts of the confusing Fae man, I had to admit that my bleary-eyed exhaustion was born more of heartache than anything else.

The most crippling part was my confusion. I couldn't understand what had happened to turn our day so sour. The kiss I'd wanted to savor forever now sat bitter on my tongue, the residue impossible to scrape away.

My mood had been irritable at best, so I kept to myself. The last thing I wanted was to deal with my mother's nonsense when I was already fending off an oppressive black cloud over my head. However, I could only avoid her so long when my stomach rioted for food, demanding supper.

When I finally emerged from my self-imposed isolation, I found her dusting the insides of the small china cabinet.

"Hello, love. You feeling better?" she asked a little too cheerfully.

"Yeah, just a long week."

"Oh, yeah? Work goin' all right?" She shot me an odd look, making me suddenly wonder if she hadn't discovered that I'd skipped work. She seemed too energetic to be angry, but I wasn't sure what else could be behind her odd behavior.

Sweat began to drench my palms, and the hunger I'd felt just moments before evaporated. "Same as always. And you—how was your day?"

My words came out clipped, but my mom was apparently too absorbed in whatever she had on her mind to notice. She picked up each cup and saucer, wiping them thoroughly before replacing them on the glass shelves. "I have good news! I think we've found a place for you and Aileen to move into soon."

Oh. Well, that was good news.

The tension in my shoulders eased, knowing my secret was still safe. Still, as I watched my mom continue to clean with abandon, the suspicion resurfaced. "Is that all that's on your mind, Mom?" I asked hesitantly.

She stalled her frenzied action and turned my way.

"Yes, just getting the place tidy for tomorrow. I have Sunday dinner plans for us, so make sure you're home."

I knew my mom like I knew my own freckles, and there was something more she wasn't saying. "What exactly are these plans?"

"My friend Moira O'Keane, her husband, and their son are coming in from Downpatrick. I've invited them over. It's important you're here, that's all." She spouted the words quickly without glancing my way.

"Is this a date? Are you trying to set me up with her son?" I blurted, hands going to my hips.

She put down the plate she'd been wiping and slowly faced me. Her features hardened with determination, making the hackles raise on the back of my neck. "You're getting older, Catronia. It's time to find you someone, and it's not like you can be with just anyone." Her words were firm, and I could see her knuckles whiten as they gripped her dusting rag.

"Of course, I can be with *just anyone*. This isn't the Middle Ages—you can't tell me who I'm going to date," I stuttered with indignation.

My mom's lips set firmly as she took a menacing step forward. "I can, and I will if needed. At one time, there were so few of us that marriage to outsiders was a necessity, but now, we are a large enough faction that the knowledge must stay within our numbers." She lifted her chin haughtily before continuing. "It has been decreed by the elders."

"What has? What the hell are you talking about?" The Druids weren't like other people, but we weren't so backward as to dictate who a person could and couldn't marry.

"Perhaps if you were responsible enough, I might be able to tell you more about our council meetings. As it is, your choice in ... *company* has not proven you to be trustworthy. When Daeglan O'Connor's father stepped down two months back, Daeglan took his seat as an elder. He's been working to restore strength to our people, which includes marrying within our own ranks."

I couldn't wrap my head around her words. I heard them and understood their meaning, but my brain couldn't make sense of them. "Are you saying I'll have to marry another Druid?"

"There are plenty of fine young Druid men to choose from. It's not exactly a hardship." Her words were firm with conviction, but her hands began to worry at the rag she held, twisting and squeezing at the terry cloth.

My nose began to sting, and my throat tightened with the threat of tears. "How could you even consider supporting a mandate like that? I'm your *daughter*," I spat harshly. "You'd have me marry someone I didn't love just to make the *elders* happy?"

Her features softened just a fraction as she took a small step forward. "Cat, I'm only doing what's best for ye."

"If that's what you think, you must not know me at all," I said in a broken voice before running from the room as the first set of tears broke free and cascaded down my heated cheeks.

I bounded out the front door with Mom close on my heels.

"You're acting like a child. Catronia! *Cat*! You best be

home by nightfall!" she hollered from the front steps, but I ignored her screeching voice.

By some stroke of luck, the evening air wasn't terribly cool, so I wandered the streets in my socks for hours. I couldn't stand the thought of going back home. I considered going to the Huntsman to stay with Rebecca, but my silly pride got in the way. I hated for my friends to know the full extent of my mother's zealot beliefs. Instead, I let the heartbreak and anger swallow me whole as I roamed the nameless streets.

I'd gone from ecstatic optimism to crushing despair in less than twenty-four hours.

Something about the extreme nature of the swing made everything feel even worse. Would Fen ever want to see me again? Would my mom succeed in selling me off like livestock?

No. Absolutely not.

I would never agree to marry someone simply because he was also born into the Druid culture. A twisted sense of duty could never prove more worthy than a chance at true love. The fact that Mom would even entertain such a possibility was nauseating.

I'd tried so hard to be the best daughter I could be. I was polite, did well in school, and followed my mother's rules. I rarely fought back against her overprotective instincts and tried to understand her perspective as a single mother when our opinions differed. Despite all of my efforts, our relationship had continued to unravel over the past few years. But this? I wasn't sure how we could ever find our way back to one another if she didn't support my right to choose my own spouse.

That was a demand I was unwilling to meet.

Maybe all of this was my fault for not putting my foot down earlier. Had I rebelled at a younger age, would she have been more apt to have given me space, or would she have doubled down and suffocated me with rules and expectations?

I had no answers except that things would have to change.

We'd reached a point of divergence, and I could no longer continue down the same path. I had to strike out on my own and show her that my life was my own. Show her that she held no more sway over me.

My first step would be to move into my own apartment.

Initially, I had entertained my mother's wishes that I move in with Aileen because it wasn't all that important to me who I lived with, and a roommate would help with living expenses. Now, I could see that wasn't an option. I would have to reject her chosen roommate purely on principle. Living with Aileen would send the wrong message. I needed Mom to understand unequivocally that I was independent of her and the Druid elders.

There was a distinct possibility that taking such drastic steps would leave me without any family. It wasn't the start in life I would have chosen for myself, but I saw no other way.

My shoulders rounded at the pain spearing through my chest.

I reminded myself that I had friends who cared about me, but it did little to bolster me at the moment. Cleaving my mother out of my life would leave a gaping wound that might never heal. Not when the separation sprang from such a bitter betrayal. Mom was choosing the Druid faith over me, and that cut deep.

My only hope was that she might come to her senses at the prospect of losing me. If she could see how confused her priorities had become, maybe then we could begin to heal.

I SNUCK BACK inside the house well past midnight. Emotional exhaustion quickly tugged me into a fitful sleep. By the time I woke the next morning, my blankets had migrated to the floor, and I'd somehow rotated sideways in the small bed.

I had decided the night before that I would attend my mother's dinner to keep the peace and give her an opportunity to see the error of her ways. Should I see no remorse from her, I would continue with my plans to find a new place to live come Monday morning. Riling her up in the meantime served no purpose.

I showered because my hours of wandering had left me smelling musty, but I didn't put any more effort than necessary into my appearance. I didn't wear makeup on a regular day, so I certainly wasn't going to change that for our *company*.

Mom never attempted to initiate a conversation. I would have been lying if I said I wasn't disappointed, though I wasn't truly surprised. I'd known my foolish hope of reconciliation was little more than a pipe dream.

With no reason to leave my room, I didn't emerge until

the front bell rang. Wearing jeans, a simple long-sleeve shirt, and a scowl, I joined my mother at the front door.

"Moira, Jimmy, it's so good to have you. Come in, please." My mother ushered in our guests, and as I rounded the corner, I gave them each a tight smile that was more grimace than greeting.

Moira was a few years older than my mom and a good deal heavier. Her husband was a large man with a rotund belly hanging over his belt. Both were dressed in their Sunday best and reminded me of the stereotypical goofy neighbors in a 1950s sitcom.

"Colleen, it's a pleasure, thank you. Let me introduce our son. *This* is Brandan." Moira put a hand on her son's narrow shoulder and gazed up at him as if he'd hung the moon.

"Brandan, it's lovely to meet you. This over here is my daughter, Catronia." She waved me over, but I stood firmly in place and nodded my hello from the other side of the room.

Brandan wasn't necessarily unattractive if you liked the tall, weaselly type. He flicked his head to toss his sandy-blond hair out of his eyes and offered a leering smirk.

Lovely.

"Come on, Colleen. You two join me in the kitchen while I finish up and let the two youngsters get to know one another." My treacherous mother grabbed her friend's hand, and they disappeared around the corner with Jimmy close on their heels.

"The house smells great—is that lamb?" asked

Brandan as he ambled over to where I leaned against the doorframe.

"Yes, roast leg of lamb with soda bread, if I'm not mistaken." My words were clipped, but that didn't seem to deter his advance.

"Mom told me a little about you. Said you like to make jewelry. Is that right?"

My mom had never seen my jewelry as a passable career, so I was surprised to find she had shared that tidbit with my chosen suitor. "Yes, I'd love to make jewelry professionally someday."

"That sounds like it would be a great little hobby." He tilted his head to the side.

Little hobby? What a jerk!

My arms crossed over my chest, a clear sign of my agitation, which he also ignored as he stepped yet closer.

"And you? What is it you do?" I asked, barely containing my irritation.

His chest puffed out proudly, signaling that I should prepare to be amazed. "I'm almost through with my finance degree. I'll be working in a bank soon enough."

"That sounds fascinating." *Hello, sarcasm.*

Brandan, too full of himself to be aware of context clues, continued on obliviously. "Yes, it's a great position to hold for our people. The elders are *very* pleased."

If I heard the words "our people" or "elders" again, I was certain I would scream. "It sounds like dinner is ready." Not waiting for a response, I blew past Brandan into the dining area.

Our parents had already taken their seats, the two

women talking animatedly while Jimmy browsed his phone.

I took the chair farthest from my mother.

As soon as Brandan sat down, Mom said a ritual blessing over the food, and we all began to make our plates. The table was made to seat four, but we managed to squeeze in all five of us with some jostling elbows and carefully arranged plates.

"Mrs. Murphy, this looks delicious," Brandan offered. "I can only hope you've passed your cooking skills on to your daughter." He winked at me in what was likely an attempt at flirtation but fell flat where I was concerned.

"Actually, I'm not a fan of cooking," I deadpanned, receiving raised eyebrows from Jimmy as he shoveled an oversized bite of lamb into his mouth.

Not to be deterred, Brandan gave a conspiratorial look at my mother. "Well, I'm sure we can work on that."

The man was unbelievable.

Every word out of his mouth was patronizing, and he was entirely too pompous to have the slightest clue. Even more upsetting, my mom ate up every word.

Smiling coyly as if she was the object of his affection, Mom simpered. "Ach, I've tried to teach her, but she can be willful, that one."

It's as if I'm not even in the room. What a fecking nightmare!

Worse than being invisible—it was as if I was an animal in a cage on display, my value being openly negotiated.

The lights on the ugly gold chandelier overhead were suddenly too bright, and I wished there had been something stronger than water in my glass. It was probably best there wasn't because there was no telling what I would have said had my tongue been any looser.

The remainder of their visit marked some of the longest hours of my life.

I did my best to keep my head down and not act out the fantasies I was envisioning. While upending the table and spewing rage-filled words at my mother might have seemed like a good idea, I would regret it later.

Instead, I considered the evening my parting gift to my mother. She didn't know it yet, but I was already gone.

CHAPTER
TEN

FENODREE

I HAD NOT BEEN SURE CAT WOULD COME FOR A THIRD VISIT, BUT she surprised me yet again. Most people would have avoided the person who had seemingly rejected them.

But not the little Druid.

I was aware she had misunderstood my reaction to our kiss. While I had not intended to hurt her, the source of my shock was not something I had been ready to vocalize. For so many years, I had been left to wonder if my magic would return to me should I ever have escaped the Shadow Lands. I had imagined every possible scenario on the spectrum—from one end where my magic was fully restored to the other where it was gone forever and everything between.

For centuries, I had waited and wondered.

The question had certainly not been forgotten upon my arrival on Earth. The first few nights after my return, I debated incessantly about finding a woman to put an end to the uncertainty. I had eventually decided that I had lived so long without magic that there was little reason to rush foolheartedly into the situation. Even more persuasive was the sizeable part of me that had been afraid of the answer.

I had delayed testing my ability to charge my old magic back to life, but when Cat's lithe body pressed against mine, the situation had unintentionally presented the answer.

Her desire had wafted off her in waves. I had not yet mentally prepared for that moment, nor did I believe Cat was the proper person to use for that purpose, but I lost myself to the sensation.

When our lips came together, all thoughts were abandoned.

I was nothing but exquisite need, desperate to devour her sweet taste. Liquid fire burned through my veins, and a long-forgotten possessive urge pounded like a drum in beat with my racing heart. I was instantly swept up in a tidal wave of hunger, that is, until a single thought broke through the lust and sealed my fate.

Not even a woman's arousal is enough to revive my magic. It is lost forever.

Once my shock registered, it was all-consuming. The heavens could have opened and rained down horses, and I would not have noticed or cared.

I had held out hope that my power lay dormant. That the cloying scent of a woman's desire would lure my power from its dark captivity and once again stir that electric current in my veins.

I was such a fool.

How long had I lived in the Shadow Lands before I learned that hope was nothing more than self-torture? I knew that lesson better than anyone. Yet somehow, I had made this one exception for myself. I had clung to the hope of my power returning despite the absence of any logical facts to support the notion.

I did not leave my room at the inn for days after my discovery.

At first, I was mired in self-loathing over my foolishness for having constructed a false reality for myself. An imaginary future I had no right to cling to. But after I grew sick of my own petulance, a new source of resentment took shape.

I was furious at myself for the hurt I had caused Cat.

She had done nothing to earn my displeasure, yet I had discarded her with ruthless insensitivity. I began to wonder if she would return, and the possibility of her loss brought on an astonishing degree of shame and remorse.

How could I possibly have formed an attachment to anyone after being so accustomed to isolation?

I had spent weeks with Rebecca and Lochlan, and while I had regretted their departure, I did not feel a fraction of the crippling remorse assaulting me at the thought of losing Cat. I had only spent a handful of days with her. How was it even possible?

I had no idea, but the relief I felt when she appeared at my doorstep was undeniable. If only I had known what to do about it. My isolation might not have eviscerated all my emotions, but my ability to socialize and relate to others was rusty at best.

I knew I had hurt her and wanted to correct the misunderstanding, yet I could not find the words. I suddenly felt more inept than I had since first struggling to survive in my exile.

Though I had not earned her gentle forgiveness, Cat gifted it anyway. She greeted me with a beaming smile that whitewashed over my transgressions, effectively wiping them from existence.

We spent a full day together in much the same way as we had before. However, this time, the air around us was charged with an unshakable tension. I was acutely aware of every casual touch—a brush of her shoulder or the barely-there touch of her hand against mine as she gave me the latest book she had brought.

Judging from the way her breathing hitched with every contact, she felt it too.

Any sort of tryst between us was a catastrophic idea. Cat was not the sort for anything quick and meaningless, and I was a fugitive with nothing to offer her. I had no business near any woman of quality, considering my current station in life. And if that was not problem enough, there was also her age and the fact that I was Fae and she a Druid.

The live wire buzzing between us might have presented a temptation, but it would only lead to devastation.

I swore I would use what little self-worth I now possessed to keep my distance while still preserving our friendship.

The task was not easy.

She arrived each week as regular as the tide, and I

spent the days in between thinking of nothing but her return—the exquisite torture of having her close yet knowing she could never be mine.

Upon her sixth visit, she arrived at my door in a dress the exact shade of her enchanting green eyes. The unexpected visage when I opened the door struck me speechless. I had yet to see her in a dress as she favored more practical attire. The summer frock was simple yet designed perfectly to give a hint of cleavage. It clung to her trim waist before gently flaring from her narrow hips. The soft fabric was cut just above the knee, and her heeled sandals arched her ankles and calves to mimic the delicate lines of a porcelain teacup.

She radiated femininity and grace, and I was utterly spellbound.

I could hardly remember my own name, let alone the strict boundaries I had set for myself.

In a daze, I watched my outstretched fingers thread through her soft curls. Her guileless emerald eyes peered up at me with the untouched purity of a mountain valley too remote for settlement. Thick green grasses and fluttering butterflies and a life-giving creek babbling over rounded gray stones. In her eyes, I could see the promise of happiness and overflowing joy ... that was, until a shutter came crashing down, closing her off to me and stealing it all away.

What had happened? Why had she suddenly erected a wall between us?

"I am sorry," I murmured. "Did I upset you?"

"No, it's not you." She eyed the empty hallway, reminding me of my lack of manners.

I stepped back and invited her inside, itching to touch her as she ghosted past me. She drifted over to the table and chairs, but instead of sitting in her regular spot, she stood at the large window and stared vacantly outside.

"Before I left to drive out here, I had a fight with my mother." Her voice sounded hollow, and I was instantly alert.

Had her mother discovered Cat was helping a Fae man?

I hated to think my presence would cause discord between her and her mother. As much as it would pain me, I would rather Cat cease her visits than be the reason the two had a falling-out.

She collected her thoughts for some time before she began to explain, eyes still cast unseeing out the window. "Two weeks ago, my mother tried to set me up with a Druid man. Her behavior was odd, and when I pushed for answers, she told me that the elders had decreed that Druids must marry within our own people." Cat's voice was toneless, void of emotion and chillingly calm. "I didn't say anything to you before because I was still trying to process it myself. I've been looking for an apartment I can afford on my own and making arrangements to move out of my mother's house. I refuse to allow someone else to choose who I'll marry. I'd been able to avoid talking about it with my mother these last two weeks, but this morning..." Her breath caught. "This morning, I told her I wouldn't comply with the elders, and we fought," she choked out. "We said the most *terrible* things." Her words faded to shuttering sobs.

I quickly encircled her shaking frame, pulling her close against me, my body curving protectively around hers.

When she melted into me, seeking comfort in my presence and trusting me with her burden, I felt a single word resound deep down in my soul.

Mine.

I hated to see her in pain and felt an inexplicable responsibility to protect her from any and all threats. My need to shield her was so great that I could vanquish an army if it meant restoring the light in her eyes.

These were dangerous thoughts, yet I could not escape them. I even had trouble releasing her when her breathing settled, and she was ready to continue talking.

"I can't do it." She lifted her teary eyes to mine. "I can't let my life be controlled like that. I've made a decision. I'm leaving my family." Her last words were no more than a whisper.

I swiped my thumbs gently under her eyes through her river of tears. "There is nothing more precious than the life we have each been given. This life is your own, precious Cat, and no one else's. You are right to demand your freedom. I only wish it did not come at such a high cost."

She stared so deeply into my eyes that I thought she must see parts of me foreign to even myself. Then she did the last thing I had expected.

She kissed me.

ELEVEN

CAT

My time with Fen was a brilliant sunny day in the middle of an arctic winter. I wanted to bask in his warmth and bottle up every hour of sunshine I could to take with me back to the frigid tundra that was the current state of my life. There had been a strong possibility he would reject my advance, but I had to take the chance. I had to have one more taste of his delicious warmth.

Fen had been keeping his distance, but I noticed how his eyes devoured me when I first arrived. The sweep of his gaze had been a physical caress down the length of my body, stealing the air straight from my lungs.

He was just as affected by the pull between us as I was, regardless of his odd reaction after our first kiss. I didn't know what had happened. I didn't have to. I knew how I felt, and I was confident he felt the same. That was all that mattered.

Not my family or his past.

Not our ages or races.

None of the arbitrary parameters society used to define an acceptable relationship.

I was sick of letting other people tell me what to think and how to feel. I wanted to be free. I wanted to finally give in to the overwhelming desire I felt toward Fen. I'd used all my strength in the battle with my mother and had no fight left.

I allowed the whispers of should and should nots to fall silent.

When it was only Fen and me in the room—no fears or consequences clouding the air—it was easy to lift my hands behind his neck and bring his lips to mine. Effortless and natural and blissfully euphoric.

Fen's arms tightened around me, making my heartbeat skip at an erratic pace. Our lips and tongues danced together in an ancient rhythm ingrained in our very beings. We tasted, tested, and explored. His hands kneaded my back and bottom while mine roamed from his short hair down the column of his neck and over his broad shoulders.

After a long moment, but not nearly long enough, Fenodree pulled back, resting his forehead on mine. He didn't have to sever our contact completely for me to feel the extent of his withdrawal. He was retreating, but I had no idea why.

"Please don't pull away," I whispered softly.

"Cat, you are so young, and right now, you are heartbroken and lost. These things have clouded your judgment." The rasp in his voice did funny things to my insides, and it was hard to think when his fingers trailed from my temple down to my jaw.

But this moment was too important for anything less than perfect clarity.

I felt it in my bones. A precipice. A turning point that would become a line of demarcation in my life.

These precious minutes would play a crucial role in the roadmap of my life.

"I'm not too young to know what I want, and right now, that's you," I told him in a calm but firm tone. "If you don't want to be with me, I understand, but please don't deny me because you think you know what's best for me. That's what my mother is trying to do, and right now, I need to be the one making decisions."

Something almost feral flashed in his eyes before his lips crashed down on mine. He lifted me in his arms in one swift motion, turned us to the bed, then lowered himself over me. My body pressed down into the soft mattress under the weight of his larger frame, and I relished the sensation. I fit perfectly beneath him, my hair fanned out around me on the white cotton duvet.

"You tempt me in ways I cannot comprehend," he whispered against my flushed cheek after grazing his teeth down the length of my neck. "You have one last chance. End this before we lose ourselves."

"We can't possibly be lost if we're together, and I'm not going anywhere." I accented my emphatic response with a roll of my pelvis, seeking friction to ease the incessant ache between my legs.

He hissed, closing his eyes and lowering his face to the crook of my neck. He only hid for a second before a growl rumbled from deep in his chest, and his lips again found mine.

"I do not deserve this." His teeth tugged at my lower lip.

"That's for me to decide."

He only grunted in return, shifting his weight to rest beside me and allowing his free hand to roam the length of my body. His fingers skated along the outside of my breast, down my ribs, and made me writhe with sensation. When he reached the length of my exposed thigh, he slowly trailed his hand up under my bunched skirt.

"There are so many reasons this should not happen, but I cannot deny you. Not when I want to taste you so badly." He watched my face intently as his hand neared the searing heat at the apex of my thighs.

When his palm cupped my sex over my silk panties, I thought I might come with the slightest movement. His touch on my sensitive core was infinitely more electrifying than my own touch had ever been. My body screamed for more.

I rolled my hips, pressing myself into his hand. The breathtaking sensation drew a moan from my lips as my head pushed back into the mattress.

"That's it, take what you want from me," he rumbled as he rocked his palm against my weeping core.

My thighs fell apart, eager for more.

Fen lowered his mouth to the sensitive skin just below my ear to nibble and suck. "How could I have ever thought of you as a child? You are a sensual siren, and I am hopelessly lost to your call."

The fabric beneath his deft fingers became drenched

with my arousal, and my breaths came in uneven pants. When he stopped only briefly to remove my underwear, my swollen clit throbbed at the loss of his touch. "More, Fen. *Please*, I need more."

He swirled his finger around my entrance before drifting up to the bundle of sensitive nerves, and then back down in a circuit of pleasure. Round and round, he teased before dipping his finger inside me and drawing a breathy gasp from my lips. I had hardly adjusted to the sensation when he began to pump his finger in and out, curling the digit up with each movement to tap on that delicious spot inside me.

I swore nothing could ever feel more perfect than his fingers stroking me.

I was wrong.

Minutes later, he clasped his mouth over my core, licking and sucking as his finger continued its rhythmic motion inside me, and the sensation unraveled me. Almost instantly, my legs began to twitch and shake. My belly tightened, and my hands instinctively massaged my swollen breasts.

It was the most euphoric, perfect moment of my existence, and it was growing. Building. Cascading like an avalanche down a mountain, I was no match for this force of nature.

Fen swirled his tongue around my swollen nub with a guttural growl, and the vibrations sent me hurdling over the edge.

Pleasure tore from my throat in an unabashed cry like a tea kettle billowing with steam. The release was so overpowering that it shook and pulsed through my body. I could do nothing but drift on the blissful waves until the perfect chaos settled.

Fen continued to gently lap at my center until he'd drawn out every ounce of the orgasm from my quaking body. "That was just as breathtaking as I had imagined." He licked my essence from his lips and moved back up the bed to pull my languid body against his.

When I recovered enough to hear over the ringing in my ears, I let my hand drift down to his tented pants and pressed my palm against him.

He took my hand in his, placed a tender kiss on my palm, then set it back on his chest.

I raised my head so that I could see his face. "What about you, Fen? I want to make you feel good, too."

He squeezed my hand, his gaze warm and content. "Trust me, that was for me just as much as it was for you."

I wasn't fully convinced, but I wasn't going to force the issue, so I returned my cheek to his chest and nestled against him.

"I am so sorry about your family," he murmured into my hair. "I wish I could do more to protect you from the hurt they are causing, but I doubt there is much anyone can do that will ease that ache."

My situation was somewhat easier to think about in the aftermath of so much pleasure. I drifted my hand back and forth across his chest as my thoughts wandered. "I never imagined that I would need anyone to protect me from my own family. All my life, I've been taught ways to stay safe and protect myself from the Fae. But as it turned out, my mother hurt me in ways deeper than any Fae could have. She's the one person who was supposed to be on my side, no matter what." My voice cracked on the last words, emotion finally getting the better of me. Before I could travel any farther down that dark road, the mention of protection had me lifting my head and smiling softly at Fen. "Actually, that reminds me of something I brought for you." I slid from the bed and crossed to where I had dropped my bag on the floor.

Fen sat up cross-legged on the bed, and I bounded back over to sit across from him, our knees just touching.

"I made this for you." I held out my open palm to display a dark leather band embellished with detailed markings.

"The protection rune," he said under his breath as he lifted the strap from my hand and brought it up to examine more closely.

"I made one for Rebecca a while back, and it helped her in a battle against some Red Caps. There's not a ton of power to it, but it might help if you find yourself in a struggle. I want to keep you safe, too." My eyes dropped to my hands as my insecurities resurfaced.

"Cat, this is stunning. You truly do have an artistic gift." He placed a hand behind my neck to pull me closer before pressing his lips against my forehead. "Thank you, my little Cat. You are a gift to me in more ways than you could ever know."

CHAPTER

TWELVE

CAT

The pieces of my new life were falling into place. Days after the devastating fight with my mother, I'd secretly lined up a new place to live. I hadn't told Mom my specific plans, but she would find out soon enough. Once she told the elders about my rejection of their mandates, I could safely assume I would no longer be welcome among them. It was only a matter of time before I would be cast out of the only family I'd ever known.

Considering what I'd learned about recent leadership changes among the Druid elders, severing ties might have been inevitable. The more I learned about the Fae, the harder it was to align myself with people like Daeglan and their zealot teachings of fear and hatred. I just wished that group didn't include my mother. Breaking away from her would be the most painful part, but I saw no way around it.

Fortunately, not every Druid saw life in terms of black and white.

Fergus was a prime example and one of the few Druids I hoped I would still be able to call a friend after I walked away. I had even considered keeping my job at the museum because of him but had decided I would need to make a clean break. Living my new life in the shadow of my old one would be that much harder on everyone involved. With that in mind, I lined up a job at a local clothing store that would help me get by until I figured out a long-term plan.

Knowing my life would soon be turned upside down, I was more inclined than ever to seek out the pockets of happiness I found in Strabane. In Belfast, I was constantly confronted with the reality of my problems. When I was with Fen, it was like the two of us were marooned on an island where nothing could touch us. Being with him on an intimate level just days before had only intensified my need for him. I hadn't even lasted a whole week before I gave in to the incessant pull and called in sick from work.

When I was away from him, I spent the majority of my time thinking about him. I understood why he and I would likely never have a future, but that didn't stop me from fantasizing about the possibilities. A series of one-in-a-million scenarios that I had no business entertaining.

He was a Fae man, having lived hundreds of years of a life I couldn't even fathom. The chance that we settled down like a typical, happy couple was inconceivably low. Yet ...

"Did you hear me, Cat?" came Fen's voice, penetrating my tormented thoughts.

"What? I'm so sorry. I guess I zoned out."

"Nothing to be sorry about. You have a lot on your mind. I just asked how things were with your mother," he said cautiously as we walked along the sidewalk toward the center of town. The day was overcast but not unpleasant. There was no threat of rain, and the temperature was relatively comfortable—the perfect day for a walk.

"Not much has changed. I rented an apartment and can move in two weeks. I also found a new job that I'll start about that same time. I haven't told my mom yet, and I don't want to think about how she'll react when I do. To tell you the truth, I'd rather not talk about any of it. I'd much rather hear about you instead," I suggested softly.

"You will have to be more specific. Not that I am all that entertaining, but I would not know where to begin."

"Okayyy. I do have something I was wondering about, but I don't want to upset you if it's a sensitive subject." I glanced at him beside me, and he gave me a wary but encouraging nod. "I was wondering how is it you're still immortal if you don't have magic anymore?"

His eyes lifted to the trees above us as he breathed deeply. "I debated about that a great deal in the early years. Would I begin to age? Would I heal if gravely wounded? The aging question was only answered with time, and my healing ability was put to the test on a number of occasions when my hunting skills proved less than stealthy. I did not heal as quickly as I had before my exile, nor was my healing as drawn out as a human's. I attributed my continued immortality to two possible sources. Either the Fae retain a latent amount of magic, or my ability was owed to the magic found in the land itself."

His answer was contemplative, even clinical in nature, considering the subject matter was his life expectancy.

"So if your immortality was owed to the land, and now you're here on Earth with less magic than in Faery, would you become mortal?" I asked the question quietly to prevent others from hearing and because the subject itself was a delicate matter. I hoped the subject wouldn't upset him.

He nudged my shoulder with his and gave a tight smile. "I cannot return to Faery, so there is little I could do about it even if I did become mortal. Either way, I do not believe that will be a problem, nor am I one to borrow troubles."

His comment had effectively ended the conversation. Even though I still had more questions, I kept them to myself for the time being. We walked the following few blocks in silence, each lost in our own thoughts until I spotted a small brown terrier being walked by a young man on the opposite side of the street. Its little legs raced to keep pace with its owner, and I giggled at the sight. "What an adorable puppy," I said wistfully.

Fen eyed the scraggly-haired dog with confusion as we passed. "When I lived on Earth before, the dogs were much larger and more wolf-like. They were used for hunting and protecting livestock. What is the purpose of such a tiny animal?"

"It's a pet. We keep dogs and cats and a number of other animals, almost like members of the family," I explained.

"Do you have a pet?" he asked curiously.

"No, although I always wanted one. My mom never

wanted the fur in the house. Do they not keep pets in Faery?" I asked.

He glanced at me coyly. "The animals of Faery are not something you want to bring into your home on purpose."

"Well, that's intriguing and somewhat terrifying."

"No more intriguing than the things here on Earth."

"Like what?"

"Like that building," he said, pointing toward the local bus station. "I have seen those large, box-like vehicles before and often here at this location. What is its purpose?"

"Those are busses, and that's the bus station. Anyone can buy a ticket to ride on the bus if they don't have their own car. It's much too far to walk to other cities, or even from one side of a single city to the other, so busses are provided to get people where they want to go."

"Anyone can ride on these *busses?*" he asked appraisingly.

"Yes, so long as you pay for a ticket, but they're not expensive. The idea is that most anyone should be able to afford a bus ride."

He eyed the opposite side of the road where passengers loaded onto a departing bus. Yet another experience I saw from a new perspective because of my time with Fen. I loved being a part of his exploration, which was precisely why I had planned our morning outing.

When we reached our surprise destination, I stopped and held my arms out broadly. "Here we are!"

He glanced up at the kiosk and studied the brightly lit sign. "What is a 'cinema'?"

"It's like watching a program on television, only much

bigger. They show movies, and people pay to go watch the movie," I tried to explain.

Fen stared back at me blankly.

"Come on, you have to experience a movie at the theater at least once." I grabbed his hand and pulled him to the ticket booth. "Two for the ten o'clock showing of *Spider-Man*." I exchanged my money for the tickets and then pulled Fen inside the building. "I've wanted to see this one. It's a superhero movie with a love story—a little something for everyone. Come on, we need to get our seats so we don't miss the previews."

"Superhero? Previews? Sometimes I am not certain that we speak the same language," he said in bewilderment as I dragged him into the darkened theater.

A weekday matinee meant we had the theater to ourselves. We selected the perfect seats, though my gaze was primarily trained on Fen. The moment the lights dimmed and the first preview cued up, he went inhumanly still. The light from the screen reflected off his wide eyes, and I began to fear that I'd made a horrible mistake.

Just as I leaned in to tell him we didn't have to stay, a childlike grin pulled wide across his face. He watched the screen with pure, unadulterated wonderment. His joy was mine, and the smile he wore was just as rare and beautiful as a full double rainbow after a storm. It was a gift I wouldn't soon forget.

We watched several previews before Fen leaned in close. "Thank you for sharing this with me. It is much louder and more intense than I would want all the time, but it is also fascinating. I have never seen anything like it," he stage-whispered.

"The theater can be the perfect escape when you need a break from reality. I love going to the movies, and I'm really glad you like it."

Fen hooked his hand behind my neck and pulled my lips to his in a quick but passionate kiss. As we pulled apart, our eyes locked for a heated moment before we both turned back to the screen.

For the next two hours, we laughed and cheered, his hand never leaving mine.

CHAPTER

THIRTEEN

FENODREE

I HAD BEEN BACK ON EARTH FOR OVER A MONTH. WITH EACH added day, I took another step toward establishing a new normal for myself. However, a growing sense of foreboding undermined my ability to settle in completely.

When I first met Cat, a voice of reason whispered a silent warning to keep my distance from her. I broke down and ignored the dangers when Cat had come to me so upset. But like a tiny pebble nestled inside my shoe, the unease grew as time progressed.

My impending departure date neared.

I could not stay in Ireland forever. My current hiding place was too close to Belfast for me to stay for any real length of time. I knew how frequently the queen sent her scouts to keep tabs on the human world. It had been one of those scouts who had discovered my relationship with Hilde.

Leaving Ireland would mean leaving Cat. The mere suggestion made my temples ache with frustration. Had her subtle curves and full lips been the extent of the lure, leaving would not have been an issue. Her refreshing perspective on life, her resiliency and determination, and all the other remarkable qualities she possessed that presented a problem.

Gods be damned, I never should have allowed her to visit alone.

My reluctance to part from her was clawed at me incessantly. Not only did I want to be near her for my own selfish reasons, but I despised the thought of abandoning her when her relationship with her family was in such turmoil. I knew what it was like to be forced from those you loved. The coming months would be difficult, and I did not want to add my own departure to that burden.

Another voice, dark and selfish, slithered into the back of my subconscious.

Take her with you.

However, logic easily deflated that idea as soon as it formed. I was an exile on the run. Not only did I have nothing to offer but I was also a danger to anyone with me. As much as I wanted to entertain the suggestion, how could I ever justify bringing Cat with me? Nor would I have asked that she leave Rebecca and Ashley behind. Those women meant the world to Cat, and I would not ask that of her. During this time of estrangement from her family, it would be even more crucial that she be near her friends for support.

I could see no way around our separation, and the

realization made me feel hollow in ways even the Shadow Lands had not.

I tried to convince myself that Cat was not particularly special. I repeated it like a mantra, telling myself that any woman would have captured my interest after such a lengthy abstinence.

It was no use. I could not even pretend to buy into such a ludicrous assertion.

Not a single thing about Cat was ordinary.

Her looks were beyond stunning. Her thoughtful nature and devoted loyalty to her loved ones were defining qualities of her admirable character. The fortitude she had exhibited by rejecting her family's beliefs was evidence of her unusual strength of spirit. Even when strapped with burdens, Cat still found ways to appreciate the small beauties in life. Cat was remarkable in every way.

Knowing how much her mother had hurt her made me want to find the woman and pull out her intestines one inch at a time. She did not deserve to live if she could not appreciate her daughter's utter perfection.

If it was not for the fact that her death would hurt Cat, the woman would already be dead.

No matter how many times I analyzed the situation, I concluded that Cat would be best staying in Belfast with her friends and establishing a new life for herself. She was young and resilient. Once I was gone, she might be sad for a time, but she would quickly rebound. She was not the type to stay down for long.

The more I thought on the matter, the more confident I was about my next course of action.

Cat would not be pleased. I considered leaving before

her next visit so that we would not part after a fight, but I quickly realized that would be the coward's way. And the more I thought about it, the more clearly I saw my situation from Cat's perspective. By deciding what I thought was best for her, I would be doing exactly what her mother had done—deny Cat the right to choose for herself.

Who was I to think I had the right to steal her choices from her?

Cat deserved every freedom life on Earth could afford. As much as I would be torn over any decision she made, the choice would still be hers.

Stay here in Ireland with her friends or embrace a life on the run with me.

My head thunked back against the wall.

I had no idea what she would do, but I was man enough to accept the consequences of whatever she decided. The next time she came for a visit, I would present her with the options and hope to the gods that I did not regret either of our decisions.

CHAPTER

FOURTEEN

CAT

I'D HAD SUCH A GREAT DAY WITH FEN THAT I DIDN'T MAKE IT home until after dark. Aside from our walk and the movie, we sat in a park enjoying the afternoon before eating dinner at a local café. The day had been one of the best in my memory and had me smiling the entire way home.

Fen wasn't the type of man to be overly expressive, but it meant what he did show was one-hundred-percent genuine. Considering all the upheaval in my life, I was incredibly grateful for his honesty. That was not to say he didn't leave plenty unsaid. A man as complex as Fen wasn't going to share his every thought, but I never had to wonder if he truly meant what he said. If he said he enjoyed the movie, then he enjoyed the movie. He wasn't saying it just to make me feel good.

The same went for our kiss before I left Strabane.

His eyes had consumed me like I was the very air he breathed.

Fenodree cared for me, but I wasn't sure to what extent. The only thing I could be certain of was how hopelessly lost I was for him. I couldn't imagine my heart belonging to a more worthy individual, but that didn't negate the complicated nature of a relationship with him. Fen would have to leave at some point. What would happen then?

I wasn't ready to entertain the difficult possibilities, so I assured myself we still had plenty of time before a choice would need to be made. It was far easier to wrap myself in the warm memories of our stolen moments together than to face the harshness of reality.

By the time I got home, I had almost forgotten about my strained relationship with my mother. Not entirely forgotten, but enough to offer her a small smile when I walked into the house and found her sitting in the living room.

If I had thought we might put aside our differences for one night, I had been sorely mistaken. My olive branch was met with an arctic stare.

"Where've you been, Catronia?" Her words were velvet menace, instantly putting me on guard.

My mind raced, wondering just how much she knew. "I went to dinner with a friend after work. Why? What's wrong?" I forced myself to remain calm, hoping her question was merely a product of her overprotective instincts.

"Fergus called today, said you've been sick quite a bit lately and wanted to ask how you were feeling. You don't look sick to me, so tell me, Cat, where were you today?"

The cold steel in her voice sent a shiver of unease down my spine.

I had already known I would have to part ways with my mother, so her learning about my deception wouldn't change my plans. However, I had hoped I could make the separation as painless as possible by playing it off as the need for a young woman to go her own way in life. If she knew what I had been up to over the last month, she would never forgive me.

"I have a friend who's been in a rough spot lately, so I've been helping her out. I'm sorry I didn't tell you. She needed my help, and I didn't know what else to do." I gave a story as close to the truth as I could offer and hoped to infuse enough sincerity in my voice to assuage her suspicions.

"And this friend, she wouldn't happen to be Fae, would she?"

"No, but would it matter if she was?" A sliver of defensiveness crept into my voice.

Stepping around the corner from the kitchen, Daeglan O'Connor joined my mother across from me.

My hands tingled with nervous energy, and my stomach surged into my throat.

Daeglan wasn't a particularly large man, but the intensity in his eyes and harsh lines of his face made him an imposing figure. When his callous eyes met mine, every hair on the back of my neck stood on edge.

"It matters a great deal, Catronia," he offered in a tone meant to reassure but instead came off as condescending. "They're a vicious race of beings, and we don't want you getting hurt."

"*We?* Mom, why is he even here? He's one of the main reasons I don't want to tell you anything because I know you'll just go telling him like you did about the sword. You want me to trust you, then keep him out of our business."

A fissure of unease softened her features, her eyes pleading with me. "He's here because I don't know what else to do to make you see reason."

"*Reason?* You mean you want me to be an anti-Fae fanatic like him? Well, that's too bad because I refuse to hate them just because you tell me to."

Daeglan's eyes met my mother's, and they shared a silent communication that made me blisteringly angry. He was the reason Mom and I had grown apart, and I hated him for it.

When she looked back at me, there was an apology in those hazel eyes I knew so well.

I looked back and forth between them as a raging river of panic began to course through my veins. Something was about to happen, and every instinct I had screamed at me to *run.*

I glanced toward the front door but only got so far as a single step before Daeglan whispered the words to an enchantment. I slammed up against an invisible barrier, and my momentum instantly halted.

The edge of a fine circle of salt teased the tips of my toes, just out of reach. A trap. They had planned this before I'd even arrived, preparing a spell to contain me the second I didn't cower to their demands.

"Mom, what are you doing?" I breathed, mounting fear choking off my voice.

She turned to Daeglan, grasping his arm firmly. "Wait,

maybe she'll tell me the truth. I'm not sure this is necessary."

"Colleen, we talked about this. It's crucial we know just how deeply they have warped her mind," he responded firmly.

To my horror, my mother nodded in resigned acceptance.

"What are you talking about?" I hissed, pounding on the invisible barrier between us. "No one has warped my mind! You're *insane*!"

Daeglan approached, and to my surprise, he reached easily into my prison. He grabbed my wrists before breaking the salt barrier and yanked me toward the sofa.

I hollered out as he roughly shoved me down on my stomach, his knee pressed into the small of my back. With my hands bound behind me, I had no leverage to pose any physical challenge. The best I could do was strain and curse, hoping my mother would come to her senses.

"What the *fuck* are you doing? *Get off me!*"

He grunted with the effort to restrain me but kept the upper hand. "We may not have the Sword of Light, but we have other means of learning the truth."

The cold pinch of cuffs clamped around my wrists.

"Mom, please don't do this," I begged with a sob. My anger had begun to give way to desperation and gut-clenching fear.

I did not know these people.

My own mother was suddenly a stranger to me. The woman who had raised me never would have stood by idly while I was mistreated.

The swish of a switchblade being opened resounded in the room, and my racing heart stuttered in terror.

"What are you doing? Please don't do this. Momma, *please* make him stop!"

My cheek was smashed against the couch cushion with my head facing the room, giving me the perfect view of my mother. Hand over her mouth, eyes glassy, she stood motionless as Daeglan O'Connor began to slice into my forearm.

I cried out in pain, but he continued, unfazed.

"This is a truth rune, not unlike the one we wear on our necks," he said almost reverently as if he was a professor offering a lesson to eager students.

Burning pain seared up my arm as his blade etched the intricate lines into my flesh.

I no longer struggled as my muscles locked in a bone-chilling terror I had not known existed. Fear struck so deep in my heart that I no longer felt it beating.

"Cat, who were you with today?" Daeglan asked solemnly.

An excruciating silence filled the room, as if not one of us was breathing.

Magic stirred inside my chest, and I fought against its all-consuming compulsion. My lips quivered, and I choked on a sob from the frustration, but I was not strong enough. "Fenodree, I was with Fenodree."

Tears ran over the bridge of my nose and pooled on the sofa cushion.

"Is Fenodree Fae?" he continued the interrogation in an eerily calm voice.

"Yes," I whispered.

Then he paused briefly. "Is Fenodree a man?"

I closed my eyes as my lips moved of their own volition. "Yes."

How could my mother do this to me?

The betrayal of our bond.

The violation of my trust.

Regardless of her intentions, I could see no way to forgive her for her complicity in this assault.

I silently prayed for the questions to end. If there was a God, he wasn't listening.

"Do you have feelings for this man?"

Sobs wracked my body, both for my situation and for the danger my words might bring to Fen. "Yes," I whispered helplessly.

My mother released a pained sob and turned her back to where I lay.

"He's a good man," I pled with them frantically.

Daeglan grunted above me. "That's what they want you to believe. He's befriended you, but all he wants is to use you. Have you been intimate with this man?"

"*Yes*," I hissed with renewed anger. "But that's none of your goddamm business!"

"Don't you see, Cat? He's *feeding* from you. That's what they do. They lure humans in just to feed from our energy." Daeglan had lowered himself until his steely gray eyes met mine. His dark hair flopped over his forehead, and spittle sprayed my face from the force of his convictions.

I refused to offer them any unnecessary information about Fen or any of my friends, so I kept my mouth shut. Daeglan might have been able to force me to answer questions, but I didn't have to give him any more than that.

Seeing that he could not shake my resolve, he turned to my mother. "Colleen, you know this can't continue. It's worse than we ever imagined. Let me take her. Time away will do her a world of good to realign her priorities."

Let me take her.

I felt as though the devil himself had reached inside me and squeezed the air from my lungs.

The weight of Daeglan's knee on my back and the bloody rune on my skin no longer registered. I was no longer flesh and bone with nerves and feelings. I was pure, unadulterated terror because when I looked at my mother, resignation shone in her eyes.

With a single nod, she sealed my fate.

FIFTEEN

CAT

A BRIGHT LIGHT GLOWED THROUGH MY CLOSED EYELIDS, enraging my aching head. I lifted a sluggish hand to cover my eyes and tried to figure out what was going on. I was curled up on a cold concrete floor, and I felt like I'd fallen from a four-story building.

Had I gone out with friends and gotten so drunk I'd blacked out?

That didn't sound like me. I racked my brain but couldn't recall any parties or nightclubs in my recent past.

Despite my raging headache, I peeked my eyes open to see where I was and hopefully figure out what had happened. My surroundings were unfamiliar. Not that there was much to the small room—solid white with no windows and no furniture. I lay on a concrete floor, my teeth chattering with cold and unease.

Where the hell am I?

I sat upright to get my bearings and realized that I was wearing an unfamiliar thin cotton nightgown. A glance underneath told me I still had on my own panties, which was a small relief. As I examined the gown further, my eyes caught sight of an open wound on the underside of my forearm. A symbol carved in my skin, swollen and only partially scabbed over.

Flashes of memory assaulted me one after the other—my face pressed into the couch, a forced interrogation, a treacherous nod.

Rolling to the side, I vomited up what little I had in my stomach, retching even after nothing would come up.

Daeglan O'Connor had taken me.

He'd changed my clothes while I was unconscious. Had he done more while I was helpless?

Shivers wracked my entire body.

I sat against the wall with my knees pulled into my chest, desperately trying to get warmer. My throat was coarse with thirst, and I wondered how long I had been out. Even more frightening, how long would I be kept here? What did Daeglan have planned for me in this prison? Did my mom know where he had taken me? Was she with him? Would Rebecca or any of my friends be able to find me?

The deluge of questions raced through my mind and spurred my heart rate to a steady thrum. The blood pumping into my brain and warmth flooding into my limbs brought a surge of clarity.

What am I doing cowering against the wall like a lost child?

My jaw clenched with mounting anger. The melee of

emotions competing for dominance inside me bowed obediently as rage took control.

There's a door here, and you haven't even tried *to open it.*

I chided myself that Rebecca never would have been so pathetic. I scrambled to the door and confirmed that it was securely locked.

I gathered as much spit in my mouth as I could muster and spat it onto my open palm. Dipping my right pointer finger into the glob, I used the moisture to draw the rune for 'open' on the back of the door. As soon as it was complete, I tried the handle again with no luck. "Why isn't it working?" I hissed to myself. I screwed my eyes shut and whispered a chanted incantation, hoping it might give power to the magical symbol. Just as before, the door remained locked.

I pounded my fists against the thick wood. "*Daeglan!* You can't keep me here! This is *kidnapping*—my friends will come looking for me." I hollered until my throat burned with strain.

When I stopped for air, I heard the distinct tread of footsteps on the stairs. I stepped back from the door, a trickle of fear diluting my concentrated anger. But as Daeglan entered the room and my eyes landed on the face I hated with a passion, my fury returned full throttle.

I braced my legs and used both hands to swiftly draw out an elemental wind rune in the air before me. When I swept my hands forward to send the power of the rune toward Daeglan, nothing happened. I frantically pressed forward again and again, but the blast of air I had expected to summon never appeared.

"Calm down, Cat. Your runes won't work in here."

Daeglan stepped inside the room and closed the door behind him.

Of course. I should have known he would have warded the room again magic.

"Where did you take me?" I skittered away from him when he walked past and placed a yellow bucket in the corner of the room.

He painted a placating expression on his face and slowly ambled back toward the door, hands clasped behind his back. "Where is not important. It's the why that matters. You're here for your own good. The length and condition of your stay will be entirely up to you. As you've probably guessed, the room is warded against the use of magic. Although, as the creator of the ward, I am exempt from its power."

"You can't just keep me here. People will notice I'm missing."

"That's been taken care of, so don't expect some grand rescue. Those *people* you were associating with don't care about you. You aren't like them, and they aren't going to risk themselves to save you. That is why it's so important for us to remind you that *family is everything*. Your priorities have become skewed, and we're going to realign them." He stood within arm's reach but made no attempt to get any closer.

"Family doesn't kidnap you," I bit out insolently.

Daeglan just smirked. "Soon enough, you'll understand."

A bolt of panic rocketed through me when he turned for the door.

"*Wait!* I need water and a bathroom," I pleaded, desperation pitching my voice high.

He peered at me over his shoulder. "I've given you everything you need for the moment." His head tilted toward the corner of the room where the yellow bucket sat.

My brows drew together harshly. "You can't be serious." I gaped at him.

Daeglan raised a single brow and closed the door without another word.

Moments after he left, as I stood stunned in the middle of my prison cell, a musical chant filled the room. The sound wasn't altogether unpleasant, but the volume was just slightly above what I would have considered comfortable, especially considering my head still ached from whatever he'd used to knock me out.

Is this really happening? Am I stuck in some kind of nightmare?

I was never a fan of Alice and her Wonderland, but how else did I explain what I was experiencing? These things didn't happen outside the movies. Why would my own family kidnap me? To keep me from the Fae? The only way that made sense was if they meant to keep me there forever because I would just go back to my friends as soon as I left this place.

The whole situation was baffling.

My mother might have agreed to send me off, but she wouldn't allow Daeglan to keep me here for long. I was certain of it. In the meantime, if Daeglan wanted me to squat in a bucket and listen to loud music, I could do that.

He wasn't going to get to me that easily.

I stomped over to the bucket and hovered as I relieved my aching bladder. Of course, it wasn't until after I'd gone that I realized he never brought me any toilet paper. Spitting out a litany of curses, I chose to use my gown to dab myself dry rather than letting the drips of urine run down my leg. The worst part was the smell. Even if I could have ignored the damp patch on my gown, there was no escaping the acrid scent of urine in the small ten-by-ten room. I had needed to go, but now I wished I'd held my bladder just a bit longer.

Returning to my place on the floor where I'd initially woken up, I listened to the music. I couldn't make out the words being chanted, but after minutes stretched into hours, it was clear that I was listening to the same song on repeat. The repetitive chanting was enough to lull me into the first stages of sleep until the volume spiked and the lights in the room strobed blindingly.

The first time it happened, I nearly jumped out of my skin. After several rounds of being jarred awake from the explosion of light and sound, I became rabid with anger.

I paced the room like a feral tiger, talking to myself and occasionally screaming out to my captor. I pounded on the door and yelled threats at my absent jailer. It didn't matter if I lay down or paced, yelled, or remained quiet, the product was the same. I was trapped in a living hell.

Endless hours passed without food or water.

My body tired from the lack of sustenance, but my battered senses could not allow me the escape of sleep. I finally ceased my pacing and lay on the floor with my back against the wall, eyes staring at the tiny debris on the concrete. I had no idea how long I'd been unconscious after he took me, but I guessed it had been close to twenty-four hours since I'd woken up. I likely had been without food or water for close to two days, considering my belly's hollow ache and parched throat. Even my eyes burned from a lack of tears.

As the warmth leached from my body into the concrete, the bitter chill of the room seeped into my bones.

When I was young, and my nana was still alive, she used to moan about her joints aching when the weather would turn. As a child, I couldn't comprehend her complaints, but sitting on the frozen concrete in my thin cotton gown, I began to understand her pain.

I knew I would generate body heat if I moved, but I had no energy to make the effort. I desperately wanted to sleep through the discomfort, but the barrage of changing lights and sounds denied me even the tiniest reprieve.

Why is he doing this? How long can I take this torture? Will I make it out of this room alive? Will I ever see Fen again?

Fen—the man who had survived hundreds of years of harsh conditions.

My heart broke for him all over again. What inconceivable hardships had he endured throughout his exile? If he could survive his trials, I would survive mine. I would not give up, even if just for him.

I resorted to what had worked so well for me back home when my worries weighed me down. I submerged myself in the memories of my times with Fen. If I couldn't escape physically, I would do so mentally. I relived his kisses and our walks, our discussions of books and our shared meals.

It was with Fen in mind that my body finally succumbed to the relentless exhaustion.

Daeglan's return to the room stirred me reluctantly from the blissful numbness of slumber. While I was able to catch a few hours of sleep, it wasn't nearly as much as my body required. I felt like I could sleep forever. My eyelids were sandpaper scraping across my irises. My lips were similarly chapped to the point of cracking, and my tongue stuck to the roof of my mouth.

I made no effort to raise myself from where I lay on the floor until I noticed the bottle of crystal-clear water he held in his hand. The sight sharpened my muted senses, and I realized that the music had stopped. I sat up and stared longingly at the precious water he dangled carelessly in his hands.

Daeglan wore different clothes than he had on his last visit, which was different from the day he'd taken me.

Two days? Does that mean I've been gone for two days?

I hardly had the energy to process the implications and instead focused on the man who held my life in his hands.

"Water, please," I croaked weakly.

He squatted down to where I sat and stroked a hand gently along my hair. "You can drink, but you must earn it."

My stomach twisted with revulsion as I dared to wonder what I would need to do to earn my water. "Please, I just need a drink."

"It's nothing onerous. I have no desire to hurt you. All you must do is tell me why you're here," he encouraged.

"You kidnapped me."

He tilted his head chidingly. "Cat, why are you here?"

What answer was he looking for? Goddammit, I need water, and he's playing games?

My mind fuzzy and my emotions still roiling, I lunged for the bottle. Just as my fingers touched the cool plastic, the back of Daeglan's hand slammed across my face, sending me careening to the floor.

"Please don't make me hurt you, Cat. You must learn that *family is everything,* and I am only doing what's best for you." He reached down to caress my head, where I lay sobbing at his feet. "I see you're upset. We can try this again later."

I whipped around at the loss of his touch, clamoring for his retreating feet. "*No*! Please, don't go. I'm so thirsty, *please...*" I cast my eyes down, grasping his hand in mine without care for anything but my desperate need for water. At that moment, my dignity and the injustice of my situation were inconsequential.

Daeglan lowered himself back down to squat beside me, and with two fingers, he lifted my chin so that our eyes met. "You must not waste my time," he said in a gently warning tone, and I was surprised at how guilty I felt at his words. "I will ask you one more time. Why are you here?"

I closed my eyes and wept silent, tearless sobs.

He gave me a minute to collect myself, and when I reopened my eyes, I told him what I suspected he wanted to hear. "Because I befriended the Fae."

Daeglan smiled warmly, and my veins buzzed with excitement that I had given him the right answer. "That's a good girl." He brought the water bottle up between us, and I lifted my shaking hand to take hold of it but was quickly admonished. "No, no. Let me do it."

I didn't care if I licked the water off the ground so long as I could wet my parched throat. He raised the bottle to my lips and let me have three swallows of the delicious liquid before pulling the bottle back.

"Please, I need more. I'm still so thirsty," I begged worriedly, afraid the small drink was all I would be allowed.

He held up a single finger to silence me. "Why is befriending the Fae wrong?"

"Because they're dangerous."

We both knew I didn't believe my words, but if that's what it took to get water, I'd tell him the sky was pink and pigs could fly.

Again, I was rewarded with a series of swallows.

"Who is your family?"

"My mother." Another drink.

"And who else?" he asked with a raised brow.

"The Druids." My answer was on the verge of being a question of its own, but I was nonetheless rewarded with more water.

I had downed a majority of the bottle before Daeglan pulled it away. "That wasn't so hard, was it?" he chided softly.

I wiped a stray drip with the back of my hand but otherwise gave no response, my eyes staying glued to the bottle and its remaining contents.

"Not too much. We don't want to upset your stomach."

His words reminded me that water was not the only thing I needed. "What about food? I'm very hungry, too."

"The rules are the rules, Cat." With his non-answer, my jailer stood and left me alone in my cell again.

My thirst had not been completely sated, but the much-needed water in my belly allowed my body and mind to lower its panic level. Aside from being back-handed, I wasn't in terrible shape. He hadn't violated me or beaten me severely. I was given water and was not left in the elements.

My confidence levels rebounded, and I assured myself that I could make it through this. Rebecca would come looking for me, or I would find a way to escape.

One way or another, I would get out.

As if triggered by my rebellious thoughts, the room filled with the recording of a woman's voice. It would seem I had graduated from chanting and was now to suffer through an endless lecture. Her monotone voice droned on for hours, repeating a speech about the importance of family and the danger of outsiders.

I curled up on my side against the wall, but just as before, the moment I started to drift off, the room would erupt in a cacophony of screeching noises and flashing lights.

Hours into the onslaught, I gave in to my tears yet again.

How long will this go on?

I couldn't imagine my mind could take the torture for days, let alone for weeks on end.

My faith that I would find a way out suddenly seemed

foolhardy. I grappled for that sense of confidence that only hours before had come so naturally, just to come up short.

Instead of being dragged into the quicksand of hopelessness, I returned to my thoughts of Fen. For hours, I relived our time together, and when I ran out of memories, I created new ones. Before long, the daydreams began to feel real. I struggled to recall which scenes in my head had actually happened and which were fantasy.

Then I realized that I didn't care and surrendered myself to my imagination.

CHAPTER

SIXTEEN

CAT

Stabbing hunger pangs radiated from my stomach, drawing me yet again from sleep. As if that wasn't bad enough, I needed to pee again, too. I tried to tell myself it was a good thing—urine meant my organs were working—but adding to the stench in my cell sounded revolting.

After much deliberation, I decided that maybe emptying my bladder would help ease the ache in my belly. It would be a distraction at the very least.

I dragged myself to the yellow bucket and squatted as best as I could on shaking legs. Unable to hold myself, my legs slowly lowered me until I balanced precariously on top of the bucket. There was still no toilet paper, so I dabbed myself dry and returned to my spot against the wall.

The room was eerily silent and notably warmer than it had been, but I wasn't about to question my good fortune.

I closed my eyes and quickly began to drift until the opening door caught my attention.

Daeglan had returned.

He carried a wood chair to the center of my room and sat. He wore different clothes, yet again, and I wondered if it was a new day or if he was playing with my mind.

Could I tell the difference? Does it matter?

I made no move to acknowledge him. He was only a few feet away, holding a ball in his fist.

Wait—not a ball.

My stomach growled out ravenously at the heavenly scent of bread. Daeglan had a dinner roll in his hand.

My muddled thoughts sharpened with laser-like focus. Saliva pooled in my mouth, and I lifted myself up to sit cross-legged before him, eyes glued to the roll.

"Come just a bit closer, Cat." He motioned with the roll, and like a dog on a leash, I scooted myself to sit just inches from his legs. "That's good. First, we need to clean up your arm."

I placed my arm with the truth rune carving into his outstretched hand. I tried to behave so as not to risk being denied, but I was so desperate that sitting still was a challenge.

Daeglan pulled a tube of ointment from his pocket.

A hiss slipped passed my lips at the sting from the cream, but I didn't pull away. If I did exactly as he asked, I'd get to eat. My body felt hollow and weak, and I was ashamed to think of what I would be willing to do for that roll.

When he was done, Daeglan pinched off a piece of bread and held it just out of my reach. "Family is everything," he said clearly before giving me an expectant look.

Family is everything.

Where had I heard that before? And then it hit me ... Aileen. She hadn't wanted me to lie to my mother, but when I said that we were family, she agreed and commented that family was everything. Such a benign statement, but taken together with her odd behavior in recent years, I had to wonder if I wasn't Daeglan's first victim.

How many others had there been?

My already aching belly clenched painfully, drawing me back to the bread in Daeglan's outstretched hand. I swallowed the excess saliva, along with my pride.

"Family is everything," I repeated mechanically.

I wanted desperately to deny him the compliant behavior his torture was designed to elicit, but I couldn't. My mind was stretched thin with lack of sleep, unable to overrule the demands of my starving body.

Daeglan grinned at me proudly and placed the bread in my open mouth like a bird feeding its hatchling.

The roll was not particularly special, but to my starving mouth, it tasted like the finest fare. I practically swallowed without a single chew and held open my mouth in hopes of another bite.

He held up his next offering and lifted his chin in wait.

"Family is everything," I responded in automaton fashion.

Again, I was rewarded.

He fed me bread, and I fed him words until the roll was gone.

I was so relieved to have something in my belly that my guilt at complying was lost in the recesses of my mind. It would have been more worthwhile had the meal filled me, but the small morsel had only whetted my appetite. My eyes scanned his hands and pockets for any sign of a second course but came up empty.

"That's all for now. Remember, I will always provide what you need. At the moment, you don't *need* any more food," he explained as he sat tall in the chair. "From now on, there will be rules you must follow. For every question you ask, the temperature in your room will be lowered for twenty-four hours."

"What?" I gasped out in astonishment.

His lips pursed, and he glowered down at me with disappointment. "That's one," he said in warning.

Now that I'd had food and a tiny bit of energy had seeped back into my ragged body, my simmering anger returned.

I'm not allowed to question him? Who does he think he is?

I could envision myself scratching wildly at his stony eyes and sharp cheekbones, but I didn't move a muscle. He possessed all the power in the situation, and I wasn't about to make things worse for myself. Instead, I bit down on the inside of my cheek as he continued.

"I'll bring you food and water. You'll eat as you have been instructed without hesitation or question. Three times a day, we will have meditative sessions together. Should you disobey me in any way, you will be punished. Do you understand?"

Meditative sessions? Again, I had to wonder if I had slipped into a rabbit hole and ended up in an alternate dimension. My mind was whirling with so many questions that I almost didn't notice Daeglan waiting for my response.

"Yes," I offered automatically.

He nodded and rose from the chair, making his way toward the door.

"Wait! Please, can I have some water before you go?" The words were out of my mouth before I realized what I'd done.

"That's two," he said without looking back. The door closed behind him, and the lock clicked into place.

How stupid could I be?

I felt like slapping myself for speaking without thinking first. The room wasn't as cold as it had been when I first arrived, but it certainly wasn't warm. How much would he lower the temperature? If I'd asked two questions, did that mean it would be lowered for forty-eight hours, or would he simply make it twice as cold? Regardless of the answer, I would be miserable either way.

Just as I suspected, the room temperature was noticeably cooler in a couple of hours. The chanting music had resumed, and I became so wretchedly tired that I feared my mind would fracture.

I found myself chanting in a trance along with the disembodied voices. The wordless sounds had no meaning, but I knew their rhythm by heart. I could see sounds in vibrant oranges and reds twisting and turning before me like the lens of a kaleidoscope.

My throat had already been dry, and after countless minutes, perhaps hours, of chanting, my voice faded to a hoarse whisper. Lost in the cadence of the song, my lips continued their wordless motion until Daeglan returned.

As he entered the room, it occurred to me that the chanting had stopped, although I could have sworn I still heard the chorus of voices in my head. I shook myself from my stupor and felt my chest shudder with a half-broken sob when I spotted the bottle of water in Daeglan's hand.

He brought the container to my cracked lips without the pretense of games, and I felt the sudden urge to hug the man. The sensation was overwhelming and disconcerting. I wasn't going to act on it, and I had no idea how to process it, so I pushed it to the back of my mind and tried to pretend it never happened.

He allowed me to drink nearly the entire bottle in a series of calculated sips.

Relief swelled in my chest like soda bubbles filling a glass, the foam threatening to overflow. The pressure was overpowering, and I had to fight back a sob with deep, steady breaths.

"It's time for your meditation." He glanced at the wall opposite the door, and I followed his gaze. Where there had been white plaster moments before now showed a projected image. I searched the opposite wall and then examined the ceiling where the end of a projector protruded beside one of the lights. The two were close enough that I hadn't noticed it before.

"Wha—" I clamped my lips shut, swallowing the question I'd nearly asked.

Daeglan lifted his chin but did not otherwise comment on my near slip. "You'll need to follow along with the video. It's a calisthenics routine. Normally, this would be an easy task, but I understand you won't be up for much yet, so we'll start slowly." He slipped his hand into his pocket, and the video began to play, sound filtering into the room.

I sat dazed for a moment glancing between the video and where Daeglan stood leaning against the door. My mind was suffering from the lack of food and sleep, making my thoughts sluggish at best.

"Cat, are you disobeying me?" he asked with a warning tone.

I scrambled to my feet in the center of the room, my head spinning with the sudden movement. I managed to stay upright as the darkness around the edges of my vision dispersed.

The video instructor was a middle-aged woman with a round face and a voice I might have said was patronizing had I not been in such great need of reassurance and affection. She encouraged me to squat as if I was about to sit in a chair, then stand and repeat.

As the video progressed, images of dead people would briefly flash on the screen, and a narrator would describe the manner of their deaths. Each of them had been killed by the Fae, or so they wanted me to believe. The video would then continue as if nothing had happened. The woman would direct me to a new pose to be held until the next picture appeared.

After what had to be nearly an hour, my atrophied muscles were close to complete fatigue, and I could hardly look at another image of a dead body.

Meditation, my arse. This was just another form of torture.

He wanted to break me, and that enraged me.

I wanted to go home. I wanted my mother, and that made me even angrier.

She let this happen to me. My mother had sentenced me to this hell.

I glanced back to where Daeglan stood idly, and all rational thought left me. All I knew at that moment was that he was the source of my pain. I had to stop him. I rushed at my captor and shoved him to the side as hard as I could before grasping for the door handle.

I had woefully misjudged my weakened state.

My shove had hardly set him off balance, and he was instantly back, blocking my exit.

"No, no, *please* let me go," I choked out with a sob.

"Cat," he admonished as he took hold of my shoulders and forcibly moved me away from the door. "I told you there would be consequences if you disobeyed." His head shook slowly back and forth before he released me and leaned down to take hold of the yellow bucket. "Privileges are only for those who deserve them. Hopefully, next time, you'll remember that lesson."

I gaped in stunned disbelief as he walked away, taking my toilet with him.

No, nonononono. This can't be happening. Where am I supposed to go to the bathroom?

So far, I'd only had to pee, but after eating the bread, it was only a matter of time before I'd need to do more than that. Was I supposed to just shit on the floor?

I had to hand it to him. He didn't have to beat me or say hateful things to bend me to his will.

Daeglan O'Connor was an expert at humiliation and manipulation.

I could only imagine that when he broke someone, they would be thoroughly shattered in a way no beating could ever achieve.

I could feel myself cracking.

Hairline fissures weaving their way through my psyche, and I'd only been in his hands for a matter of days.

Sliding down the wall, I collapsed into a heap on the floor. I listened to the woman lecture until I memorized her speech by heart. Eventually, the inevitable sensation of my bowels contracting drew me from my trance. I had assumed when the moment came that I would be humiliated to defecate on the floor. But as it turned out, I was too exhausted to muster any emotion at all.

I went to the corner of the room where my toilet bucket had been, for no reason other than habit. From the start, I had designated one of the walls perpendicular to the door as my sleeping space, and even though the size of the room did not allow for distinct areas, I considered the far corner as my toilet. Ingrained concepts of decency were hard to break. Logically, in such a small room, it didn't matter where I went to the bathroom. In my addled brain at that time, it only seemed right that I pooped as far from my bed as I could. The fact that my bed could have been any section of floor in the room was irrelevant.

I leaned my back into the corner and slid myself down until I was doing a wall sit. I didn't cry or clench my fists in anger. I did my business in a detached haze, then returned to my designated sleeping area. What ended up being more upsetting than the act itself was the fact that the smell made me hungry.

Thirst and hunger. My constant companions.

My only companions.

I'd never realized being alone could be so painful. Again, my heart broke for Fenodree. Thoughts of him were the only thing to break through my cocoon of numbness. But instead of the heartwarming comfort his image had previously summoned, now his memory evoked heart-wrenching sorrow and longing. Just the recollection of his face had me clutching my knees tighter into my chest to stave away the pain.

I SAT ALONE for so long.

At least, it felt like ages. I had no way of knowing.

The lecture stopped, and I slept. The chanting began, and I chanted.

I became a robot, a machine going through the proper motions.

Each hour that passed, the hairline cracks fragmenting my mind splintered and expanded like the surface of a frozen pond in spring.

By the time Daeglan returned, I was no longer sure I was the same person.

I made no effort to move from my spot against the wall. The only evidence that I was affected by his presence was the slightest flutter of my heartbeat.

For the first time since I'd arrived, Daeglan came to my side and sat on the floor with me.

I didn't turn my head toward him or acknowledge his presence except with a single whispered word. "*Please*."

He gently turned my face toward him and lifted a bottle of water to my lips.

When he pinched off a bite of bread between his fingers, I offered without prompting, "Family is everything."

Daeglan ran the back of his fingers down my cheek in a gentle caress before offering me more water. His barely-there touch felt like the warmest embrace, and I longed for the comfort it suggested. For several minutes, he fed me by hand and gave me water without a word between us, and the reprieve from my misery was a balm to my aching soul.

Gratitude bubbled up inside me. Gratitude to be fed, to quench my thirst, to be cared for.

The emotion expressed itself in a single tear down my cheek.

He softly swiped at the moisture with his thumb, and I leaned into his hand cupping my cheek. In a swift motion, Daeglan lifted me onto his lap and cradled me in his arms. I pressed my forehead into the crook of his neck and shed silent tears. Somewhere in the back of my mind, I knew that this man was the enemy, but I was too broken to care.

The comfort that he offered was all that mattered.

"You are an amazing creature, Catronia," he murmured into my hair. "I know you'll find your way home ... to your mother and to me. We can be a family together."

Together.

I should have wanted nothing to do with the man, but all I could focus on was that together was not alone.

OVER THE NEXT FEW DAYS, we developed a routine and, even more importantly, an understanding. My bucket was returned and replaced with a clean version at each visit. I did as I was asked, performed my meditations, and answered Daeglan's questions as I should. I gave him no reason to punish me, and I found I received water, regular bread rations, and a few hours of uninterrupted sleep. The intervals of sleep were not exactly regular nor were they frequent, but it was enough to prevent total exhaustion.

As some of my strength returned, I looked forward to Daeglan's company. The hours alone were maddening in a way I couldn't have expected. A simple touch or an exchange of words with my captor was the highlight of my days. I knew it was wrong, and I wanted to be strong, but I had trouble remembering why.

CHAPTER

SEVENTEEN

FENODREE

A FULL WEEK PASSED AFTER MY LAST VISIT FROM CAT WITHOUT A word from her. While she had not previously gone more than a week between visits, her life was much fuller than my own, and I was confident she would return as soon as she was able. Unlike her, my life consisted entirely of observing those around me. I had little to distract me, so thoughts of her were my only occupation. I found I missed her presence even more than I would have expected. That point became painfully clear when I opened my door to a knock and found Rebecca standing outside my room.

"Ouch! It's good to see you too, Fen," she said teasingly at the frown that had inadvertently tugged at my lips.

"Hello, Rebecca. I had thought when I heard the knock that it would be Cat," I tried to explain as she joined me inside my room.

With a glance back at me, she arched an insinuating

167

brow. If she had intended to scorn or tease me with her look, her efforts were futile. I had lived too long to care what anyone else thought of me.

My thoughts and actions were my own, and I would apologize for neither.

"It has been longer than normal since her last visit. Is she well?" I asked as we both sat at the small dining table.

"She's spending the month with family, according to Fergus. She has an aunt on the coast somewhere, and I guess her mom and her visit in the summers." Becca smiled brightly as she explained. She clearly had no reservations about Cat's whereabouts, so I tried to calm my overactive imagination. "You don't look convinced," she prodded.

I let out a sigh, something I rarely did anymore. The behavior was expressive rather than a necessary bodily function, and I had been broken of making any unnecessary noises in the Shadow Lands.

"She was having problems with her mother. I was simply concerned that her absence might be related to those issues." Plus, I was somewhat surprised she would have left on an extended trip without telling me on her last visit.

"She hadn't mentioned any trouble to me. What's going on?" she asked with genuine concern.

I explained Cat's marriage dilemma and described the arguments between her and her mother. My intuition whispered that something was not right, but there was no evidence that Cat was in actual danger nor that her time with me had played any role in her delayed visit.

It was more likely that I was projecting fears borne

from my own experiences. I had been forced to watch as Hilde was beheaded by the queen's guard. She died merely because she had loved the wrong man, and that guilt colored my perceptions. I was not sure I could support the burden of knowing I had played a role in harming yet another woman I cared for.

Rebecca listened earnestly to every word, her brows deeply creased. "She never said anything to me about her mother or marriage. I knew her mom was strict, but telling Cat who she can marry is a whole other level of crazy. Not that arranged marriages don't happen, but I didn't peg them as the type. Hopefully, she and her mom just went away to spend some quality time together to talk things out, but I'll try to check on her."

"I would appreciate that, thank you." I bowed deeply and considered how my fortunes had changed since Rebecca appeared in my life. Before her arrival, I had believed my life in the Shadow Lands to be fulfilling. I prided myself on my survival skills and ability to adapt. However, the reintroduction of friendship into my life had made me suspect that all those years in Faery, I had simply been coping rather than living.

When Rebecca and Lochlan had gone home after their stay with me, I knew something was missing. Not even a successful hunt gave me the satisfaction it once did. I tried to ignore the niggling disquiet I felt, but it was there with me, always. I preferred not to think about what I would have done in response to the hollow feeling had Rebecca not returned for me.

I'd spent hundreds of years on my own, yet one small taste of companionship had rocked my foundations to the core. Even more significantly, my time with Cat had given me something I had not even realized I was missing—a purpose. Before, my life had been purely about survival, but what had been the reason to continue surviving? An existence without any impact on the world around me would hardly have been any life at all.

While I had no other options, I had convinced myself that surviving was enough. Now, I realized that believing survival had been enough was itself a product of my survival. It had merely been another technique I had used to get through until my life could begin again.

Looking forward to each of Cat's visits and knowing I could bring a smile to her face or comfort her gave me a purpose for being. Even the most solitary humans will keep dogs or cats to reinforce their sense of purpose—someone to provide for, share experiences with, and care for. That was the true foundation of a fulfilling life.

Personal, intimate connections were a vital element of living ... of thriving.

Some men saw wealth or power as their purpose, but those things were merely the tools used to draw people to them, to give them a reason to be wanted. Strip away the societal expectations and overdeveloped ego, and each of us would find that there was only one thing that mattered.

Our purpose for living.

Each man's purpose might be different, but it was always essential to finding fulfillment. I had begun to get a taste for my purpose, and no matter how unlikely it seemed, all signs pointed at a certain redheaded woman who beguiled my every sense.

When I was around her, I could not get close enough. I

wanted the feel of her soft body against mine, her honeyed taste on my lips, and the light that lit up her face when her eyes met mine. When we were apart, my mind constantly turned to thoughts of her—what she was doing, whether her family was being cruel, or whether another man might be pursuing her. I counted the minutes until I might see her again when I could be reassured of her safety and happiness.

In my younger years, adventure had called to me, but Hilde had been the reason for my aimless wandering. The moment I laid eyes on her, nothing else mattered. She had been my purpose. Lifetimes had passed since those days, and I was no longer the same man, but I recalled the sensation well.

I had a new purpose in life, and her name was Cat.

CHAPTER

EIGHTEEN

CAT

I knew I should sleep at every opportunity I was given, but I had so little time for my own thoughts that I lay awake under the lights amidst the endless chanting. It was surprising how thoroughly Daeglan could fill my time while I was stuck in a prison cell for twenty-four hours a day. Between lectures, lessons, meditations, and sleep, I hardly had the time or mental energy to think.

The best I could tell, I had been with Daeglan for at least a week. I had rebounded somewhat with food and rest, but he still kept me balanced on the edge of that cliff. One misstep and I was punished, my haggard state compounding the effects of those punishments.

My feelings toward Daeglan changed like the winds. One minute, I hated him with a fiery passion, and the next, I would watch the door handle in anticipation of his presence. Had I not been aware of the drastic changes in

172

my perspectives, I would have said I was becoming schiz-ophrenic. As it was, I recognized when the pendulum swung, but I could do nothing about it.

The days bled together as one discomfort morphed into another. With each hour, my hope for escape waned. At times, my outlook was downright bleak. Doubts that I would ever be free seeped into my mind. As much as I fought them, they still took root like an insidious virus infecting my thoughts.

As I lay on the floor, cheek against the smooth concrete, I battled those doubts. I came back to Daeglan's claims that Fen had used me to feed his magic. Fen had said he'd lost his magic because of his inability to feed while in the Shadow Lands. I had seen no evidence to suggest he had regained his powers during my time with him. Would he have kept that from me?

Trust me, that was for me just as much as it was for you.

I recalled the words he'd spoken after giving me an orgasm, analyzing them from a new perspective. Could he have meant my orgasm fed his magic? Was that what he'd gained from our intimacy? Would I have known if he'd fed from me? If he did feed from me, was that all I was to him?

The ugly thoughts weighed heavily on my chest.

If I couldn't even trust my own mother, what made me think I could trust anyone else? Was anyone even looking for me? Rebecca and Ashley and the Huntsmen—did they wonder where I'd gone? Or were they too busy with their own lives to notice my disappearance?

Then a startling realization came to me.

This was their fault.

Had I never befriended them, I never would have

ended up in this room. They were off enjoying their freedom while I lay broken on a cold basement floor.

Before I could rid myself of the dangerous train of thought, a voice whispered in my mind.

I wish I'd never met any of them.

THE NEXT TIME I woke, Daeglan was entering the room. He carried a blue foam pad the size of a beach towel and a yellow quilted blanket. My heart thrummed with excitement at the prospect that these things were for me.

Please, please, Lord, let these things be for me.

I hurried to my feet and offered a hopeful smile to Daeglan.

"Hello, sweet girl. You have been doing so well that you've earned a reward. However, you must remember to keep the blanket folded when not in use. Those are the rules." He gave me a pointed look, and I nodded vigorously to reassure him I would do everything he asked. A blanket would be a godsend, and I couldn't imagine risking its removal.

"That's my girl. I know you won't let me down." After setting the bedding down where I typically slept, he wrapped an arm around my shoulder in a side hug.

The embrace caught me off guard. I had no idea what to think. All I knew was that the feeling of his touch was the best thing I'd felt in ages. I relaxed into him for the count of several deep breaths as he held me against him.

When he pulled away, the loss of warmth made my eyes sting with unshed tears. My emotions were even closer to the surface after wasting valuable time for sleep on pointless thinking. I was constantly on the verge of exhaustion.

"Daeglan, is there any way I could please have a little more time for sleep? I'm so terribly tired."

He pursed his lips and shook his head with disappointment. "Cat, you know the rules."

Stupid, stupid girl. What have I done?

I had done so well, even earning a reward. Then I went and threw it all away by asking a worthless question. "No, please. I'm *so* sorry, it's just that I'm so tired. I wasn't thinking straight." My voice cracked as I begged for forgiveness, but my words fell on deaf ears.

"The rules are the rules," he said.

I nodded, my eyes cast down as a trickle of tears broke free.

Daeglan walked toward the door, but to my surprise, he didn't leave. Instead, he brought a new bucket into the room, one that was heavy with its contents. "It's time for you to bathe. Remove your gown; you may leave your underwear," he instructed tonelessly.

An emotion shoved to the background of my mind made a sudden resurgence.

Fear.

During the prior week, I'd been good friends with anger and frustration, sadness and worry, hate and even relief. My emotions swirled in a constant maelstrom, but with the establishment of routine and structure, I had forgotten about fear.

Most of the tasks put forth by Daeglan were not terribly cumbersome, so there was little struggle convincing myself to comply. This new demand made me terribly uncomfortable, but I did not want to risk punishment by disobeying. I had already earned one punishment since he arrived. Would I lose the new gift of bedding if I refused him?

With trembling hands, I lifted my gown over my head.

Goose bumps perched on my exposed skin, and my shoulders curved inward as I crossed my arms over my naked breasts. I made no attempt to lift the sponge from inside the bucket. I had not been instructed to do so, and taking it without permission would be breaking the rules.

"Very good, Cat. Perhaps, if your bathing continues to go well, I might overlook your slip from earlier."

I lifted my questioning eyes to his but could read little in their depths.

We stood in the middle of the room by a small drain. Daeglan wrung out the sponge and began to wipe me clean, starting with my arms and back. The water was deliciously warm, and the sponge was soft as it swept over my neglected body. He was thorough in his task, removing the grime with firm but tender strokes.

I wanted to know why I couldn't bathe myself, but there was no way I would ask the question.

A part of me wanted to shut off my mind from his touch. I was ashamed to admit just how good his ministrations felt. I should have been repulsed but couldn't muster the emotion. Instead, I felt gratitude. In order to enjoy the attention without the accompanying guilt, I imagined it was Fen tending to me—Fen's strong hands lifting my hair from off my neck and wiping down my shoulders. Fen's stoic strength caring for me and keeping me safe.

The delusion almost worked when I kept my eyes tightly pinched shut. But the moment my arms were pulled to my sides, my eyes flew open, and I was confronted with the ugly truth. It was not Fen's warm eyes gazing down at me. Not his hands on my body. Instead, I met Daeglan's clinical gray eyes with a muffled sob.

"Cat, I've told you before, I have no desire to hurt you. That means intimately as well, so you need not fear me. This is no different from when your mother bathed you as a child. We are *family*." His stare was more intense than I'd seen in some time, but it did little to ease the horror of the situation.

I nodded obediently as he continued with his task.

This time, I kept my eyes open.

Having Fen with me, just to have him ripped away, was more painful than simply persevering. I would have to stop seeking out his image if I was going to survive this ordeal.

Daeglan was true to his word and did not touch me in my private areas, but that did not mean the experience was any less traumatizing. I was a grown woman stripped of every freedom. I was given no choices and no right to independent thought. My body was not even my own.

CHAPTER

NINETEEN

CAT

I couldn't fathom how long I'd been down there—ten days? Two weeks? More? It felt like it could have been months, but that wasn't right. I had no way of knowing an exact length of time, and something about that uncertainty added to my mania.

My mind battled against itself at every opportunity. I was two people fighting for control of one body, and I was no longer sure who was the real me.

The warrior inside me grew more feral every day, raging about finding a way to escape. When she ran the show, we were disobedient and belligerent. Punishment always followed, and it only fueled her fury.

The survivor insisted that we must comply with Daeglan's demands if we were to tolerate our time there. At first, the survivor was given free rein under the pretense that I would soon be rescued. I had told myself that I only had to get by until help arrived. The warrior insisted that was not the best course of action. More and more, I was inclined to believe her.

The two voices quarreled incessantly.

If I didn't get free soon, I feared I might lose myself permanently. It terrified me.

I was my only hope, and hope would be my greatest asset.

Without hope, I had nothing.

WHEN DAEGLAN ARRIVED for my next ration of bread, my warrior was firmly at the helm. Despite her hostility, she remained calm and calculating as he entered the room. She grasped the importance of a well-planned attack and how failed attempts only left us weaker than before.

Daeglan provided us with only as much bread as we needed to keep us functional and no more. Our bones began to protrude from sallow skin. Even with the sleeping pad we'd been given, sleeping on our side was uncomfortable because our insides felt hollow. As often as we could, we slept upright against the wall, knees pulled into our chest to ease the empty ache in our belly.

This feeding was like all the others. We ate out of his hand like a household pet, reciting his teachings on command. He had made us into his bitch—a dog trained to eat, sleep, and shit when instructed.

My warrior seethed with barely contained rage.

When Daeglan brought the bathing bucket into the

room, my warrior went silent as she quickly constructed a plan.

"*This*," she cooed in a purring whisper, "*may be our best chance.*"

My survivor was nowhere to be heard, relegated to the recesses of my mind.

Pleased to be of one mind for a change, I let myself fully become the warrior.

I squared my shoulders as I removed my soiled gown, unbothered by my nudity. Let him see my flesh. It was not who I was inside.

"I'm so glad to see you are becoming more comfortable with me. You've been doing very well, Cat. I've spoken with your mother, and she may come to visit if you continue to progress." He wrung out the sponge and began scrubbing my shoulders and back as I stood perfectly still in the middle of the room.

Had he not been so consumed with his inappropriate activities, he might have questioned the unusual steadiness of my hands.

The warrior suffered no nerves or anxiety; she was confident in our abilities.

I'd had more sleep and food the prior day than I'd had since arriving, although I was sure it would not be reflected in my appearance.

Daeglan's pointless scrubbing would do little to improve my condition, but cleanliness had little to do with his bathing me. The entire charade was just another power play.

He was a worthy opponent. I would grant him that.

He had taken into account the tiniest of details—from

the size of the room to the pure white walls, his frequency of feedings, the low-level nutrients he provided, his carefully measured words, and his application of comfort at pivotal moments.

He was a master tactician.

And I was a merciless warrior who would fight him until the end.

The only sound in the small room was the dripping of water and the swishing noise the sponge made as it brushed across my skin. My nostrils flared on a deep exhale as Daeglan lowered himself to wipe my legs. He may not have been aroused by my body, but I knew his power over me excited him in a perverse way. Whether it was ego, or something much darker, Daeglan relished his ability to crush the human spirit.

His disgusting proclivities fanned the flames of my rage, making my fists clench until my ragged nails dug into my palms. Almost as bad as his actions was the fact that he fully believed what he was doing was right. His twisted mind was warped enough to think he was helping me. Me and how many others? If I didn't stop him, how many more would follow?

I waited patiently for him to inch his way around until he was in the perfect position. Lost in his perverted fantasies, he never noticed me eye the bucket's handle. With speed faster than I thought myself capable, I whipped my hand out and grasped the handle. Swinging myself in a full circle, I flung the water-filled container in a wide arc toward his head like an Olympic hammer throw. I loosed a feral battle cry and felt a surge of ecstatic joy when the heavy bucket collided with his head.

Despite my limited strength, the well-placed blow sent my captor reeling backward. Without pause or hesitation, I released the bucket midair and darted for the door. Yet another success, it swung open, and I scrambled up the wooden steps.

Light peeked under the door to the basement, and I could almost taste my freedom. Almost. I was near the top when a strong hand clasped my ankle and yanked me viciously back down several steps as if I was nothing more than a doll.

I cried out in furious frustration, kicking and flailing with every ounce of energy I had left.

Daeglan towered over me, eyes feral and blood dripping down from a gash on his temple. "You're so strong, so *willful*. It's a good thing I love a challenge," he purred. He had me firmly trapped with my back painfully pressed against the steps, his face twisted in sick pleasure over the prospect of breaking me.

My breaths came in heaving pants as terror took control of my system.

"You've resisted my teachings so much longer than the others, but we have no deadline. We can stay here together as long as it takes." His lips pulled back in a sinister leer, and I knew I had lost.

Neither my warrior nor my survivor made a single peep.

Despite my best efforts, my escape attempt had failed. Now, I was more alone than ever, caged by the devil himself.

I had been defeated, and I wept for my loss.

What I did not realize at the time was that defeat was

just another word for hopelessness—the acceptance of a current state of being without expectation of improvement.

Defeat.

Conquer.

Vanquish.

They were all finite and absolute.

They left no room for exception.

For hope.

CHAPTER
TWENTY

CAT

Elizabeth Miller. Eighteen years of age. One of the latest in a spree of murders by a Fae known as a Fear-Gorda. Elizabeth worked at a local pub before she was brutally tormented to death. The Gorda forced Elizabeth to live out her worst nightmares, then fed from her terror, causing a complete adrenal failure...

The woman's voice continued with the list of atrocities committed by the Fae. Horrible, terrible things. For hours, most likely days, I'd listened to the account. Women. Men. Children. Victims of barbaric crimes.

If I could have wept for them, I would have.

But I couldn't.

I could no longer weep for anyone, including myself.

My punishment for attempting to escape had been severe, and it was all my fault. Bound in a wooden dining chair, naked and cold. I was a captive audience for the broadcast of Fae crimes played on an endless loop.

Gauging the passage of time was nearly impossible. Daeglan had entered on four occasions, each instance providing half a ration of bread and some water. I had not been allowed out of the chair once. For seemingly endless hours, I sat in a cold puddle of my own urine. Sores formed where my wrists and ankles had been tied to the chair, and every muscle ached from lack of movement.

How naïve I'd been in thinking my condition could not get worse.

Until I challenged his authority, Daeglan had allowed me a host of freedoms. It was amazing how little we appreciated the things we had until they were gone. And I only had myself to blame. Had I not broken the rules, I would have had a padded bed, a toilet, and the freedom to move about.

The only reason I was tied up was because I could not be trusted.

As Daeglan said, it was my choice how I was treated. If I acted in a manner worthy of trust and affection, I would receive it. It had been my own doing.

In those endless hours, I took what little comfort was available.

Rocking.

I rocked back and forth in the chair, just a few inches of movement, but it set me adrift to bob and float above the ocean of pain. I was an untethered buoy cast out into the far reaches of an angry sea. Its foaming fingers tried repeatedly to pull me under, but as long as I continued my rhythmic sway, I slipped free of its painful grasp.

As a buoy, I had no thoughts or feelings.

There was no Cat or Daeglan.

No Druids or Fae.

There were no teachings, no rules or rewards.

No dreams or fears.

On my ocean, there was only nothing.

I DID NOT SPEAK for several days after being released from my punishment. Not until I was instructed.

I had to start my re-education from the beginning, earning back each of my freedoms. This time, I walked through the process easily and without defiance.

I never would have believed I could have withstood so much for so long, but I had survived. At least some part of me survived. The experience had been transformative.

I was no longer the same, yet I was not something new.

I was amorphic. Without shape.

In the days after my punishment, I could feel myself testing the form of Daeglan's words, seeing how I might fit inside his mold. Without structure, my edges were blurry. I longed for the comfort of defined parameters. I used to have a shape, but I could not remember how to find it. There was only one place where I found peace, and I longed to return.

As I lay on the floor, eyes unseeing on the well-lit ceiling, I returned to drift on my ocean. The buzzing fluorescent lights faded away, and I could no longer hear the chanting voices around me. There was no cold concrete floor nor a foul-smelling bucket. Floating on my vast ocean, I entered a state of utter peace and disconnect.

I never wanted to leave.

But that was not in the cards for me.

A buzzing chatter disrupted my heavenly escape, and the solace of darkness started to fade.

No, don't go!

I could not hold on to it. Desperately, I grasped for the numbness, but instead, there was pain. My cheeks. My cheeks stung and burned.

Slowly, an image began to take form before me.

Eyes, stone-gray eyes. Daeglan.

I examined his face to find he was worried.

Why is he worried?

"Oh, Catronia. Thank *God* you're back." He lifted my limp body into his lap and held me as he rocked back and forth.

The rocking felt much like my ocean.

Being in Daeglan's arms was almost as good as my ocean. Warm and secure.

Daeglan had given me that.

His hand stroked my matted hair, and he softly whispered words of love and reassurance.

With Daeglan, I was no longer adrift.

I molded perfectly into his shape.

CHAPTER
TWENTY-ONE

FENODREE

THE NAGGING SENSE THAT SOMETHING BAD HAD HAPPENED TO Cat persisted until I could take no more. It had been three long weeks since I had seen her, and my hands twitched to be near her, to assure myself that she was safe.

Rebecca had come back and attempted to reassure me that Cat was with her mother; however, I could not cast aside the feeling that something was horribly wrong.

For hours, I paced the length of my room, debating what I might do or if I should do anything at all. In the end, I decided that I had spent too long relying on my instincts to ignore them now.

I needed to find Cat. In order to do that, I would need Rebecca's help. I thought briefly about using the phone to contact her but quickly banished the idea. Rebecca had attempted to reassure me twice that Cat was not in danger —if I was going to force the issue, I would need to do so in person. Plus, I was not the type to allow others to perform a task that was of vital importance to me. If Cat was last seen in Belfast, I would go to Belfast.

I set out the modern pack I had acquired and threw inside a change of clothes along with a few necessities I might need. There were still piles of clothes Rebecca had supplied me with left in the drawers, but I had no means to carry them nor the desire to take them with me. Once I was ready, I retrieved the card Rebecca had given me in the event I might need to find her.

The Ulster Museum, Belfast. Her place of employment. That would be my first stop.

It was midmorning when I arrived at the bus station. Cat had told me on one of her visits that it would take several hours to walk to Belfast. I did not have that sort of time. Despite my aversion to riding in modern vehicles, I would have to purchase a ride on a bus to get to Rebecca.

Urgency and apprehension crawled under my skin as I exchanged my money for a ticket and then waited for my assigned vehicle to arrive.

The inside of a bus was far less confining than a car. I still preferred horseback, but the freedom inside a bus was an acceptable compromise. A thin layer of clouds blanketed the sky, softening the daylight just enough to be gentle on the eyes. Several of my fellow passengers slept, but I was too anxious to rest.

Once we arrived, I asked the driver how I might get to the Ulster Museum. His instructions had been relatively simple, and I was relieved to find that in hardly any time at all, I stood before a large stone building with a sign in front reading *Ulster Museum*. On a normal day, I might have stopped to study the impressive structure, but Cat was too important to set aside for even a minute.

The young woman at the front desk summoned Rebecca. Within minutes, she was hurrying over to my side, her features drawn with alarm. "Fen, what are you doing here?" she hissed quietly. "Durin and Parisa are likely in town. You know what will happen if they see you." She grabbed my arm and dragged me inside a small room with poles lining the walls.

"Rebecca, you must listen to me. Something is wrong with Cat. I know she would not have left for this long without a word." I took hold of her arms in my firm grip to ensure she understood my urgency.

She chewed on her bottom lip and eventually nodded. "I know. Ashley had a vision last night that Cat was in danger. She hasn't been able to learn how to tell if a vision has already happened or when it might come to pass, so I have no idea of the timeline. I've tried to reach her all morning with no luck. Let me tell my boss I need to leave, and we'll go see what we can learn at her house."

I had thought reaching Rebecca might relieve some of my anxiety, but her news only multiplied my concern. Something terrible had happened, and I prayed we were not too late.

CHAPTER

TWENTY-TWO

FENODREE

"You wait in the car. I don't want you to be seen," Rebecca ordered as she opened the car door.

"I am coming with you. It is not up for discussion," I responded curtly.

Rebecca glowered at me over the top of the vehicle but said nothing further. We both walked up the path to a small single-family home in need of repair. From what we could see through the front window, the house was well cared for on the inside.

Rebecca rang the doorbell and knocked, but no one came to the door. She looked helplessly at me as if we were out of options, but I was not about to let a trivial lock keep me from finding Cat. I moved Rebecca aside and slammed my shoulder into the door, which gave easily in its old rotted frame. My momentum carried me inside, where my eyes landed on a broken circle of salt near the entry, along with blood splattered on the wood floor not far away.

"Is that blood?" Rebecca asked in a hushed whisper, craning her neck to see around me.

I stepped over the salt to examine the rest of the house, Rebecca sticking close behind me. We cautiously examined each room, finding nothing else out of the ordinary until we reached Cat's room.

"Cat's purse," murmured Rebecca, eyes glued to the satchel bag set on the bed. "She wouldn't have left her purse. It's the only one she uses, and she takes it everywhere."

"I knew something was not right. It has been weeks, so it will be even harder to track her." My words were clipped with frustration, but the emotion would do me no good. I had to focus on finding Cat.

"When you first told me you were worried about her, I tried to reach her by dream walking but never got through. I don't know if she was too far away or if something was keeping me from reaching her. I hadn't tried to connect with her like that before and figured it may have just been her truth rune that prevented the magic."

One of Rebecca's unique gifts was the ability to pull another person's consciousness into a waking dream. It was exceptionally useful for communication purposes but had its limits. The variables were too numerous to pinpoint any reason for Rebecca's failed attempts.

"You did as much as anyone could," I assured her distractedly. "There is one remaining room. Once we have searched it, we can plan our next steps."

The final bedroom belonged to Cat's mother. It

contained no personal items, indicating the woman had taken her belongings.

Cat's mother had left intentionally, but had Cat gone with her?

"Here's what I suggest," said Rebecca after we had examined the entire house. "I say we go to Fergus and see what else he can tell us. He's a Druid, but he's one of the good ones. He might be able to help."

"I have no better ideas, so please, lead the way."

Rebecca drove us to a tall building containing numerous homes within, much like the hotel where I had been staying, except Fergus's home was much larger and more luxurious than my room had been.

"Rebecca, what a lovely surprise. Is everything all right?" A petite man with vibrant red hair opened the door in a flamboyant manner. His eyes roved from the top of my body down over every inch of me, a hungry gleam in his eye. "Where do you girls find such gorgeous specimen?"

Rebecca choked on a cough. "This is Fen; he's a friend of mine."

Ignoring his odd comment, I offered a polite nod as Rebecca rushed on with her explanation.

"I'm so sorry to stop by unannounced, but we're really worried about Cat. I know you said she was on a trip with her mom, but we stopped by her house to check on her and found disturbing evidence that Cat may be in danger."

"Whatever are you talking about?" Fergus asked, sobering as he ushered us into his home.

"There was a salt circle in the living room along with blood splatter," Rebecca explained.

"That is odd, but not exactly evidence that Cat's in danger," responded Fergus warily.

Rebecca elaborated on the list of concerns and described the marriage debate recently developed between Cat and her mother, including the mandate that Druids marry other Druids.

Fergus sighed loudly, mouth pulled down in the corners. "A faction of Druids has gained strength in the last year. These Druids hate the Fae and have been lobbying to take a more aggressive role against them. Daeglan O'Connor is the leader of this group—he was the man who tried to beat you to the Sword of Light at the British Museum of London. I can only assume the concept of forcing Druids to marry one another was a product of his design because I assure you, there is no such mandate. I don't agree with his beliefs, and I think there are enough of us to keep him from taking over the council. However, he's still dangerous. He's also a childhood friend of Colleen, Cat's mother. Some weeks ago, I caught Daeglan at the museum talking to Cat."

Rebecca shot a worried glance at me, equally disturbed by the new information. "Fergus, do you have any idea where they might have taken Cat? We don't believe they've been in the house for some time, and it appears Colleen packed a bag when she left."

"Cat's aunt lives on the western coast. It's entirely possible they're with her. There's also the possibility they went to one of Daeglan's properties. I can't recall the exact locations, but I know his family has property out in County Donegal."

"Is there a way for us to find out the address of that

property?" Rebecca asked, her voice exhibiting the same reserved optimism I was battling. I doubted we would find Cat easily, but it was difficult not to foster hope at the hint of progress.

"I can get you Colleen's sister's address. As for the others, you'll have to wait until tomorrow. The Public Registry Office has indices where you can search the deed records and should hopefully be able to find the land his family owns. But keep in mind, my suggestion about Daeglan is just a guess. I have no way of knowing for sure if he has anything to do with this." His worried gaze danced between Rebecca and me. He might have made an odd first impression, but I was quickly learning why Rebecca spoke of Fergus with such high regard. He cared a great deal about Rebecca and Cat.

She offered the older man a smile. "Thank you, Fergus. You've been an amazing help."

His lips thinned, and he dropped his chin a fraction. "I just wish I had recognized there was a problem. Colleen has always been rather ... protective of Cat. I never imagined she would have gone this far, but so much has changed ever since you showed up. Much of the change has been good, but as for Colleen, outing the Druids to the Fae has only heightened her paranoia. I fear she may not be thinking logically, which means it would be hard to predict what she might do. I wish I could be of more help."

Rebecca reassured Fergus that he had helped us tremendously, and we said our farewells.

The next day, we were at the doors of the Registry Office the moment they opened. With the help of one of the clerks, we were able to come up with three pieces of land owned by Daeglan O'Connor's family. This had not been an easy task as half of Ireland carried the surname O'Connor. It was well into the afternoon when we pulled out a map and began to make a plan.

"Cat's aunt lives all the way in Clifden, easily the farthest, so I'd suggest we make that the last stop. It looks like the County Donegal properties are all spread out and will take travel time to get to each. I suggest we hit the Ballyliffin property first, then make our way around to Falcarragh before hitting Teelin," she said as she outlined the route on the map with her finger.

"Agreed. However, you sound as though you plan to come with me on this journey, and that is not possible," I told her.

Rebecca screwed up her face in annoyance. "Of course, I'm coming with you. Cat is my friend, too."

I leaned in close to keep others from hearing. "I understand that you want to help, but you cannot come. I cannot risk anyone finding out about my escape, which means we cannot chance you being followed or Lochlan looking into your disappearance. Not to mention the fact that you could not sneak up on a target if it was already dead. In case you forgot, I have heard you trouncing through the Shadow Lands and know just how conspicuous you are. Practically my entire life has been spent hunting, and I hunt alone."

"And how will you get there if we don't take my car? What if they use magic against you? What if you're outnumbered?" she pushed back defiantly.

"I can travel the same way I managed to get to Belfast, and Strabane before that. And as for the Druids, do you not think I have faced more vile creatures with much worse odds already in my life? We do not have time to argue over this. Your presence will hinder my abilities, and I am not willing to take that chance. I am going alone." I stared at her emphatically, watching as competing emotions crossed her face.

Rebecca stood at the table we had been using, eyes searching the nearby shelves for answers. Eventually, she let out a resigned exhale and brought her eyes back to mine. "The only way I would agree to that was if you took a phone and agreed to keep me informed. I don't want to dream walk and risk disrupting you during a dangerous situation. Do you even have your phone with you?" She raised a haughty brow, and I took a small amount of pleasure in retrieving the device from my bag.

"Charged and ready." I illuminated the screen, punched in a simple text to Rebecca, and had the phone back in my bag by the time her phone chimed.

"I thought you had refused to use the phone," she groused.

"I had refused, except in the event of an emergency. *This* is an emergency."

THE FIRST TWO properties were utterly abandoned, with no chance anyone had stepped foot in them for years. With travel time between cities and then my journey into the countryside to check each house, I had lost two days.

My nerves were strung tighter than the strings on my bow.

On my bus ride to Teelin, where the third property was located, a well-bred man in a suit sat near me, clicking his writing instrument incessantly. It took all my restraint not to put his head through the window.

I was now on foot, nearing the location of the third O'Connor property. So far, the unpaved road along the Irish coast was equally as isolated as the other properties, making me wonder if I had wasted time on yet another dead end.

The land was perched on a bluff above the crashing waves of the northern sea. The bright green shade of the grass-covered hillside was still visible in the muted twilight hours, though I took little notice. My thoughts were entirely focused on my task.

I crested a sizeable hill and saw a stone cottage near the cliff's edge. At the sight, my steps faltered, and air rushed from my lungs with the crushing disappointment of seeing yet another dilapidated structure that showed every sign of having been long abandoned.

The gray stone looked porous with age, and I was skeptical that the crumbling shingle roof would keep the rain out, let alone survive a good storm. A wild overgrowth of scrub bushes covered much of the outer façade, making it hard to even locate the entrance. There were no vehicles out front, and no lights shone through the windows.

Advancing closer felt like a waste of my time, but I had not come this far to be anything less than thorough in my search. Senses on high alert, I continued my approach.

TWENTY-THREE

CAT

When I was young, my mother took me to the Dublin Zoo. As most children do, I loved seeing all the animals, but my heart hurt to see the wild creatures kept in small enclosures. Standing outside the wire cage of a large eagle, I began to cry for the bird that was in such a small aviary it didn't have enough room to fly.

My mother took me aside and explained that the bird's wing had been broken when it lived in the wild. He had been rescued by conservationists, nursed back to health, and provided an easy life where he could not be harmed. Even if he'd been able to fly again, his life at the zoo was infinitely easier than in the wild, where he had to fight daily to survive. Now, he was well cared for and would live a much longer, happier life.

I took another look at the majestic bird as he sat unbothered, his glossy feathers shining in the sun, and realized that there was truth in her statement. Mother Nature could be cruel and unfair. In the zookeeper's hands, the wildlife was kept relatively free of disease and allowed to enjoy their lives without the constant threat of death lurking around every corner.

I had accepted her explanation as a child, but only now did I truly understand the freedom such a life provided. There was security in knowing that I was safe and unburdened by the multitude of daily decisions that plagued my life before.

Those days had been so painful that I had buried them deep inside me. I did not think of them. Instead, I celebrated all the blessings around me. At the top of that list was my family because *family is everything*.

I did my best not to disappoint my mother and Daeglan. They were my world. They wanted the best for me and provided for me in every way. I was given a new gown with warm socks and a book of my own. If I did fall short of their expectations, I understood that I must be punished because *the rules are the rules*.

I had not actually seen my mother since I had arrived at my new home over a month ago. Daeglan explained that she was visiting her sister and might come to see me if I continued to improve. For some reason, the possibility of seeing her made me sad, and I was unsure why. I didn't share those feelings with Daeglan because I knew they were wrong.

Family is everything.

Daeglan spent time with me often, helping me settle into my new routine. I derived enormous comfort from knowing exactly what I should be doing without any uncertainty or ambiguity. I did as I was told, and there was no suffering or troublesome anxiety over decision-making. By allowing Daeglan to guide me, I had made my life so much better.

As was our routine, Daeglan had brought me my evening meal just as I grew hungry. My ration still consisted of bread, but I was given a portion of butter, and the ration was all I needed to sustain myself. I ate every bite. Once I was done, I started my bedtime stretches to stay healthy and sound. I had memorized the stretching routine, but the instructional video still played in the background. I had not yet earned the freedom to be left to my own thoughts, so the chanting and lectures remained a part of my life. They didn't bother me terribly, but I looked forward to a time when I might earn Daeglan's complete trust.

I was midway through my stretches when a loud crash sounded from above. My heart leaped into my throat at the sound. There were never any loud noises, aside from the music and chanting. I tried to tell myself that I was safe in my own home.

Daeglan always keeps me safe.

But the noise was extremely unusual, and it frightened me so badly that I had trouble continuing with my routine. Stretching out in a warrior pose, I did my best not to disappoint Daeglan by failing to stretch properly. However, I could not shake the sense of unease that had the hair on my arms standing on edge.

Footsteps thundered down the stairs outside my room, and I stumbled to press myself against the back wall as far as I could get from the door. Daeglan burst into my room, his always perfectly coifed hair ruffled in all directions. But that wasn't the most upsetting part. My heart pounded against my ribs as I took in the crimson stain spreading down his shirt.

The shiny black handle of a knife protruded from the right side of his upper chest, just below his shoulder.

Bile rose in my throat as I stood frozen against the wall.

"Catronia, come here quickly." His voice was hoarse with strain.

I instantly did as he said, reaching for his outstretched hands. "Daeglan, you're hurt," I whimpered through stuttered breaths, making sure not to ask what was happening. It was not my place to question.

"The Fae are attacking. You *must* be strong. This wound may prevent me from using spells to protect us, and I have no idea how many of them are out there." His face twisted in pain, beads of sweat dotting his forehead. "I'll do my best to defeat them, but you must be prepared. If they capture you, they'll try to twist your mind. *Do not let them.* Remember, *family is everything.*" He held my arms tightly, and with his last words, he shook me with the strength of his convictions. When he did, a surge of blood oozed from his chest, and a jagged sob clawed past my lips.

Family was everything, and my family was in grave danger.

"Get behind me," Daeglan commanded as he whipped around toward the door.

I didn't argue.

Daeglan wanted what was best for me and would

protect me. He was even using himself as a human shield, prepared to give his life for me. From behind him, I peeked at the deadly man who prowled into the doorway of my room. He was tall with dark features drawn into a sneer. He looked brutally savage.

Even more frightening, he was familiar.

He must have been on one of the videos Daeglan showed me to teach me about the dangers of the Fae. Seeing a Fae in the flesh, knowing the atrocities he was capable of, made rational thought flee from my mind. A monster had forced its way into my home and attacked my family. The Fae truly *were* out to destroy and murder, ripping families apart.

"How did you get inside the cabin past my wards? Those wards should have kept out anything Fae," Daeglan bit out with his hands up at the ready.

"Child's play." The man glared at Daeglan before his eyes fell briefly to where I hid behind him. A look of disgust twisted his features. "What have you done to her?"

"I've kept her safe from scum like you." After his hissed response, Daeglan swirled his hands before him and sent a surge of energy blasting into the man.

The force sent the intruder flying back against the wall outside the room, the collision crumbling the sheetrock behind him. The man remained on his feet, but just barely. When he stepped forward dazedly, he touched his hand to the back of his head, his fingers coming away coated in blood.

While the man was seemingly stunned, Daeglan initiated a second assault. The blast hit directly where the man still held his hands out before him. To my utter astonishment, the blast never reached him. Instead, a thunderous clap sounded in the room, and the leather band tied to the man's wrist fell to the floor.

Time came to a stop as I stared at the lifeless leather and its markings artfully inset into the grain. I knew immediately that I had made the bracelet. The memory was fuzzy, but I was certain I had crafted the piece.

Why would the Fae man have my bracelet? Had he taken it from my home? From my mother? Had the Fae man hurt my mother?

I clenched the back of Daeglan's shirt, more afraid than ever, as time snapped back into motion.

Taking advantage of Daeglan's surprise, the man charged. He punched Daeglan with a sickening crunch, sending him flying to the side and leaving me helplessly exposed.

I rushed backward with a cry until I reached the safety of the far corner.

Daeglan was my family, and I was terrified the man would kill him. The Faerie was so large and barbaric looking with beady eyes and rippling muscles.

What could I do to help? I couldn't just stand against the wall and watch the men fight.

Daeglan recovered from the blow, standing tall and yanking the knife from his shoulder. From where I sat huddled, I could see the profile of his blood-stained grin. "You think your powers make you better than us? You think you can control and kill us with the slightest whim?" He accented his words with a wild swing of his knife.

The Faerie easily danced out of reach as Daeglan took swing after swing.

"We have powers of our own, did you know that? The wards around this room prevent you from using your magic within these walls. How does it feel when the tables are turned?" Daeglan spat out angrily.

"Those wards are not to protect against the Fae. They are there to keep Cat your prisoner. Do not twist the facts. There is only one monster here," seethed the intruder, lunging so fast he blurred as he grabbed Daeglan's hand.

He knows my name. The monster used my name. How could he possibly know who I am?

I was unable to ponder the issue further as the two men grappled for the knife. Daeglan's face contorted with effort while the Faerie appeared practically unfazed. He was going to kill Daeglan if I didn't do something. I had to at least try.

I flung myself forward and latched onto the Faerie's back, wrapping my arms tightly around his neck.

"Cat, *stop* this," sputtered the Faerie, still locked in a struggle with Daeglan over the knife.

I used what little strength I had to protect my family the only way I knew how.

But it wasn't enough.

The man shoved Daeglan away, then folded himself forward until I was flung from his back onto the floor. He leaped over me, then swept his foot out, knocking Daeglan off balance.

The next minute passed as if in slow motion.

I could see exactly what was about to happen. Despite the seemingly infinite moment, I could do nothing to stop it.

Daeglan's arms flailed to right himself, but it was no

use. Without the proper leverage, he was unable to defend himself. The Faerie seized Daeglan's hands, joining the two in a deadly dance. Like a toppling domino, Daeglan's back raced to the floor with the man above him, forcing Daeglan's knife toward his chest. The two men slammed to the ground, Daeglan flat on his back with the knife plunged deep into the middle of his chest.

"*No!*" I screamed hysterically, tears filling my vision.

The man lowered his face just inches from Daeglan's. "I have seen the faces of hell, and I hope you rot there eternally," the man hissed viciously. He shoved himself away from Daeglan, whose head lolled to the side lifelessly.

"*Daeglan!* Please, no." I rushed to his motionless body, my shaking hands skating over his slack features. My breaths came out in rushed pants as the mounting tears began to pour down my cheeks.

Daeglan was dead.

The tether to my anchor had been severed, and I was again adrift.

Where would I go? What would I do?

Family was everything, and my family was dead.

CHAPTER

TWENTY-FOUR

FENODREE

IT HAD BEEN FORTUNATE THAT YEARS OF PRECAUTIONARY INSTINCT had me drawing my knife well before approaching the run-down house. Still unused to the ambient noise, I was taken off guard when a man rushed me from behind. He had the advantage of surprise, but that was nothing compared to my centuries of well-honed survival instincts.

I easily dodged the heavy rock he swung at my head, and in one swift motion, I extracted my knife and sank the blade deep into his shoulder.

The man doubled over, using the motion to scoop up a handful of dirt that he flung at my face. Blinded for some minutes, I was unable to prevent him from fleeing, but I knew he would not go far.

Cat was here. It was the only explanation.

Once I was able to clear the dirt from my eyes, I

cautiously approached the cottage. Before entering, I walked the perimeter to ensure I was familiar with my surroundings. I assessed the number of rooms and looked for other inhabitants through the grimy windows. Only after I was comfortable proceeding did I try the front door.

The lock had not been turned, but a series of runes lined the doorframe. Among them was the protection rune. I decided to gamble that the spell was not harmful and pushed open the door. As I tentatively pressed my hand through the doorway, I felt a sharp tingling sensation but was otherwise not repelled by the spell. Once I stepped fully through the entry, the feeling of pinpricks ceased.

The living space was not as dilapidated as the outside façade but was sparsely furnished, making me think the structure was not used as a home. A television-like screen displayed an image that appeared to be Cat talking with the man I had stabbed. She clung to him as if he was a friend rather than her captor. The entire situation had me on guard, and I continued to assess my surroundings. I was not foolish enough to run headlong into a trap.

I found the main level empty, but a doorway led to a set of stairs descending into an underground space. I could identify two voices coming from below, and after seeing the image of Cat and my attacker, I was fairly certain the two were alone in the room below.

Unlike the rest of the cottage, the space below ground was modern and sterile, not to mention outfitted with an impressive lock and solid metal door. The realization that he had constructed an underground prison was unsettling, but the sight of Cat cowering behind the bastard was downright infuriating.

When her eyes met mine, there was no recognition, only fear and hatred.

My body hummed with indignant rage.

What must she have suffered to undergo such a drastic change?

The fool thought his chances were better because I could not use magic. I had spent hundreds of years compensating for my lack of magic in a world filled with the most malevolent magic in existence. I developed what strengths I had—stealth, strategy, evasion, and hand-to-hand combat skills.

His feeble attempts at fighting me off were laughable. The only reason I hurried things along instead of taking out my rage and battering him to a pulp was because Cat entered the fray. My sweet, innocent Cat had attacked me like a feral wolf going for the jugular. I was terrified she would get hurt in the fight and knew I had to end it. Had it been up to me, I would have kept him in the room and made him suffer ten times what she had been forced to endure.

Sinking my knife into him and watching the life drain from his eyes was one of the most satisfying moments of my long life. I only wished it had not been so short-lived. The broken cries wrenched from Cat were a splash of cold water onto the fiery rage burning inside me.

Seeing her kidnapper dead, my strong Druid princess shattered into a thousand pieces.

The hatred and fear she had initially greeted me with would have been preferable to the vacant, feral glare she cast my way after she backed herself into the room's far corner. Knees tucked beneath her chin, she curled into a ball, hiding her eyes beneath untamed red curls.

I slowly stepped forward, hands held up placatingly to show her I meant no harm. "Cat, I am here to take you home. He cannot hurt you anymore."

The moment I stood within her reach, she lashed out like a wounded animal. Arms and legs thrashing, she viciously screamed wordless threats.

I quickly retreated, hoping to keep her from harming herself. Standing on the opposite end of the room, I had no idea what I should do. "Will you talk to me, Cat?" I asked softly, my words filling the tiny room.

She made not a sound in response.

Releasing a sigh filled with a month's worth of pent-up fears, I stepped forward and began to lift the dead body off the floor. Cat rushed at me with a second round of rage-filled screams as she clawed at any part of me she could reach. The moment I dropped the body and stepped back, her attack subsided, and she withdrew back to her corner. Her breathing remained harsh from exertion, and before long, her heaving breaths morphed into heart-wrenching sobs.

For nearly a half-hour, she wept.

I would have given anything to hold her while she was so obviously in need of comfort. I lowered myself to the floor instead. If I could not go near her, I would sit as close as she would allow me.

The Cat I had grown to know was lost, but I was going to do everything in my power to help her find her way back.

ONCE CAT HAD CRIED herself to sleep, I disposed of the remains of Daeglan O'Connor. The bastard would receive no burial; he did not deserve peace in this life or any other. I threw his corpse over the cliffside and into the churning ocean waters, walking away without a second thought.

Despite the overwhelming guilt it created, I had locked the door to Cat's cell to ensure she did not run from me while I was gone. I took my time walking back, thinking about my next move. There was no way we could leave with Cat in her current state. Furthermore, I could not release her from her underground prison until I could trust that she would not run. If she had to remain in her room, I would stay with her whenever possible.

On my way back to the house, I set wards around the perimeter of the seaside cottage, resorting to the use of magic I had sworn I would never use again. I could not guarantee other Druids would not come looking for Daeglan, and Cat needed to be protected. The blood magic warding spell was the best way to do that.

I kneeled on a patch of rocky soil and took out a small vial of blood from my pack. The blood had belonged to a Shadow Fae who had been butchered and sold for parts. The spell required sacrificial blood, which was not always easy to come by when needed. I had kept the vial with me for just such an occasion, despite knowing its use might be catastrophic.

I poured the blood into a small bowl I had found inside, then swiped at the wound on my head to draw out a small amount of my own blood. When I touched sticky wet, I was surprised to find that my wound was still producing fresh blood.

I had not stopped bleeding.

I had expected to find dried, crusted blood that I might use, but the wound still seemed fresh.

Continuing with the spell, I mixed the blood together and said the incantation I had used once before to ward my home back in the Shadow Lands. The words were in the original language of the Shadow Fae, and I could feel their dark power seep into my body.

Continuing to repeat the spell, I coated my feet in a layer of blood and then began to walk in a circle around the small seaside cottage. When I reached the spot where I had begun, the magic sealed the ward, and a burning pain scorched a path from the souls of my feet up to the center of my chest.

I dropped to my knees, curling in on myself to ease the blazing flames inside me. I had never experienced such pain when I had used blood magic in the past. Fear unlike any I had known shook me to my core.

I needed to extinguish the smoldering heat inside me.

Fumbling with shaking hands, I took out a bottle of water from my pack and poured its contents into my mouth but immediately spit the rancid-tasting liquid to the ground.

The pain was so excruciating that I was tempted to crack open my own chest to douse the flames inside me. I was certain that I was burning from the inside out, and at any moment, a raging fire would leap from my chest.

I screamed out in desperation, throwing my head back in agony.

When I looked back down at the ground, the small bowl of blood caught my eye.

The blood, yes, the blood is what I need. That is the only thing that will ease the searing pain.

I took the bowl in my shaking hands and lifted it halfway to my mouth before freezing mid-motion.

This is wrong. I cannot give in to the temptation.

My hands shook violently as I battled with myself.

Ever so slowly, I tipped the bowl to spill its contents onto the dry ground. The pain did not subside, but I still breathed in a relieved breath that I had not drunk from the bowl.

For long minutes, I lay in a ball, wishing I would simply die.

The pull to lick the precious blood off the ground was more than I could bear. I had to remove myself.

Rising on trembling legs, clutching my middle, I staggered toward the house. With each step I took, the blood's power over me lessened. I stumbled more quickly, desperate to flee from its grasp. When I reached the cottage, I flung the door shut behind me as if my pursuer might try to follow me inside.

Hands on my knees, I heaved deep cleansing breaths. My chest still ached, but the pain was much more manageable than minutes before. Once I regained control of my breathing, I lifted my shirt to examine my chest. There was no physical manifestation from the use of the magic, but it had left its mark regardless.

I would have to remove blood magic from my dwindling arsenal of weapons. If I were to attempt such a spell again, I did not think I would survive the effects.

TWENTY-FIVE

CAT

WHEN I WOKE, I WAS INSTANTLY WARY OF THE HAUNTING silence that filled my room. Curled on my side, I peeked through my curtain of hair. No longer curled up in the corner, I had been moved to my bed and covered with my blanket.

Had the Fae man moved me? Had he done anything else while I was asleep?

A sliver of fear skated across my skin as I looked at where the man lay sleeping against the door, preventing me from escaping.

I didn't know where I'd go even if I did try to run.

Daeglan was gone, both his presence and his body. I'd made it clear that I did not want him removed, but the man must have taken him while I slept. Daeglan's loss was a constant ache in my chest. What would I do without him? He brought me food and provided for me in every way. He was my protector, and I was lost without him.

While I avoided those painful thoughts, my eyes were drawn back to the Fae man. I studied his dark features, now eerily soft in sleep. The peaceful way he lay made him seem almost harmless, but I knew better. What I couldn't figure out was why he still felt so familiar.

As if he sensed my attention focused on him, his eyelids lifted, and our gazes locked. Neither of us moved a muscle as we assessed one another. I wanted to hate him, but I was too tired and overwhelmed to muster any emotion at all.

An image took shape in my mind's eye as I stared at the man. A river. Not a river, the dark green water of a canal.

The vision was gone just as quickly as it had appeared, and I had no idea what it meant or where it had come from.

I didn't like the unknown.

Structure and order were paramount to me. The image inside my head was rife with perplexity, making me want to bury it away where it could not bother me.

"Are you hungry?" the man asked in a voice raspy from sleep.

There was no way I was going to answer him. He had taken Daeglan from me, and while he had not yet hurt me physically, the emotional pain he had caused was traumatic enough.

He accepted my silence, leaving the room without another word.

I had hoped he would leave me in peace so that I could

seek out the comfort of my swaying ocean. However, my luck was still against me. Not only could I not connect with the dark waters, but the man returned within minutes, drawing me back to my painful reality.

When he entered the room with food, I told myself I would not touch it. But before long, I caught the scent of not only bread but several other delicious items, and my stomach grumbled loudly in response.

I sat up and scooted back against the wall as the Faerie approached. The man lowered himself to sit across from me, allowing room between us but still sitting closer than I would have liked. He slowly extended an outstretched palm, presenting an orange as an offering.

I made no move to take it, and his hand retracted.

Unperturbed, he peeled the skin back from the orange, releasing a tart citrus scent throughout the room.

Daeglan had only ever given me bread to eat. Wanting more than what I had been given felt like the gravest of violations, but the sweet, tangy smell of the orange made my stomach clench with hunger, and saliva pooled in my mouth.

Again, he held out his hand with wedges of the fleshy fruit set on his palm.

Why is he doing this? Why doesn't he just kill me and get it over with?

The image of his outstretched hand made my head swim with confusion. I was so utterly exhausted, physically and mentally, that my mind swam with deja vu. I had no energy to even guess at his intentions or succumb to the fears that whispered darkly from the back of my mind. Without the unease holding me back, the temptation of the orange was too great. I told myself that my body required sustenance if I was to live, and Daeglan would have wanted me to survive.

I slowly extended my hand before snatching the fruit from his open palm.

I sniffed at the orange, my eyes watering from its pungent scent. When I bit into the tender flesh, the burst of flavor on my tongue made my jaw ache painfully. Still, I greedily consumed every bite I was offered.

Not once did I take my eyes off the savage. Just because I was starving did not mean I trusted my captor. Unlike my meals with Daeglan, the man did not limit my consumption, and I was soon uncomfortably full.

The rules are the rules.

Daeglan always knew best. He fed me as much as I needed and no more. Left to my own devices, I had already broken the rules and was paying the price.

Oh Daeglan, what will I do without you?

The weight of my situation came crashing down upon me. The sadness of despair, paired with my full belly, made my eyelids dangerously heavy. I did not want to sleep with this man in my room, but I was afraid I had no choice.

"Sleep, Cat. You are safe here; I will not harm you," the man said softly as he stood and walked from the room.

His words and actions were so confusing. Saying kind things, giving me food, and not going near me—everything he did was seemingly compassionate—but I knew better than to fall for his tricks. Daeglan warned that the Fae would try to twist my mind. Any kindness this man might show me was manipulation and nothing more.

CHAPTER

TWENTY-SIX

FENODREE

THE LOOK OF WONDER ON CAT'S FACE WHEN SHE BIT INTO THAT orange made me feel just as relieved as I felt homicidal. I was all too familiar with the sensation of tasting a long-denied food again for the first time. Between her enjoyment of the orange and her nearly skeletal frame, Daeglan had clearly denied her proper nourishment.

Her physical health would need just as much recovery time as her battered mind. I was enormously pleased that she had eaten and was starting the healing process. Her inner conflict was evident, and I had not been sure her hunger would win out. Cat had practically fallen comatose as soon as she finished eating.

For long hours, I watched her sleep. I could not fathom how anyone could bear to mistreat such a peaceful, breathtaking creature. Not just anyone, but her own people. She had been punished for her ability to empathize with those around her, to see past race and stereotypes.

The similarity to my own situation with Hilde was not lost on me.

How was it that in a thousand years, people, whether Fae or human, had not progressed past the blindness of prejudice? Underneath the fancy clothes and advanced technology, everything was still the same.

Hatred rooted in fear and ignorance.

I had to actively refrain from allowing anger to foster my own hatred. However, there was one individual who deserved my wrath. Daeglan had given his life for his crimes, but Cat's mother had yet to answer for hers. If she had anything to do with Cat's imprisonment, her life was forfeit as far as I was concerned.

Startled from her sleep, Cat woke with a gasp. Her eyes danced around the room as she sat up, and her nostrils flared with the sudden rush of adrenaline.

I remained still, allowing her time to calm herself. Once her breathing returned to normal, I took the plastic water bottle sitting next to me and rolled it across the room to where she sat. Her hand shot out to stop the bottle's momentum, but she did not pick it up, not at first. Instead, she held my gaze, another debate waging inside her. Eventually, the tense showdown ended, and she drank reluctantly from the bottle.

"Cat, do you remember what happened? How you came to be here?" I asked gently.

She continued to take sips from the bottle, seeming to ignore my presence.

"Your mother and Daeglan brought you here to teach

you to fear the Fae, but that is not who you are. Your best friend Rebecca is Fae, as is your friend Ashley and others."

Cat shook her head, brow furrowed, but still, she did not meet my eyes.

Encouraged that she had engaged with me, even if just to deny my words, I continued. "Daeglan brought you here to warp your thoughts and turn you against your friends. These people are not your family—" The moment the words were out, it was clear that I had hit a nerve.

Cat whipped her head toward me, eyes blazing and teeth bared. "*No!*" she growled fiercely before flying in my direction. A far cry from the cowering girl in the corner, this Cat was seething vengeance. Hitting and kicking, she raged against me with every ounce of strength she possessed.

I clasped her wrists and tugged her down to the ground, forcing my weight on top of her to subdue her attack.

"I do not fault you, Cat. Get out all that hurt. I am so sorry for what they have done to you." My strained words fell on deaf ears as she struggled beneath me, screaming and hissing her fury.

"You don't know," she screamed. "You don't know what family is. You're just a heartless animal. I *hate* you," she cried out with one last frenzied assault. As her words quieted, so did her fight. Her bare foot slapped limply on the smooth ground as her chest heaved gasping breaths and her eyes slid off to the side. Her straining muscles eventually went limp beneath me, and tears began to flow from her eyes.

After a moment, I released her hands, bracing myself

for the possibility of a second attack. To my surprise, she did not resume her assault or scurry away. She merely rolled herself into a protective ball.

Taking a chance, I slowly snaked my hands beneath her and lifted her into my arms.

She did not latch her arms around me or fight me. I took a couple of steps to where her bedding lay and set her down on the blanket.

I was well aware that her outburst had not been about me or my words. Rather, it had been a defensive response to her psyche battling the inner conflict created by what I had said. Regardless of how hostile they became, our exchanges would be the trail of crumbs she would use to find her way home. And until she did, I would be with her every step of the way.

CHAPTER

TWENTY-SEVEN

CAT

THE FAERIE FINALLY LEFT ME ALONE, THE WAY I LIKE IT. I HAD started to think he would never leave as he sat vigil at my door. I had raged against him and his ugly words. Raged against the confusion and the hurt, against my sadness and longing to feel safe. I raged against all the feelings that blurred together like a swarm of angry wasps.

I was finally blessed with soothing numbness in the wake of so much emotion. Maybe that was why I couldn't rouse the appropriate fear of my inevitable punishment.

Such behavior would surely not go unpunished.

Yet he hadn't enforced any consequences so far. The room was still comfortably warm, and nothing had been taken from me. He hadn't lashed out in any way.

This man wasn't family, and he certainly had no reason to be kind to me, which was why his behavior was so confusing to me. If he was going to punish me, why had he carried me gently to my bed?

I had felt unexpected security in his arms.

Something about his woodsy scent soothed my riled thoughts. For a fleeting second, I had hoped he wouldn't put me down. Yet as soon as the thought materialized, it was quickly dashed away by waves of guilt. How could I be anything but repulsed by a Fae man's touch?

I deserve to be left on the cold concrete.

The thought spurred on a memory of lying on the freezing floor in agonizing pain. The flash was so vivid that it stole my breath and sent a phantom ache through my belly.

The rules are the rules.

The pain I had endured in my lessons had been brutal, but the punishments had been my own fault. Hadn't they? If I had followed the rules and behaved, there would have been no need for discipline. Daeglan was my family, and he was only doing what was best for me. It just so happened that what was best for me resulted in immeasurable pain.

Other images tried to surface, but they were vague and terribly confusing. The onslaught frightened me, each image instigating more questions than the last. I was torn between wanting answers and needing to hide from the assault of information. I couldn't sort it all myself, and I was not allowed to ask questions.

I sat up, and my body began to rock back and forth in the hopeless pursuit of clarity, but even my rocking was of little comfort. Just as I began to feel panic wrapping its icy tentacles around me, the door slowly opened.

For a moment, my disoriented mind expected to see Daeglan. Instead, my eyes fell upon a bronze warrior as he entered my room. My body stilled, and I tilted my head with muddled confusion as I stared at the familiar man. Tears blurred my vision, and my heart began to pound relentlessly against the walls of my chest.

I was lost and confused and utterly terrified, but in spite of that, I knew one thing for certain—this man before me was not evil.

TWENTY-EIGHT

FENODREE

"Fen?" her tiny voice called out.

Never could I have imagined the exultant emotions I would feel at the sound of my name on someone's lips. She remembered me.

I grinned broadly at my sweet Cat, but she dropped her eyes and curved in on herself. Her response was not unexpected, but a small part of me had hoped for more.

She was still far from healed.

"Are you hungry?" I asked her gently.

Her hesitant eyes met mine, and she gave the slightest hint of a nod.

"Good. I will get us some food and be back in just a moment." I offered another small smile before heading upstairs.

Besides food, I gathered some toiletries, a blanket, and a book I had found in one of the closets. I carried the items down to the basement and was able to approach Cat without her pulling away in fear. "I found this book upstairs and thought I might read to you." I held up the tattered copy of *The Lion, the Witch, and the Wardrobe* as I sat down near her. "I do not have any idea whether it is any good, but it sounds like one of your adventure books."

She began to nibble on her food and made no objection to my suggested reading, so I opened the book to the first page.

"Once there were four children whose names were Peter, Susan, Edmund and Lucy. This story is about something that happened to them when they were sent away from London during the war because of the air-raids. They were sent to the house of an old Professor who lived in the heart of the country. ..."

I read to Cat for hours until my voice grew hoarse, and I had to stop. She stayed awake and appeared to listen but never said a word.

"I think it is best if we get some rest now. Would you like to go upstairs and use the washroom first?" She had only used the bucket up until that point, but I was sufficiently encouraged by her progress to attempt a brief trip to the toilet upstairs.

Her eyes danced between me and the door before she shook her head vigorously back and forth.

"All right, I will step out for a moment and let you have some privacy, then we can get some sleep." I stepped into the stairwell, closing the door behind me but not locking it. After a few minutes, I returned to find her curled up on her bedding under the new blanket I had brought.

I emptied and rinsed the bucket, and before closing

the door of her room upon my return, I flipped the light switch in the stairwell to turn off the lights. As I lay in front of the door, the silence was broken by the increasing cadence of Cat's racing breaths. I jumped back up and opened the door to turn the light on.

Cat's eyes were rounded in terror. Her only movement was the erratic rise and fall of her chest as she panted in obvious panic.

Gods, I wanted more than anything to hold her in my arms and comfort her. "We can leave the lights on. Does that sound better?" I asked her huddled form.

Her pleading eyes lifted to mine. "Yes, please."

We slept as we had the night before, each of us on the floor with the glaring lights above us. However, the atmosphere in the room was entirely different. When I arrived at the cottage, we had been on opposite sides of an enormous chasm. Standing across from one another at its widest point, we were so far apart we could barely see one another. Each of our interactions moved us further along the edge of the chasm to narrower segments. I still could not reach her fully, but she had seen me, and it was only a matter of time before we found our way back together.

The brain was quick to heal under the right circumstances. It would have taken time for her to give in to Daeglan's manipulation, but I knew that bandage she had wrapped around her mind to protect herself would soon peel away. The exposed wound would hurt, but that would enable the real healing to begin.

The following morning, after we had relieved ourselves and shared breakfast, I began to tell Cat the story of our meeting and wound my way through each of our encounters. I described how she had taught me runes and brought me books and food. I told her about our walks and how excited she had been to take me to the movies and how terrified I had been of riding in her car.

For nearly an hour, she sat unmoved as I walked her through our memories together. I made no mention of her mother or anyone else in her life. Steering clear of anything painful, I focused on all the beautiful moments we had shared.

I was not sure I had gotten through until a single tear trickled down her pale cheek.

TWENTY-NINE

CAT

"The first time you visited me by yourself..." Fen continued with his thoughts. "When I opened the door and saw that you had come alone, I was stunned and beyond irritated. You were so young and exceptionally beautiful, and I was shamefully tempted. I had hoped that you would have been scared enough not to return after your first visit because I knew somehow deep down that you would undo me."

As I listened to him tell his story, the scene played out like a silent movie in my head. It was surreal to have images unveiled in my mind that had been hidden from me just moments before.

My own memories were taken from me.

"You brought muffins for me," he said, "and then babbled endlessly about whether I should eat them. I wanted nothing more than to shut you up with my lips on yours. You were undiluted innocence and everything I should not want. Yet between visits, you occupied my every thought. When I had you near, you captivated each of my senses until they could focus on nothing else."

Fen detailed every warm and beautiful moment we had shared together, and I recognized them for the truths they were. The veil that had concealed my memories pulled away, and one by one, my pieces fell into place.

Had his recollection merely exposed each of the occasions he spoke of, the reclaimed memories would have been much easier to enjoy. However, along with all the warm moments he described, other memories crept back into my consciousness.

Bad memories.

Ugly memories.

Memories I wished could have stayed forgotten forever.

I relived the heartbreaking disappointment of watching my mother surrender me to Daeglan O'Connor. I recalled my mother slapping me and the forced dinner with her chosen suitor. Even darker, I remembered waking in Daeglan's prison and each passing hour of torture that had broken me into a shell of my former self. There to carry with me forever was the searing pain of a rune carved into my arm. At the reminder, I dropped my gaze to where the skin on my forearm was pink and gnarled.

The physical reminder was too much.

I turned to the side and purged my stomach of its contents as the flood of memories bombarded me.

I remembered. Everything.

Fen held my hair away from my face and rubbed

soothing circles on my back, but it didn't take away the excruciating pain of remembrance.

Eventually, my stomach ceased its revolt, and I sat back to take in my surroundings with new eyes. The awful prison I had somehow taught myself to call home.

Daeglan had done this.

He'd warped my mind until I'd forgotten who I was.

That was when the sobs started. Heaving, cathartic sobs wracked my body.

Fen scooped me into his arms without a word and carried me swiftly up the stairs. He sat us down on a small sofa, still holding me firmly to his chest. He said nothing. No words were going to fix what had happened to me. He simply held me, and I clung to him as if he were life itself.

I couldn't fathom how I'd let myself forget such an extraordinary man. Not just forget. I had demonized him. I was horribly ashamed.

"I'm so sorry," I whispered.

Fen pulled back to look at my face. "There is nothing to be sorry about."

"I let Daeglan win. Let him change me in so many ways. I was so horrible to you—attacked you physically and verbally."

"No," he responded firmly. "Your mind did what it needed to adapt to the terrible circumstances forced upon you. There is no shame in doing whatever it takes to survive."

I gazed into his penetrating eyes and read his earnest belief in his words. "What did you have to do to ... adapt when you were sent to the Shadow Lands?" I asked softly.

I never would have asked such an invasive question before, but I needed to know I wasn't alone.

"Too many things to even recall all of them—drinking my own urine, sleeping inside the carcass of an animal to stay warm. Perhaps one of the most embarrassing was happening upon two animals mating and sneaking close to try to feed my magic on the male's release." He lifted a brow and smirked at me. "That bit of information can stay between you and me." His features sobered before he continued. "I believe only people who have experienced the desperation elicited from a survival situation can fully relate to someone who has experienced the same. Not to say others cannot be empathetic, but there is no way to comprehend what goes through the mind unless it is something you have lived through yourself."

We held each other's eyes, and I realized that this man had come into my life for a reason. Rebecca's arrival, my mother's treachery, and Daeglan's actions were all stepping-stones that led me to this exact moment—a tidal wave of events, each building on one another. There had been no way to escape the storm, but persevering through its aftermath might be manageable under the glowing light of a silver lining.

Fen was my silver lining.

"Now that you've regained your memories, I assume there is no threat of you trying to run?" Fen asked with a hint of humor.

Unable to share in his levity, I frowned in response. "Where would I go? I have no home anymore."

He pulled me against his chest, running an idle hand

over my matted curls. "If there is anything I have learned in this life, it is that home is not a place."

I nodded against his chest, and after a moment, my eyes were drawn to where the sun streaked in from the nearby window.

"Would you like to go outside for a bit? We have not finished our book, and I would like to know what happens to the children in Narnia. I could read to you outside," he suggested warmly.

"That sounds nice. First, I'd like to use the toilet. I don't ever want to see another bucket again." I gave Fen a small smile, the first since my return, and he grinned widely in response.

I cleaned up in the bathroom and put on a fresh gown Fen had brought me. When I stepped out into the bright midday sun, I could feel its warmth down to my bones. It was the first time I had felt fresh air in over a month, and the salty breeze invigorated my skin.

Fen laid down a blanket on the grass, and we spent the next few hours reading, eating, and enjoying the cool breeze coming off the cliffs. Not only was the story a perfect distraction from my own muddled thoughts, but listening to Fen's soothing voice relaxed my muscles that had been rife with tension. Everything about that afternoon was perfect, yet I couldn't shake the haunting sadness that loomed over me.

I felt as though the darkest, most vile parts of humanity had touched me and left an inky stain on my psyche. What I had experienced would forever color my perceptions of the world. How did I continue to see good in others when I knew just how evil people could be? I couldn't imagine I'd ever be free of the cynicism and doubts that developed from my captivity.

"Fen, do you think I'll ever go back to being the same person I was before all this happened?" I asked vacantly as I stared off at the distant sea.

"These things change us, and there is no going back. I doubt much will be the same, but that is not necessarily bad. In fact, sometimes, different can be very, very good." The sincerity in his voice had me looking back to meet his eyes. Even more than his words, the emotion in his gaze wrapped me in warm reassurances.

That night, Fen put me to bed on the cushioned softness of a mattress piled high with blankets in a proper bedroom. We left the small bedside lamp on, and for hours, I tried to sleep. Aside from my overactive mind attempting to process all that had happened, I could not get comfortable. The bed and blankets were like sleeping in a mound of melting marshmallows. Eventually, I sat up with the intent of finding something to read but instead found Fen lying asleep on the floor in front of the door. Without overthinking it, I went to where he lay and lowered myself to the ground.

Fen's eyes opened, and he pulled me into his arms, my back to his solid chest. His hard body behind me and the ground beneath us gave me the security I needed to fall into a dreamless sleep.

THIRTY

FENODREE

Sleeping with Cat in my arms was immensely satisfying. What I had said about home not being a place had been true, and at that moment, when she lay against me, I was reminded of what it felt like to be home. I only hoped that I could offer her that same sense of belonging once she was fully recovered.

Cat was far from healed, but she progressed faster than I would have expected. Her inner strength was inspiring, and I was sure it would not be long before she would be ready to return to Belfast and confront what had happened. I wondered what that would mean for her and for us. Before Cat had been taken, I had been willing to walk away from her, if only for her own good. But now, I was not sure even that was sufficient reason.

I was mesmerized by the woman. Even my own safety paled compared to my need to be near her. I could not imagine ever walking away. The thought itself was repulsive. While I realized it was no longer an option for me, I also knew Cat might still reject me. As I had told her, she was no longer the same person. As far as I was concerned, that metamorphosized woman was even more magnificent than the striking girl she had been before. However, there was no way to know how those changes would affect her feelings for me. Only time would tell.

I spent the next morning chopping wood for the fireplace as evenings could get cool. The activity was cathartic, and I imagined what might have happened had I not followed my instincts to seek out Cat. The image of Daeglan O'Connor had me slicing into each log with a furious force. The wretched excuse for a man had taken so much from her.

When we first met, Cat had seemed naïve with a child-like innocence. Now, I realized what a gift that was and would have given anything to see that optimistic gleam in her eye. The violation of her mind and trust had stolen any innocence she had once possessed.

I flung down my axe with the force of my frustrations, splintering a log into pieces.

"What did that log ever do to you?" Cat's soft voice asked teasingly.

I turned back to see her wrapped in a blanket, hair blowing in the morning breeze. "Sometimes, it is hard to control my own strength." It was not typically in my nature to be playful, but with Cat, I found myself capable of anything.

She smiled warmly, but the light never quite reached her eyes. "I was wondering, when do we go back to Belfast?"

"Whenever you decide you are ready."

Her face was wrought with uncertainty, teeth nibbling on her bottom lip. "Does anyone know where we are?"

"I have been texting Rebecca to keep her informed. I let her know that you were safe and needed time before we returned."

"You texted?" she asked with astonishment.

"Do not look so surprised," I scoffed with feigned insult.

She shook her head with a slight smirk. "I didn't think you'd ever use that phone."

"Nor did I, but some things are more important." I held her brilliant green eyes for a long moment before turning back around to finish my chore. Placing one of the last few logs onto the stump, I easily sliced the wood in half.

"Fen, you're bleeding," said Cat with worry.

I turned to her before glancing down at my body.

"No, on the back of your head. I could see blood shimmering in your hair."

I touched the spot gingerly, and my hand came away wet and sticky. "Ah, that is the injury I sustained from Daeglan's blast. I suppose my activity opened the wound. I do not seem to be healing like I used to." My voice had taken a solemn tone, and the corners of my mouth turned down.

"What does that mean?" she asked in a small voice.

"I cannot say for certain, but I have a guess. I have thought a good deal about why Daeglan's wards did not keep me from the cottage. It makes the most sense that they were meant to keep out Fae, and I am no longer sufficiently Fae to have triggered them."

"You're becoming human?" Her breathless words drifted on the morning breeze.

"It would appear so."

THIRTY-ONE

CAT

EACH DAY, I WAS REMINDED MORE AND MORE OF WHO I HAD been before Daeglan took me, and each night, I lay in Fen's arms and contemplated who I'd be going forward. I wasn't the same person, and I didn't think I would be ever again. But with Fen, I didn't feel like I had to be who I was. It was enough just to be.

One night, I turned in Fen's arms so our faces were a breath apart. I hadn't fully thought my actions through; I simply felt the need to thank Fen for everything he had done. His masculine scent enveloped me as my eyes met his—musk and smoke and absolute acceptance.

He searched my face questioningly, and in response, I lifted my lips to softly brush against his. He tightened his strong arms around me, and we both gave into the heat of our kiss.

He tasted even better than I remembered.

His touch was a jolt of electricity to my battered senses, sparking them back to life. My skin tingled, and my heart raced at the welcome feel of pleasure. I reached down to cup his hardening length through his pants, making Fen press against my hand with a groan.

But before we could get carried away, he pulled back, his breaths shaky and shallow. "We cannot do this, Cat. Not until I know it is because you truly want it, and not because you are lost or unsure what else to do."

Feeling chided, I said nothing in response and curled in on myself.

Fen pulled me against his chest as tears threatened to overflow my watery eyes. I thought I'd wanted to be with him, but once he'd spoken, I questioned my own motives. His denial had not upset me so much as my own uncertainty about myself. Would I ever know myself again? How could I learn to trust again if I didn't feel like I could trust myself?

The only thing I felt I *could* trust was Fen.

Despite the short time we had known each other and the dangers to himself, he had come for me. He had killed for me. Even at my very lowest, he had stayed with me and was helping me heal.

Fen wasn't just my silver lining; he was my lifeline.

Don't you see, Cat, he's feeding from you.

Daeglan's venomous words came back to me, and I hated that my mind gave the statement any merit. But once the thought had taken root, I could not escape it. I was ashamed to question Fen's motives, but I needed an answer. I was also pissed at how afraid I was of merely asking any question. Fen was not Daeglan, and I was no longer a bird in a cage.

I took a steadying breath and spoke into Fen's chest. "I want to ask you something, but I don't want to hurt you."

He gave me a gentle squeeze. "I doubt anything you could ask would hurt me."

"I know everything Daeglan said was a lie, so I shouldn't give anything he said credence, but he claimed that you were only with me to feed from me. His claim was absurd because you didn't even have your magic anymore, but when I was half delirious, I recalled you saying my release was as much for you as it was me, and I started to wonder." I glanced up in his arms, an apology in my eyes. "I'm so sorry to doubt you, but I want to trust you, and it's something I need to understand."

His eyes grew sad, and he placed a tender kiss on my forehead. "There is nothing to be sorry about. I should have talked to you about it all earlier when we shared our first kiss, but it was more upsetting than I expected. I understood that my magic was likely gone, but I had held on to more hope than I realized. Before a Fae feeds his or her magic, as arousal builds between a couple, the energy calls to them. The energy can be felt building to a crescendo, the power pooling, ready to be claimed. That first time we kissed by the canal, my blood hummed with need, and I could feel your desire, but there was no magic. I did not need you to climax to know at that moment that my magic was gone for good."

"If you weren't feeding from me, how was my orgasm as much for you as it was for me?" I asked with confusion.

"Spending a lifetime alone puts many things into perspective. Making you feel good, giving you pleasure and comfort, was just as satisfying as any release of my own could have been. I am not led by my cock as most young men are. Solitude teaches you that what two people share between them is infinitely more gratifying than five seconds of release. That day was about you, and it made me feel good to give that to you." His voice had gone husky by the end of his explanation, and I could feel his length still hard against the apex of my thighs. "And now it is time for us to sleep before all this talk of sex makes me do something I will regret," he grumbled as he gently tickled my ribs.

I giggled against his hard chest, and not long after, I drifted into sleep in his warm embrace.

THIRTY-TWO

FENODREE

Cat was still asleep when I woke early the following morning. She slept long hours, likely in need of rest for her recovery. After more than two weeks of healing, her bones did not protrude as harshly from her skin, and her smile appeared more each day.

When I first met Cat, I had thought her personality was so different from Hilde. Cat was subtle and demure at times, and I had incorrectly associated those qualities with weakness and immaturity. Hilde had made her strengths obvious to all around her—with brash confidence, she proclaimed her spirited strengths for all to see. Where Hilde had been the solid, thick trunk of a giant oak, Cat was the delicate system of roots anchoring the tree to the ground. Both contained great strength. One was just more obvious than the other.

Watching Cat battle against the effects of her suffering

was an inspiring display of strength. She did not wallow in self-pity or allow Daeglan's manipulations to control her thinking. Each day, she took another step forward, shaking off his chains and continuing on a path she paved for herself.

I did what I could to support her, but she had to do most of the heavy lifting.

That morning while she slept, I took the time alone to walk along the cliff's edge and explore a distant glen of trees. The area was breathtakingly beautiful. I had enjoyed my time at the cottage for my own selfish reasons as much as I was glad to be there for Cat. The fresh air and open skies suited me infinitely better than the bustling activity inside a city. I needed to live in a place without the constant commotion and less concrete than green grass. The mere thought of returning to Strabane or Belfast was suffocating.

Drawing me from my thoughts, I caught a high-pitched mewling sound. I closed in on its source and found a tiny gray-and-white kitten huddled alone in the tall grasses. I was not extremely familiar with cats, but it was clearly very young, which meant its mother was likely nearby.

Searching the area, I walked in circles around the kitten, eyes peeled for a mother cat. As I walked, the mewling continued, but there was no sign of its mother. I returned to the ball of fluff and lifted its tiny body in my hands, looking into its gray-blue eyes. "Perhaps you are just what Cat needs to help her heal."

The kitten cried out loudly, making me laugh at its fighting spirit.

"Yes, I think you two would make quite the pair. Cat said she always wanted a pet, and you, as it would seem, are without a home." I held him against my chest and made my way back across the grassy hillside.

When I returned to the cottage, I found Cat sitting outside with a blanket wrapped around her shoulders.

"What do you have there?" she asked curiously.

I held out the ball of fur that had fallen asleep on my way back. "I found this little fellow all alone off near that cluster of trees. I searched all over for its mother but never found her, so I thought, perhaps you might be interested in taking on an orphan. A cat for Cat?" I lowered the groggy kitten into Cat's waiting hands.

She cooed at the small animal and brought it to her face as it lifted its head and yowled. "Oh, Fen, he's adorable. Thank you." Cat lifted her face to me, flashing a brilliant grin that lit all the way to her eyes.

If I hadn't been lost for the woman already, seeing the look on her face at that moment would have sealed my fate. I might as well have handed over my heart instead of a kitten because it was no longer mine.

The incredible redhead sitting at my feet owned me, heart and soul.

Unaware of my disorienting revelation, Cat stood and wandered back toward the house. "I've been thinking about it, and I'd like to see Becca. A part of me would like to stay here forever, just you and me, but I know that's not realistic. It's been almost three weeks, and I'm feeling much better, so I think it's time." She gazed back to where I stood shell-shocked behind her.

"Um..." I cleared my suddenly tight throat. "Yes, I can

text her now, or you can call her yourself if you would like."

She rubbed the furry kitten against her freckled cheek. "You can text her. I think I'll see what I can find for little Bilbo here to eat."

"Bilbo? You're naming him after a hobbit?"

"He was a great adventurer, just like this little guy." She waltzed inside the cottage with new purpose and vigor. To see such happiness on her face, she could have called me Bilbo for all I cared.

THIRTY-THREE

CAT

LITTLE BILBO WAS OLD ENOUGH TO BE WEANED BUT JUST BARELY. I fed him small bites of meat and plenty of warm milk every few hours, including several nighttime feedings. Fen sat with me in the dark during the first two wakings, but when I saw his exhaustion upon the third, I persuaded him to stay in bed. After weeks of catching up on my sleep, missing a few hours was no problem for me.

Just before dawn, I slid beneath the blanket beside Fen, snuggling into his warm embrace with Bilbo nestled at my lower back.

"How is the little monster?" he rumbled in a sleep-filled voice.

"He is *not* a monster. He's a perfect angel, and he's doing excellently." I huffed playfully.

"Good to hear."

"I'm sure you were worried."

"I could hardly sleep all night. Oh wait, that was because the mongrel needed to eat every hour."

I whacked his arm, and we both chuckled quietly before settling back down. "Fen?"

"Hmm?" he answered sleepily.

"If your magic is gone, and you're not healing, your immortality was likely tied to the Shadow Lands. If being here takes away your immortality, won't you need to go back to Faery?" I'd been thinking on the matter all night, terrified of his answer.

"There are more important things than immortality. I have lived many lifetimes, but none of it compares to my time with you. I would gladly live a human existence if I could spend my days with you."

He believed what he said, making my chest swell with love.

I surged up to press my lips to his, wanting to be as close to this man as possible. I needed to breathe him in, have him on my tongue and in the air all around me. I grazed my teeth along his jaw and kissed my way down the column of his corded neck.

"Cat, slow down," he panted in a gravelly voice.

"No. I want this, Fen. I want you, and you have to trust that I can make that decision for myself. I love you. I loved you along the canal and on our walks. I loved you at the theater and sitting under the stars. My love has only grown since you saved me from Daeglan. It breaks my heart to think I could have forgotten that love. I don't ever want to deny it again. Please don't push me away." I peeled back my layers and offered him everything that I was.

My devotion, respect, gratitude, and desire.

They were his.

Fen pulled away and stood, but before I could argue, he swept me off the ground in his strong arms, kissing me senseless as he walked us to the bed. When he pulled back, those eyes that had been so mysterious when we first met now shone brightly with unadulterated love.

"I cannot deny you anything. Even from the day we met, I told myself to stay away, but I could not heed my own advice. I was drawn to you—the dazzling light of your spirit. It calls to me unlike anything ever has before. Every hour and every minute in your presence, I learn more facets of that beauty until your light eclipsed even the sun. It blinds me such that I can see nothing else, only you." He lowered me onto the soft mattress, easing himself on top of me.

We kissed and explored each other freely with no hesitation or doubts. Our pasts and inhibitions were discarded along with our clothing, and nothing was left to come between us.

He was my Fen, and I was his Cat, and that was all that mattered.

Fen met my eyes, and his twinkled with humor. "You know, it has been quite some time for me. I may embarrass myself the first time around."

I softly traced my hand along the line of his jaw, touched that he was being open and honest. "I have no experience to compare it to, so you have nothing to worry about."

His eyes darkened, and his gaze dropped to my jaw.

"He didn't ...? I did not want to hurt you by asking, but Daeglan didn't...?"

"No, by some small mercy, he didn't. I was mistreated in every other way, but never that."

Fen's eyes lifted back to mine, and along with love swirling in their depths, there was vengeful rage. Fen was not a man to be trifled with.

"Don't let him take this moment from us. Stay here with me," I said softly as I trailed a hand along his stubbled jaw.

"You are the only place I want to be. You are my home." He brought his mouth to mine in a kiss so reverent it brought tears to my eyes. When he pulled back, he looked at me apologetically. "If this is your first time, it will hurt. I wish I could do something to prevent that, but there will be pain no matter how ready you are."

"I've known pain. Nothing about being with you will be painful," I assured him.

He prepared me with his fingers, alternating between kisses and whispered praises. He built my desire until I could take it no longer.

"What is it, Cat? Tell me what you need," Fen said on a guttural command.

I moaned at the loss of his deft fingers. "I need you inside me, please, Fen."

He lined himself up at my entrance and gently rocked the head of his engorged shaft just inside me. "Never deny you ..." he choked out before surging to fully sheathe himself inside me.

I gasped at the twinge, and we both struggled to catch

our breath. Finally, we were joined physically, just as the circumstances of our lives had bonded us emotionally.

A pulsing vein bulged on Fen's forehead as he held motionless above me.

"Are you okay?" I asked.

"Yes, I am trying to be gentle and give you time to adjust to my size. You feel so unbelievably good, and I do not want to hurt you." His voice was raw with restraint, turning me on even more than I could have imagined.

I lifted my knees to allow him deeper. "The only thing that hurts is how much I want you. I want to taste you and feel you inside me for days so that even if you're not beside me, I have you with me."

He rocked himself slowly in and out of me in rhythm to his response. "I. Am. Yours."

Fen and I made love in that little cottage by the sea. A place that had been dedicated to oppression and hate, we christened with love and the beauty of new beginnings.

THIRTY-FOUR

CAT

THE FOLLOWING DAY WAS OVERCAST, A STORMY WIND BLOWING IN off the churning waters of the northern sea. I didn't leave the bed until nearly noon. After our morning extracurricular activities, Fen took Bilbo to the living area to allow me some uninterrupted sleep, which I greatly appreciated.

Once I was up, I fed the kitten, ate a hearty breakfast, and then sat on the floor to play with the sweet boy. We had discovered that a wadded-up paper ball was about as much fun as one kitten could have. He pounced, chased, and batted the ball until his eyes could hardly stay open.

"It looks like it is time for another nap," noted Fen from where he sat reading on the sofa.

"Yeah, not a bad life—eat, play, sleep, repeat."

Fen lifted his chin in feigned haughtiness. "That is what I have said all along—the simple life is the best life. I have lived long enough that I should know."

"You mention that long life of yours regularly. Does it bother you that you've lived so much longer than I have?" I asked, truly curious how he felt.

"The Fae do not see age the same as humans because of their long lifespans. Mine may not be quite so long anymore, but my perspective is still the same. Once a Fae reaches adulthood, their age becomes irrelevant in regard to finding a partner. What matters is shared interests, mutual attraction, and all the other intricacies of a relationship. Humans focus more on age, so if anyone had a problem with the difference in our age, it would be you." As he finished, he sounded almost sad.

"Why would I have a problem? Just because society says I should? I think we've established that I don't follow social constructs well," I teased.

"Because you are young and might prefer someone who enjoys social events and doing things other young people are more interested in than I would be." There was a raw vulnerability in his words that shredded me.

I stood and joined him on the couch, sitting so close I was practically on top of him. "First of all," I said softly, "I am not an average young woman—never have been, and certainly won't be after the last few months. Second, you get excited about sunny days and indoor plumbing. If that's not a youthful heart, I don't know what is. You may be ancient, and you may have been exiled, but those things are not *who you are*. You're my Fen, and I choose you. Every part of you."

We came together in the same instant, his lips to mine and mine to his. I wasn't sure I could ever get enough of this man. Everything about him filled me with happiness.

When we finally pulled apart, his hand slipped around to the back of my neck, and our foreheads rested against each other.

"I love you, Cat. You are my reason for living."

My heart swelled with emotion. "I love you too, Fen."

His lips started toward mine again before he pulled back with alarm, eyes darting to the window.

"What is it?" I asked, adrenaline surging into my system.

Fen rose quickly from his seat and strode to the window. I hurried over to join him and saw a familiar car some distance away, nearing the house on the rocky road.

"Could you hear her car? The wind is blowing so loud, there's no way I could have heard that."

He shook his head, eyes dropping to where Bilbo now batted at our feet, wanting to know what the commotion was about. "No, I set wards around the property."

"How did you do that if you don't have magic?" My forehead creased with confusion as I stared at Fen, but he did not meet my eyes.

"It was a spell I learned in the Shadow Lands." He lifted the kitten and walked back to sit on the sofa.

I got the distinct impression he was keeping something from me. Battling the repressive urge not to ask questions, I pressed further. "What kind of spell?"

Fen finally lifted his eyes to mine, his gaze hardened steel. "Blood magic."

"*Fen*! How could you? That's too dangerous—you could have lost yourself to the magic." My voice rose louder than I had intended, worry getting the better of me.

He stood tall, arms crossed over his broad chest. "You

needed the protection. I do not regret what I did, but you can rest assured that I will not use the magic again," he offered coolly.

I closed the distance between us and pressed a pointed finger to his chest. "You had better not, Fenodree. I did not get you to myself just to lose you to mindless bloodlust." My warning hung in the air for only a moment before we both heard Rebecca approaching the house. In a much softer tone, I added, "Please, Fen, don't do anything that might take you from me. I've lived through that once. I'm not sure I could do it again."

He took hold of my finger and brought my hand back down to my side. "I cannot make any promises, but I will always do my best to come back to you." We held each other's gaze until a knock came at the door.

I somewhat reluctantly turned away and hurried to open the door. Becca and I instantly fell into each other's arms, sobbing hysterically. Ever since my memories came back, my emotions had felt like an overstuffed suitcase ready to burst. Seeing my dear friend easily triggered the waterworks, despite the anger I'd felt at Fen only moments earlier.

"I'm so glad to see you in one piece. I was so worried!" She sniffled as she held me tightly. "Fen knew—he told me from the beginning that you were in trouble. I'm so sorry it took us so long to figure it out. I'm so sorry."

I pulled back and offered my best friend a teary smile. "There was no way for anyone to know what had happened. I would never have believed it if I hadn't lived it myself."

At that moment, little Bilbo mewled to join the conversation.

"Oh! Isn't he *adorable!* Who is this?" Rebecca asked as she scooped up the kitten and nuzzled him against her cheek.

"That's Bilbo, our new kitten," I said proudly, hoping Fen noted my use of the word "our."

Becca smiled wickedly and held the small cat out before her. "You're my *precious*," she hissed in a gargled voice, just like the character Gollum from *The Lord of the Rings*.

We both broke into a fit of giggles, only to laugh harder when we took in Fen's bewildered expression, the movie reference lost on him.

For the next couple of hours, Becca updated me on all I'd missed in the past six weeks. It was wild to think I'd missed almost two months. The world had continued to go on while I was trapped in that basement. How much time would I have spent down there had Fen not saved me?

The possibilities sent a shiver down my spine.

Once we had moved on to more trivial conversation matters, Fen snagged my attention when he stalked to the window again.

"Rebecca, did someone come with you?"

Rebecca and I tensed, our eyes locked on one another. "No, why?"

Fen took two swift steps back. There at the window stood a hooded figure, the wind battering his covered form. The man's hands lifted to draw back his brown hood, revealing a terrifying face that I'd never seen before.

He was a hulk of a man, tall and broad. He kept his hair shaved bald to the scalp and had sharp jaw bones and sunken cheeks. If his goal was to intimidate with a single look,

"Durin," hissed Rebecca, pressing little Bilbo into my arms.

I whipped my head in her direction. "Queen Guin's man? The one who kidnapped you?"

Her jaw flexed as she gritted her teeth and gave a single nod. She charged to the front door with several swift strides and flung it open but stood with her arms crossed, blocking his entrance. "What do you want?" Her voice was unbending, a swell of power building in the air around us.

His thin lips lifted in a smirk as his eyes roamed across the room. "That's some very dark magic outside this place." His eyes held Rebecca's for a moment and then jumped to Fen. "You the one responsible for those wards?"

Panic seized my lungs.

The queen's man had spotted Fen and seemed to recognize him. How could that be? After all those years, how did they even remember his existence?

This was the one thing I'd feared, and now, Fen could be sent back into exile ... or worse ... all because of me. I started to open my mouth and take the blame for the wards, but I was too late.

"Yes, I am," offered Fen calmly.

"*No!*" Rebecca and I shrieked simultaneously.

Durin barked out a laugh. "I was curious where you were hurrying off to, but this is more interesting than I had expected. You have another Fae/not Fae friend—the same way you felt when I first encountered you." His eyes came back to where Fen stood seemingly unbothered. "I'm not sure who or what you are, but you will be coming back with me to have a chat with Queen Guinevere."

I lunged in front of Fen. "*No*, you're not taking him." This man didn't know Fen, but chances were, the queen would remember. I couldn't let that happen.

Rebecca slid in next to me, equally set on protecting Fen. The hair on my arm stood tall as magic sizzled in the air, and an unnatural breeze lifted her hair up off her shoulders. "You need to leave here," she hissed at the man.

"What are you going to do, Rebecca? Kill me? You think Guin would look kindly upon you and your dear friend Ashley when I don't return?" His lips lifted in a sly sneer.

Fen grabbed my arm, along with Rebecca's, and swiftly whipped us around to face him. "Stop this instant. Nothing good can come from a fight right now." He cupped my cheeks with his large hands and drew my eyes to his. "Cat, do not fight this. I am going to go with him peaceably. I am not letting you get drawn into a fight." He spoke the words fiercely; there would be no arguing with him. He pulled back and looked at Rebecca. "You both have too much to lose from defying Guin, and I will not be the reason it comes to that."

"If you go with him, I'm going too," I insisted stubbornly.

Durin scoffed in the background. "No, *human*, you aren't."

Rebecca sighed heavily, angling her back toward Durin. "I agree. This is a clusterfuck no matter how you slice it. Durin's not going to leave without Fen," she said just loud enough for us to hear, her eyes catching mine. "Cat, you need to trust me and let me handle this. You'll come with me, and we'll get help. Fen, I will get you out of this, even if it means stealing you away again."

Fen gave her a long look. "I cannot stop you from whatever it is you are already planning, but please know that I could not live with myself if either of you were hurt trying to free me."

"That's enough," barked Durin impatiently. "It's a long walk to the nearest portal, and I don't want to keep the queen waiting."

Fen whipped around angrily. "I told you I would come with you. The least you can do is give us a moment," he roared at Durin before turning back to me. He cupped my face again, his eyes searing me with a fierce intensity. "Cat, know that whatever happens, this was not your fault, just as what happened to Hilde was not mine. Circumstances are often out of our control—all we can do is try our best to find happiness in the hand we are dealt. You have been the greatest treasure I never expected to receive from this life. Every moment, all of this, has been worth whatever price I have to pay. I love you. I will *always* love you." He kissed away the tears streaming down my cheeks and then pressed his lips to mine, but I could not return the kiss.

"You sound like you're telling me goodbye. Why are you doing that? Stop, stop right now." My words were choked and broken as I fought against sobs.

Fen wrapped me in his arms, shushing my cries. "I have to go now. What happens is out of my hands but know that I will do everything in my power to come back to you."

CHAPTER

THIRTY-FIVE

CAT

I watched from the window as Durin escorted Fen away from the house. Logically, I understood what had happened had been no one's fault, but it still felt like Fen would have been safely hidden away if it hadn't been for me.

As he grew smaller and smaller, walking toward the horizon, a gaping abyss opened up inside me. There was a possibility I would never see him again, and the thought had me gripping the window ledge to keep myself upright.

"Come on, sweetie. We need to get going. It'll take them a lot longer than us to get back, but we have a lot to do if we're going to help him." Becca gave my arm a firm squeeze. "Gather up what you want to take, and let's go."

I nodded absently, too choked up to speak.

It only took me five minutes to put on some of Rebecca's clothes she had brought and gather the few items I wanted to keep. We raced back to Belfast in Rebecca's car, both of us too lost in our own thoughts to talk. Bilbo did his best to fill the silence with his frightened yowls until he finally fell asleep on my chest.

I'd been anxious about returning home, but now the only thing that mattered was saving Fen. I was terrified for him. The fact we had Rebecca—and hopefully, the Wild Hunt—on our side was the only thing keeping me from hysterics.

We arrived at the Huntsman building late that afternoon and went straight to Ashley's apartment. She wrapped me in a welcoming hug while Becca unloaded an ultra-brief explanation of what had happened with Durin.

"What can I do to help?" she asked, blue eyes glowing.

"For now, we just need you to take care of this little guy." Becca motioned to the tiny ball of fluff cradled in my hands.

I handed her the kitten. "His name is Bilbo. We shouldn't be long, but I needed to leave him somewhere while we talk to the guys."

"Of course! He's just the stinkin' cutest thing I've ever seen. And Knight has been AWOL for the last day, so no trouble there. I wouldn't think he'd hurt the little guy, but best not to take a chance."

"Is Knight okay?" I asked.

She shrugged. "I hope so. It's not like him to disappear for long, but he does have a mind of his own. There's really no telling. Don't worry about him. You two have enough going on."

"Thanks, Ash," Becca said. "We'll be in touch as soon as we know the plan."

We exchanged another round of hugs before hurrying back to the elevator in search of Rebecca's boyfriend, Lochlan. As the leader of the Wild Hunt, he was one of the few individuals with enough clout to challenge the queen, should he see fit to do so. All I could do was plead my case and hope it was enough.

"Cat, this may get a bit awkward, so I'll go ahead and apologize now," Rebecca warned as we rode in the quiet elevator.

"Why would it be awkward?"

She glanced at me sheepishly as the bell dinged, announcing our arrival. "I never told Lochlan about Fen or what had happened to you. He's not going to be happy about any of it."

"Do you think he'll help?"

She glanced warily to where I walked beside her into the main club. "We're about to find out."

Her words did not instill a great deal of confidence, nor did the look on Lochlan's face when we entered his office. Consistent with the 1920s-themed club, the office boasted mahogany bookcases, a tufted sofa, and red velour chairs. It was lush with an old-world elegance befitting the ancient Fae who owned the place.

"Hey, babe," Becca greeted in an abnormally high-pitched voice.

Lochlan took in our approach with narrowed eyes and slowly leaned back into his large leather desk chair. He was an imposing figure, tall and solid with lean muscle. He kept his blond hair neatly trimmed and had a thin layer of facial scruff that gave him an edgy playboy appearance in his tailored suit, though I'd never seen him be anything but professional and respectful.

"What's going on?" he asked, keenly aware of our suspicious behavior.

Rebecca motioned for us to sit in the two visitor's chairs. "There's a lot to explain and not a lot of time, so I'm going to need you to listen and not get upset."

Lochlan's lips thinned, and his chest slowly rose and fell with a calming breath. Rebecca launched into an explanation of how she'd helped Fenodree escape from Faery and had been harboring him in Strabane. Lochlan never tried to interrupt, but his face grew notably redder as her story continued. She told him about my arrival on the scene and how my family had attempted to brainwash me into being a good Druid soldier.

At that point, he cut in with one simple question. "Is he dead?" Lochlan's voice was positively arctic.

"Daeglan?" I asked.

His chin dipped, eyes never straying from mine.

"Yes. Fen killed him."

Lochlan's steely gaze held mine for a moment longer before wordlessly turning back to Rebecca.

She explained how Durin had followed her out to the small seaside cottage and taken Fenodree with him. "I'm so sorry for not telling you, but I was trying to protect you. I knew your involvement could put you at odds with Guin. I wouldn't be here now telling you if it wasn't absolutely necessary. We have to help him, Lochlan. He's done so much for us—training me on my magic when he didn't have to, then saving Cat from being imprisoned and tortured. He's a good man. He doesn't deserve what he's been through."

Lochlan was silent for endless thudding heartbeats. "He's Seelie, under Guin's rule. I can't usurp her power in that regard. These are delicate matters that could involve more than just Fen's life. If I piss off Guin, we could have a war on our hands."

"Would it matter if Fen was no longer Fae?" I asked with renewed hope.

"What do you mean?" replied Lochlan, his eyes narrowed. Rebecca also turned a confused face in my direction.

I glanced down at my hands, uncomfortable with the scrutiny as I began to explain. "Fen lost his magic when he was in the Shadow Lands, and he can't ... recharge it, even now. We think his immortality was a product of staying in Faery. Now that he's on Earth, he's healing, and likely aging, as a human."

Lochlan's hand came up to rub against the hairs on his chin. "There is a chance that might help, but knowing Guin, I doubt she would give up her rule over him so easily."

Rebecca's mouth snapped shut from where she'd sat gaping. "What else can we do, then? There must be something."

"Let me talk to the others. This isn't something I can decide on my own." He rose and walked around to where Rebecca now stood beside her chair. "Go back to the apartment while I call a meeting. I'll find you when I have an answer."

We started into the hall when Lochlan's voice rang out again.

"And Rebecca, we'll discuss your role in all this later." His rumbled warning had me opening my mouth to defend my friend when I noticed the heat in Lochlan's gaze.

My jaw snapped shut.

Rebecca didn't need my support. She was going to be just fine.

CHAPTER
THIRTY-SIX

FENODREE

Returning to the palace was something I had never expected to do in my lifetime. There were times I had dreamed about it—longed with all my being to be back on Seelie Lands. Now that I was there, it held none of its previous appeal. The only benefit to my return was the small degree of relief I garnered in seeing how unchanged the court remained compared to Earth. They had not adopted modern technology, no doubt at the queen's insistence. The old customs and culture still thrived.

We rode on horseback from the city gates, and I noted that women still wore long dresses and the men traditional pants and tunics. The roads remained cobbled, and the lampposts were still outfitted with magical Pinket lights. On the surface, little had changed in the time since I had left. It was a small comfort as I rode to what would likely be my execution.

Knowing that I would be killed rather than sent back to the Shadow Lands was one of the reasons I had not fought my capture. That and the knowledge that Cat was safe. Had I fought Durin, it would have been dangerous for Cat and Rebecca. They could have been hurt, but they might also have been named enemies of the queen if Durin had run and reported what had happened. All it would have taken was a simple trace for him to escape my reach. He would have the upper hand in a fight with me, and that might lure the girls into trying to help. Rebecca could not trace either. If she involved herself and broke the tenuous truce she had with the Fae queen, I could not suffer the guilt. Fighting Durin would have been a disaster, no matter how I looked at it.

I assured myself that Cat would be better off without me in the long run, despite the initial difficulty of separation.

The brutish man escorted me through the grand halls of the palace and into the enormous throne room. The numerous courtiers standing in groups, no doubt indulging in idle gossip, took little interest as we proceeded through the crowd. This very scene had played out nearly a thousand years before, and I was amazed to find that it seemed like just yesterday.

Queen Guinevere was a radiant beauty with fair skin and high cheekbones. Her long red hair was artfully woven into braids around her jeweled crown, and she wore a rich velour gown of deep purple. She held court from an impressive throne of metallic vines and sat upon a dais strategically perched above her subjects.

As I approached, a glint of recognition registered in her

eyes. "My, it's been a long time. I have to say that I am surprised you are still alive. Not many go into the Shadow Lands and live to tell about their journey." Her voice was equally commanding as it was melodic, an unsettling combination.

I refrained from offering the standard bow of respect, knowing it would do me little good. "I wondered if you would remember."

Her eyes flashed before narrowing. "You broke a coven law by taking a human bride. I used your transgression to set an example, one that was exceedingly effective. But I see your love for humans has cost you a great deal more than just your exile. You have nearly become one of them." Her voice took on an eerie cadence, catching the crowd's attention, who gasped in horror at her final statement.

I gritted my teeth and attempted to rein in my temper. "That was not so much a product of my love for humans as it was my exile. When you cannot feed your magic for centuries, the magic dies." I did not say the words explicitly, but they had been clearly implied. This was her doing.

Aware of my veiled attack, Guin's pale green eyes narrowed. "*Silence*," she hissed. "You do not want to anger me. In addition to a *human* wife, you have now committed another flagrant violation of our laws by fleeing the Shadow Lands and illegally crossing the borders of Faery onto Earth. What say you?"

"Why bother? Nothing I say is going to change the outcome here today." I glared at the callous monarch before me as the crowded room held its collective breath in an ominous silence.

Guin's lips slowly pulled back in a devious grin. "You

are right. Take him to his cell to await his execution at dawn," she said with twisted amusement. Her words had been directed at her guards, but her eyes never left mine, reveling in her absolute power.

I had expected the outcome. If she had hoped to witness me beg, she would have to deal with disappointment. I held my head high and walked without struggle between her Valkyrie guards toward the main exit. They led me down to the palace dungeon, where they placed iron shackles around my wrists and deposited me in a dirty cell.

I let out a resigned sigh and lowered myself to the ground against the far wall. The first morning after Rebecca had brought me to Earth, I had sworn beneath the breathtaking sight of the rising sun that I would never allow myself to be taken alive if I was ever discovered.

Never say never.

The gods are fickle and find amusement in making us eat our own words. I did not regret my decision, but that did not mean I would not mourn the fact that the next sunrise I witnessed would likely be my last.

During my exile, I had resigned myself to the fact that I would never leave the Shadow Lands. No matter how short, my time on Earth had been a gift I never expected to receive. I was immensely grateful that I could go to my death knowing I had been able to experience love one more time in my life.

CHAPTER
THIRTY-SEVEN

CAT

A COUPLE OF HOURS STRETCHED INTO ETERNITY AS WE WAITED
for the Huntsmen to discuss the situation. Rebecca and I
anxiously passed the time, giving Ashley the promised
explanation. The three of us talked and paced in her apartment until Lochlan finally texted.

"What did he say?" I asked, straining my neck to see
Becca's phone.

"Oh, *hell* no! That asshole thinks he'll go to Faery and
leave us here." She jumped off the couch and grabbed her
purse, throwing her phone forcefully into its depths.

"Bec, he probably knows what he's doing," Ashley said
cautiously.

Rebecca whipped around to glare at her best friend.
"And I suppose that's what you'd do if Casek told you to
sit on the sidelines? You'd be a good little girlfriend and
just hope for the best?"

Ashley arched a brow and rose from the loveseat. "Let me put on my shoes; I'll be ready in five."

"That's what I thought," muttered Becca.

Despite my worry for Fen, I couldn't help breaking out in a trembling smile. These girls were the best, and I was incredibly lucky to have them on my side.

We set up Bilbo with food and water in a bathroom, and Ashley made arrangements for one of the Huntsmen to check on him in a couple of hours. Once that was settled, we hauled ourselves up to the club level where the men had conducted their meeting. Lochlan was still talking with several of the guys. His shoulders visibly sagged as he took in our girl posse as we charged in his direction.

Rebecca opened her mouth just to be silenced when Lochlan raised his hand with a dangerous glare.

"We don't have time to argue. Let's just skip to the end where you refuse to stay behind, and I can't stop you," he grumbled.

Becca placed her arms on her hips and cocked her head with attitude. "Finally catching on, are you?"

The air around him shimmered with energy, and his narrowed eyes let off a subtle blue glow. "I'll deal with you later. I was serious when I said we didn't have time. Let's go."

A group of us raced to a local church where Lochlan opened a portal to Faery. As the window into another world opened before me, I mused that my mother would have had a heart attack if she knew what I was doing. The reminder of my mom made my heart ache, but there was no time for sadness. Fen needed me.

We crossed into a stone mausoleum-type building guarded by two imposing female soldiers. The sight of them sent an icy dread down my spine, but they made no move to stop us. Once we were all through the portal, we hurried outside.

"Is that the sunrise?" I gasped in surprise. A brilliant sun lit the sky in soft pinks and purples, not unlike the sunrise on Earth but somehow even more extraordinary. It had been late afternoon on Earth just minutes before, and the time shift was disorienting, to say the least.

"Time in Faery moves differently than on Earth. It's roughly twice as fast here," Becca explained as we made our way through the tall grasses.

"What does that mean? How long has Fen been here?"

"That all depends on how quickly Durin brought him back," Lochlan cut in.

What if we were too late? What if we made it in time, but they still couldn't save him?

Adrenaline pushed me to drive myself faster, rushing across the open field as quickly as my body could take me. Not even when we neared the imposing city gates did I slow my pace.

Lochlan commandeered horses for us, and we rode through the cobbled city streets toward the looming palace. The townspeople were outside engaged in their morning routines, and I felt like I'd gone through a time warp as women in long skirts emptied wooden buckets and men strapped horses onto antique-looking carts.

It would have all been fascinating had I been able to concentrate on my surroundings. Instead, my mind was solely focused on getting to Fen.

As we rounded a corner, the enormous palace came into full view. Tall spires and numerous turrets made for an impressive sight, but the shimmering stone reflecting the sun's glowing rays took the breath from my lungs. Only in Faery could something so beautiful exist.

At ground level, a large crowd gathered near the palace entry.

"*Fuck*," growled Lochlan before pulling his horse to a stop.

Rebecca rode with him while Ashley and I were saddled with the other two Huntsmen who had come with us. The men corralled the horses together before Lochlan issued instructions.

"I agreed to let you come," Lochlan told Becca, "but the three of you must stay in the back unseen. Is that understood?"

She nodded and dismounted from the large black stallion, Ashley and I following suit.

The three men then urged their horses to gallop the rest of the way to the crowd. We hurried toward the mob of people, attempting to see what was happening at the front of the group. Despite Lochlan's warning, Rebecca squeezed her way through the throng of bodies until we were close enough to get a look.

In the center sat a wooden platform like a small stage, and on it lay a large block of wood. A man holding a giant axe stood to one side while Fen stood on the other.

The sight of him bound and waiting for his execution made my legs give out. I clasped Rebecca's arm, and she just barely kept me upright as a stifled wail slipped past my lips.

"Keep it together, Cat. We can't draw attention to ourselves," Rebecca whispered softly into my ear.

I understood, but the panic seizing my mind prevented me from controlling my own body. My chest rose and fell with shallow pants, and tears filled my vision.

"Guin," Lochlan's commanding voice sounded over the crowd. "I hate to disrupt your party, but I'm afraid I must."

The crowd on one side parted, allowing Lochlan to casually step forward. Every ounce of the tension he had radiated just moments before was gone. His display of unflappable confidence was remarkable, and it gave me hope that just maybe he could pull this off.

While we'd waited back in Ashley's apartment, Rebecca had explained that as Erlking, Lochlan held comparable power to the queen. Significant but not equal, creating a tenuous relationship. Through the ages, the Seelie Queen and the various Erlkings had a long history of being at odds. Only once since the Hunt had been formed had the two monarchs ever brought their disagreements to the point of war. The balance of power was delicate, and Lochlan was taking a great risk appearing on Fen's behalf.

A gorgeous redheaded woman who could only have been Queen Guin stood near the palace entry. She wore a diaphanous blue gown perfectly fitted to her slender figure and a golden crown atop her head. Even from a distance, I could see her lips draw back in a malevolent grin.

"Why, Lochlan, what a pleasure to have you at court."

He offered a slight tilt of his head, far from a customary bow. "It was time I came for a visit."

"A visit? Come now. Your timing would suggest there's more to your arrival than a visit. Say your piece, so we can get on with our morning."

"I can't help but wonder why the Seelie Queen is executing a human. I don't believe humans are subject to Fae laws."

She lifted her head haughtily and stepped forward. "There is still some Fae left in him, if only a tiny bit. He is Seelie enough to fall under my rule, but even if he wasn't, nothing says I cannot kill a human if I so choose."

"I thought you might feel that way," he said with resignation as he began to walk forward along with his men behind him. "In that case, I must inform you that this man is a member of the Wild Hunt."

My heart stuttered in my chest as I processed his words.

A member of the Hunt? Was this some kind of ruse?

The men of the Hunt believed their oaths to be sacred. I couldn't imagine he would lie about such a thing. I was at a loss as to what was happening.

The courtyard went utterly silent, and the queen lifted her chin in repugnance. "He cannot be part of the Hunt. He is practically a human."

"You said yourself, the man is Seelie," countered Lochlan.

Guin's nostrils flared, and the muscles in her jaw flexed angrily. "He cannot be of the Hunt. He has not passed the trials."

"The trials exist to test a man's loyalty and skill. These

are qualities Fenodree had already proven to the brother-hood on a number of occasions. The men have voted, and the decision was unanimous. Human or Fae, he has been made a brother for so long as he chooses."

Guin glared furiously at Lochlan. "You press the limits of my good graces," she said menacingly. The air in the courtyard pricked with energy, and not even the nearby animals dared to make a sound.

Lochlan offered another bow and addressed her in a placating tone. "I understand and had hoped to avoid upsetting your majesty. This man has been stripped of his magic and everything that makes him Fae. I did not believe he would have been of any value to you. I would respectfully ask for your benevolence in this unusual situation." He had artfully provided her an out. I was highly impressed with his diplomatic abilities.

Guin stared at the imposing Erlking for long moments, giving away nothing. Eventually, her features softened, and she glided gracefully toward Lochlan. "I suppose there may be a way around this little ... tangle. You may recall, many years ago, the Seelie Queen and Erkling were united." She spoke wistfully as her slender fingers slid down Lochlan's chest.

Standing next to me, Rebecca's hand clasped my arm. "What is she up to?" she whispered warily.

Guin continued speaking to Lochlan, seemingly unaware or indifferent to the enraptured audience around her. "The Seelie suffer from the division of our great powers. If we were united, we could easily stand against any threat. In the wake of the recent threats you faced, this issue has weighed greatly on my heart. I want nothing more than for our people to be well protected." She lifted her head to stop Lochlan from interrupting. "I understand that you are currently spoken for, but that would not preclude us from all avenues of a union."

"What are you asking?" Lochlan asked with a note of warning.

She tilted her head and gave a sickly-sweet smile. "I believe a child would do the trick nicely. A son or daughter shared between the two great Seelie powers would seal the bond between us in a way little else could."

The air filled with the buzzing whispers of the crowd, and Rebecca squeezed my arm so tightly that I whimpered. I pried open her rigid fingers to relieve the ache in my arm, both of our gazes staying locked on the show unfolding before us.

"Try to stay calm," I urged her. "There's no way he'll agree to it."

Her eyes went jet black as her magic engulfed her.

After a brief silence, Lochlan finally responded in a clipped tone. "You know I cannot agree to that, nor would I if I could."

The hard angles of Guin's face returned as she slowly spun away. "This man has broken the law, and a price must be paid for his actions. His life was the price I had demanded, and I have gone so far as to offer you an alternative, yet you snub my offer."

"That was no offer, and you know it. Now you try *my* patience." Lochlan's eyes gave off a subtle blue glow, and his two brethren took a step closer to their leader.

"Hmm ... I suppose there might be ... another option," she mused coyly. "If there is to be no child, and you wish this man to live, I will require one simple conveyance." As a master of manipulation, she paused for effect. "You must give me the Sword of Light."

I stopped breathing.

I wasn't the only one. The entire courtyard remained frozen in wait to hear his answer. My eyes dancing between Fen and Lochlan, I had no idea what would happen. The sword was a massively powerful object—it could be used to compel the truth from anyone at its blade. Would Lochlan agree to surrender it to save Fen? Doing so would yield yet more power to the crown and disrupt the scales. I had no idea what his decision would be.

Only after my lungs began to burn did Lochlan answer.

"Agreed," he barked. "Send these people home and get the man down." Without waiting for a reply, he charged inside the palace.

"Oh, my God, *he's safe.*" The words drifted from my mouth in a reverent benediction.

Rebecca, Ashley, and I released our firm grip on one another. We each smiled broadly, falling into a group hug. After a moment, we separated to disperse with the crowd but did not get far before Guin's voice rang out over the courtyard.

"Rebecca, I see you back there. Don't think I am blind to your involvement in this man's escape. Consider yourself warned." Her voice was as sharp as cut glass, softened only by the promise of retribution.

CHAPTER

THIRTY-EIGHT

CAT

FAMILY IS EVERYTHING.

That much Daeglan had right. What he failed to understand was the definition of family. Family wasn't just blood relations or the group of people we were born knowing. That was circumstance. The people who make up a family are those who love one another exactly as they are. They support and encourage each other through the best and worst of times. It had been family who had rescued me from that basement, family who had risked themselves to save Fen, and family who had been helping us find our place in this world. And I didn't bear a blood relation to one of them. What they did came from their hearts and not some twisted sense of obligation. Becca and Ash and the Huntsmen—*they* were my family.

The first night of Fenodree's freedom, we had an enormous celebration dinner at the Huntsman. As I sat at one of the club's many booths, I looked at the smiling faces around us and was overwhelmed by how they had all laid down their lives for us. That was unconditional love and loyalty. *That* was family.

"How's the little guy?" Ashley asked me from across the table. "I imagine the past couple of days have been a lot of change for him—the cottage, a car ride, my place, then your temporary apartment. I imagine he feels a little lost."

"I think Bilbo's adjusting just fine. Although, he did try to suffocate me in my sleep last night, so maybe just a touch of separation anxiety after I disappeared on him."

"That's adorable. I'm not really a pet kind of person, but after having Knight around for so long, I have to admit that a furry companion isn't the worst thing in the world."

"Any sign of him today?"

The evening before, when we first returned to Belfast, she'd mentioned that the wolf hadn't been seen in a day or so. I hoped nothing had happened to him.

"No. And it's impossible to say where he might be. For all we know, Merlin is up to something and has called him away, so I'm trying not to worry." Ashley and Casek exchanged a knowing look, and he cupped his hand around the back of her neck supportively.

I appeared to have missed a good deal while I was away.

Ashley was a proud single woman when I left, and now every sign pointed to her being very attached. As soon as I had a chance, I would have to ask her what exactly had happened between her and the stoic Fae warrior.

"Merlin won't let anything happen to Knight," Becca assured us. She and Lochlan filled out our table of six. It was a tight fit in the circular booth, but no one seemed to mind. "If anything, I'm more worried about his plans for Morgan than Knight. Merlin has been off attempting to rehabilitate her, no doubt. I can't imagine why. Anyone that messed up could never be redeemed."

Lochlan downed the contents of his whiskey glass. "I would worry less about it if we still had the sword. The trade was worth it, but I can't shake the feeling that Guin orchestrated the entire exchange. She set me up, knowing I would never grant her first demand, which tells me all she really wanted was the sword. I only hope her motivation isn't anything more specific than general greed for power."

Fen took my hand in his, clutching it tight. "I hate that I have cost you such an important relic, but please know that I will be forever grateful."

Lochlan tipped his head respectfully. "No price is too high for the safety of a brother. You're one of us now, and we're proud to have you. Besides, dealing with Guin's drama is nothing new. I doubt it will amount to anything in the end."

"It looks like dinner is ready," Becca cut in, eyeing the catered buffet table set up in front of the bar.

We'd arrived early to have a drink and catch up, but new arrivals were now making their plates and filling tables. A number of guests had been invited in addition to the dozen Huntsmen that lived in the building. The club wouldn't open for several hours, so we had the place to ourselves until then, and we filled every last minute with laughter and conversation.

Now that I no longer harbored a fear of the Fae, I was more at ease than I'd ever been at the Huntsman. I felt not just comfortable but accepted. I felt at home here among my true family.

My mother and Daeglan, on the other hand, had acted in ways contrary to everything family stood for.

They had sought to change me—hurt and manipulated me—all because I didn't believe exactly as they believed. I could almost understand where Daeglan had come from. He was a zealot preparing for what he thought would be a war. But my mother? What she'd done was unforgivable. She'd put more weight into Daeglan's conspiracies than her love for me, her own daughter.

She'd committed a horrific betrayal.

As much as I hated to even think about what she'd done, I couldn't move forward until I confronted her.

Several days later, when I told Fen my plans to talk with her, he had insisted on going with me.

"There is nothing you could say that would ever convince me to let you go alone. Plus, I have some things I would like to say to her as well," he seethed.

From the malice in his eyes, I feared he had more than words in mind for my mother.

I gazed up at him pleadingly with a hand placed on his hard chest. "Fen, I know you're upset with her. I am, too. But you can't threaten her. Don't you see? You would just prove her point that the Fae are evil monsters."

"That problem is easily remedied. If she is dead, it will not matter what she thinks. Death is what she deserves."

Menacing darkness crossed his features, and I had no doubt he wouldn't hesitate to follow through with his threat.

"She's my mother," I said softly. "I know she did a bad thing, and I'm not ready to forgive her, but I also don't want her dead. If you go, I need you to stay outside and let me have this moment with my mom, please."

His jaw flexed as our gazes battled. Eventually, his eyes fell to the side in reluctant concession. Fen did not speak a word on the ride over, and he refused to stay in the car, stationing himself on watch just outside the front door.

I debated whether I should walk in or knock first and decided that I would let myself in to avoid her seeing Fen. When I did, I found my mom standing dumbstruck in the living room, her tea mug slipping from her hand and shattering on the floor. "Jesus, Mary, and Joseph, you're back," she whispered with disbelief. Her skin went ghostly white, and she looked like she had aged ten years while I'd been away.

"I wanted to let you know that I was back in town, but I'll not be seeing you anymore, at least not for a while." Despite practicing the words dozens of times in my head, my voice shook.

"What do you mean?" Panic rose in her voice, and a small part of me felt a twinge of guilt.

"I know you thought what you were doing was for my benefit, but you were wrong. It was for *your* benefit. You wanted to feel better about my safety, and it blinded you. All you had to do was love me, regardless of who I was friends with. If you trusted me to surround myself with good people and didn't let your fears overrule your judgment, none of this would have happened. What you did hurt me deeply, and what Daeglan did to me was more atrocious than anything the Fae could have ever done."

Her shaking knees gave out, and she dropped down onto the sofa. Her lips opened and closed without sound as tears gathered in her eyes. "I … I was trying to keep you safe. And then … he wouldn't let me see you … he said it was lessons … I didn't know." She stuttered as she spoke, and each word caused more pain than the last.

"Whether you knew or not is irrelevant. The thing is, you handed me over to that man with the intent to 'fix' me when there was nothing wrong in the first place. When you have a child, you're supposed to love that child unconditionally. Somewhere along the line, you let your fears get in the way of that love. I don't need to tell you the particulars of what happened for you to know that what I endured was *not simply lessons*. I'm not saying we won't ever move past this, but for now, I'm not ready."

A ragged sob tore from my mother's chest. "I'm so very sorry, Catronia," she wept quietly.

"I know you are."

That was the best I could give her.

I collected my things from my room as she looked on tearfully. Fen helped me load up the car, his silent presence the perfect support. Walking away from my mother had been heartbreaking, but I was surprised to feel a lightness in my chest as we drove away. Setting boundaries wasn't easy, but it was worth it. Life was too short to endure toxic relationships.

After settling things with my mother, I had one other person I needed to talk to. The following day, I met Aileen for lunch. I tried to talk to her about what had happened to me in the hopes that she might open up about her own experience. The moment I mentioned Daeglan's name, she gushed about what a wonderful man he was. Any attempt I made at digging deeper was met with redirection. He still pulled her strings like a marionette, even after his death.

She hadn't had a Fen or a Rebecca in her life to save her.

I felt wretched that I hadn't realized what she'd gone through. While I hadn't been aware enough to rescue her back then, I could be a lifeline for her now. If I gave her my friendship and support, maybe she too, would find her way back to herself. Either way, I promised myself that I would keep trying.

I wanted to help undo the damage Daeglan had inflicted. That meant helping his victims, but more than that, I wanted to help irradicate the fear that was making the Druid people susceptible to his brand of manipulation.

I had put hours of thought into my situation. I firmly believed that the Druids needed to change, but I doubted I possessed the requisite power to instigate the transformation. But if not me, who? Daeglan was not alone in his radical beliefs. How could I stand by and not do what I could, as little as that may be, to confront that negativity? Addressing the council wouldn't be easy, but it was something I felt compelled to do.

I'd never been the vocal sort—pushing my views on others and sharing outspoken opinions. I preferred to keep my thoughts to myself, but I felt compelled to speak up in this instance. The Druids needed to know the dangers they were courting by allowing extremist beliefs to continue. I had to tell the council of elders exactly what had happened to me. What they did with the information would be their burden.

With Fergus's assistance, I was able to call an emergency assembly of the council. There were eleven in all; the odd number would act as a tie breaker. Only invitees were allowed to attend council meetings, which meant I had never been to one. They gathered in the centrally located town of Enniskillen, each councilperson representing one of the eleven districts across Ireland. The districts held monthly meetings, which were much more informal. Those gatherings were more of a family affair, people catching up and spreading news of the latest gossip. I had been to any number of those in my lifetime and knew our local district elder well.

Uncertain about the procedure and unfamiliar with most of the other elders, I was dreadfully nervous. The only thing keeping me from backing out was my conviction that I could not sleep at night without knowing I had done what I could to instigate change.

Yet again, I had to talk Fen out of going with me. I assured him that Fergus would be with me and that I wouldn't be in any danger speaking to the group. I also explained that his presence would be counterproductive, distracting from my purpose in meeting with them. His brooding silence the morning of the meeting was a clear indication of his displeasure, but he muffled his complaints and wished me luck, albeit somewhat sullenly.

While the council opened their session and talked with Fergus inside a large conference room at a solicitor's office, I waited anxiously in the hall. It was after business hours, so no employees were present, and the main office lights remained off. Had I not known better, I would have said the scene had been straight out of a bad horror movie. Not my ideal setting for an already high-stress event.

"Miss Murphy," the unexpected summons from a stern voice caused me to jump clear out of my skin. "We're ready to get started." The matronly woman stood with the door open, waiting for me to enter.

I flashed my teeth in an attempted smile and hurried inside the quiet room. All eyes trained on me as I walked to the only vacant chair, which was thankfully next to Fergus. I settled in my seat and took in the curious stares, some more welcoming than others.

The elderly man seated directly opposite me at the far end of the table cleared his throat. "Catronia, I am Paedar O'Shae, your chief elder. It's a pleasure to have you with us today, although we were surprised by your request to come before us. You can be sure this is rather unusual." He spoke in a conversational tone, without a hint of condescension or reproach.

I took that as a good sign that the rumors of his even-tempered nature were true. That could not be said for everyone in the room. Heated glares were aimed in my direction from a number of the other attendees. The sensation of being judged had me fidgeting in my chair.

"I know it had to be an inconvenience to gather everyone so unexpectedly, and I'm truly grateful for your time," I offered sincerely.

"I understand you have some information you'd like to share with us today?" he asked, his voice cracking with age.

"Yes." It was my turn to clear my throat as I took one more look at the men and women who led the Druid people. "A months ago, I was kidnapped by Daeglan O'Connor."

The room erupted in whispers.

I let them have their moment and waited for the chatter to die down before continuing. "With the intent of re-educating me on the dangers of the Fae, he took me to a seaside cottage near Teelin where he kept me in a basement prison for three weeks."

This time, their only responses were gasps and gaping mouths. "I was physically and emotionally tortured until he bent me to his will. The only reason I resemble my former self at all is because I was lucky enough to be rescued."

"What proof do you have of this? You don't look like someone who's been tortured," said a middle-aged woman with dark hair and the hint of a sneer on her overly-pink lips.

I pulled up my long-sleeve shirt to my elbow, revealing the scar on my otherwise smooth forearm. "This was the truth rune Daeglan carved into my skin, for starters. I would be happy to show you the chair he tied me to, leaving me for days naked and forced to sit in my own urine. Or perhaps you would like to see the methods he used to keep me in a perpetual state of exhaustion, starved and dehydrated. It took me over two weeks just to shake the spell he'd put me under. I may look fine to you, but inside, I will always bear the scars from his actions."

"How did no one know of your disappearance?" asked another elder curiously.

The next words were heavy on my tongue. "My mother let him take me. She told my boss, Fergus, that I was on an extended holiday. She has been friends with Daeglan since they were young, and he convinced her that she was doing what was best for me."

"There are always two sides to a story. We should hear what Daeglan has to say about this," grumbled one of the men.

"I'm afraid that won't be possible. Daeglan is dead," I said without a hint of remorse.

After a brief stunned silence, the room erupted in a cacophony of voices. Among the sea of voices came demands that I be punished along with mumbles of good riddance.

Paedar quickly quieted his fellow elders and regained control of the room, all eyes turning back to me.

"Daeglan O'Connor was an evil man," I continued. "I have no apologies about his death. If he'd had his way, I have no doubt that the person who would have emerged from that basement would not have been me."

"Who killed him? Why are they not here to account for their actions?" demanded the woman with pink lips.

I leaned forward, slapping my hands on the table. "They aren't here because who killed him is irrelevant. Each of us who suffered at his hands knows the truth of my statements, and yes, there have been others. I came before you today to try to ensure something like this never happens again. I know that Daeglan had a following among the Druids—people who shared in his zealous beliefs. I'm here to implore you to stop their cancerous influence before it consumes our people entirely.

"For centuries, we have cultivated hate and fear as a way of life—they were the fundamental principles of Daeglan's ideology. Previously, we believed the fear was necessary and justified, but now things are different. The Hunt now knows of our existence, which has opened the door for a time of great change. Some have embraced what we have learned and accepted that the Fae are not out to kill us, but others have not. Those who continue to hang onto their contempt for the Fae do our people a disservice. That negativity makes us vulnerable to a decay of our values until the Druids are no longer recognizable as the peace-loving people we are."

I held Paedar's eyes, and I could swear there was pride in those worldly depths.

"I can't imagine any of this has been easy for you," he said softly, "and I'm sure we are all grateful to see that our next generation of Druids cares so deeply about our people. Rest assured that everything you have brought before us today will be thoroughly investigated and your concerns taken to heart. Is there anything else you would like to say while you're here?" His eyes held mine, a flinty strength in his gaze that I had not expected from him. Paedar O'Shea was tougher than he appeared.

I sucked my lips into my mouth as my eyes danced around from one face to another. "There is. I've put a lot of thought into this lately, and I know my opinion may not be popular, but I think it's important to voice it. I believe we need to ally ourselves with the Fae."

"This is madness," spat a balding man who had been less than amused with my entire presence. His outburst was not the only one.

"Please, let me finish," I cut in over the outcries. "Try to think of this logically. What do we have to lose? The Wild Hunt already knows of our existence. There would be no added danger by allying with them. Quite the opposite, what we stand to gain is immeasurable. I've grown to know the few Fae who live here in Ireland, and they are good people. I strongly believe that if the Druids had a chance to talk to them, maybe even work beside one another, it would prove to everyone involved that your fears are unfounded." I leaned forward, looking imploringly at any receptive listener. "The one tried and true way to eradicate fear is with familiarity."

"If I might cut in," came Fergus from beside me as he reached into his deep green suit jacket and pulled out a folded paper. "This is a letter given to me by Colleen Murphy, Cat's mother."

His eyes cut over to me, and my heart thudded in my chest. I knew nothing about the letter, nor the message it contained.

Fergus placed his glasses on the end of his nose and began to read aloud.

"*To the Honorable Members of the Council. My name is Colleen Murphy, and I would like to testify as to the actions of Daeglan O'Connor, and those of my own. Catronia is my only child, and I have long feared for her safety in every respect, as any mother might. However, it is with profound shame that I acknowledge that my fears themselves put my daughter in grave danger. Daeglan swore to me that he could help Cat understand the risk of befriending the Fae. I believed his intentions were honorable, but I was terribly wrong. Once he took her, he refused to let me see her. The more time that went on, I*" *knew in my bones that I'd done something horrible, but I had no idea how to fix it. I watched as he held down my baby girl and carved a bloody rune into her skin. You cannot know the shame I feel. I've included a list below of the names of Daeglan's closest supporters in the hope that I might start to repent for my wrongs. I don't know if these people were involved in what happened to Cat, but I know they were plotting with Daeglan in the forcible removal of certain council members, namely chief Paedar O'Shea.*

As for me, I will accept whatever punishment you deem appropriate. The loss of my daughter's trust has been far more painful than anything you could force upon me. I don't know that I'll ever feel safe around the Fae or see them as anything other than monsters, but that is no excuse for allowing my fears to overcome my good judgment. Please know that everything Cat says is the God's honest truth, and I'll be sorry until the day I die. Respectfully, Colleen Murphy."

Fergus folded the letter and handed it over to Paedar before addressing the elders on his own behalf. "I've long been friends with Colleen, which is how I came to have that document. I went to speak with her about how disappointed I was in her actions. I let her know that I would be here today with Cat, and she wanted to offer her support. I agree with what young Cat here has said. This is a pivotal time for our people. We have to decide if we will adapt to the changing times or bury ourselves in the past. I, for one, know where I stand." He let his words hang pointedly for a moment before giving a respectful nod and then signaling that it was time for us to go.

The room was eerily silent as Fergus and I walked to the door.

My testimony might not result in any change whatsoever, but I had taken a stand and voiced my beliefs. Speaking out gave purpose to my suffering. What I'd endured would not be in vain.

Not long ago, I'd been proud to call myself a Druid, and I hoped someday soon I would feel that way again.

EPILOGUE

CAT

BLUE WOULDN'T WORK. I'D HAVE TO USE GREEN FROSTING. I'D been baking all morning and decorating for Fen's birthday. He had explained that the Faery calendar didn't translate to Earth's calendar, so he had no idea what his birth date would be.

I took the opportunity to give him a new birthday.

It had been one month since we'd come back to Belfast from Daeglan's cottage. With a little help from Ashley's persuasive powers, I was able to get out of the apartment lease I'd signed before I'd been taken. Neither Fen nor I would be happy living in the city. As much as I would miss being close to Rebecca and the others, Fen and I needed a quieter lifestyle. We discovered a small farmhouse for rent just outside the city and decided it was perfect.

Lochlan helped acquire legal documents for Fen, and in no time, we had rented the house and moved in together. Some might have said it was too soon for such a leap, but when you had been through what each of us had, you learned a lot about yourself. I had no question how I felt about Fen—he was my world. And as it should be, I was his.

We understood each other in ways no one else could.

With that being said, I was not one-hundred percent certain how he would respond to my surprise. I inscribed a special message on the top of the cake and anxiously waited for him to come home.

Lochlan had not been lying when he said Fen had been voted in as a member of the Hunt. As soon as we returned from Faery, Fen had happily sworn his oath and been taken into the fold. The first ever human member. He enjoyed his work with the brotherhood but also looked forward each day to our secluded retreat from the world.

As for my work, I was still employed at the museum, but only part-time. Fen brought in enough income with his job that money was not an issue, which meant I was able to take fewer hours and focus on my dream. The farmhouse had a small sunroom that was the perfect size for a workshop. We bought a desk and installed shelving for all my supplies so that I could dedicate myself to making jewelry. Fergus had even suggested that I use one of the museum gift shop display cabinets to sell my work.

Spending hours at a time on my jewelry was a dream come true. As much as I'd hoped I could make jewelry for a living, I'd had some serious doubts it would ever happen. So much had changed in such a short amount of time. I had to sit back in wonder about my new life. No one should ever have to experience what I went through at

Daeglan's hands, but I was proud to know I'd come out stronger on the other side.

The front door closing startled me out of my thoughts as I put the finishing touches on the cake.

"Mmm, that smells delicious. What's the occasion?" Fen asked as he set down his keys and came over for a kiss. He had reluctantly agreed that living outside the city meant he would have to learn to drive. His only condition was to insist on selling my tiny Fiat and purchasing a spacious SUV.

"It's your birthday! I have a cake ready for you, so have a seat, and I'll bring it over." I beamed at Fen, careful not to touch the back of his neck where I'd inked his truth rune two days earlier. The skin would still be tender.

It had taken me weeks to gather the information on how to replicate the spell used on Druid children to protect them from Fae enchantment. Once I was confident I had everything right, I performed the spell, then insisted Lochlan test its effectiveness. Fen was unaffected by Lochlan's attempt to alter his memories and had no trouble resisting attempts at mental coercion.

Knowing he had at least some level of magical protection was an enormous relief. Life as a Huntsman was unpredictable at best and downright dangerous at times, especially for a human. I needed to know Fen would be around for a long time to come.

"Today is my birthday, is it?" He walked to the table and sat down.

"Yes, I figured it was as good a day as any," I said as I lit the candles. Then I retrieved the cake and carefully walked to the table, singing a brief chorus of "Happy Birthday" to Fen. "Now you have to blow out the candles," I said softly.

I set the cake before him, and he did as he was told before reading the icing message. "Happy Birthday, Daddy." His head cocked to the side as he reread the words, then brought his narrowed eyes to mine, lips slightly parted. "Is that? It can't … Surely not." His bemused gaze danced between me and the cake.

I sucked my lips in my mouth, tears filling my eyes, and nodded. "That's exactly what it means. I'm pregnant," I whispered.

Fen stood so quickly that his chair flew backward onto the ground. He paid it no mind. All his attention focused on pulling me into his arms, holding me close against his chest. "I never imagined it was possible." His hushed voice was thick with emotion.

"I didn't either, but I never had a period after the cottage. I haven't been to a doctor yet, but the test I took was pretty certain. You're not upset, are you?"

He pulled back to peer into my eyes, his face warm and full of love. "Upset? Cat, you have made me the happiest man in the world. I never thought I would have children. I never thought I would have any of this."

I beamed up at him as I choked on a sob. "I was so nervous to tell you. I know it's all happened so quickly, but I can't imagine doing this with anyone else."

Fen's face lit with a brilliant grin, and he lifted me into his arms, whooping in delight. He spun me around several times before setting me down and dropping onto his knees. He reverently placed a shaking hand on my flat belly. "I never imagined my life could be so wonderful. Thank you."

I pulled him back up to his feet with a wobbly smile. "What are you thanking me for?"

"For you, for everything." His lips sought mine in a kiss so achingly sweet that my lungs forgot how to breathe. But with Fen, I never had to fear. As if he knew his effect on me, he gave me his breath and jumpstarted my heart back into motion.

He lifted me just long enough to set me on the table. His legs pressed between mine, our hands and tongues and teeth a tangle of need, but Fenodree's phone rang in his pocket before we could go any further.

Fen groaned loudly, his teeth nipping my bottom lip. "That's Lochlan's ring."

I grinned, still amazed at how quickly he'd assimilated to the modern world. Granted, I'd had to program the numbers and ring tones, but he now used the phone without complaint.

"Better answer it. He wouldn't call if he didn't need something."

Lips crooked down in the corners, he pulled the device from his pocket and answered. He kept me anchored in place, close enough to hear Lochlan's voice on the other end of the phone.

"Fen, I need you to come back here, and you'll probably want to bring Cat since the other women will be involved as well."

"What's going on?" Fen's body went rigid.

"Knight's returned, and he's asking for our help."

"Asking for help? How does that work? Isn't he a dog?"

Fen's brows drew tightly together.

A long pause preceded Lochlan's answer.

"Not anymore."

My jaw hinged wide open.

Knight isn't a wolf anymore? How? Could he change at will? Why does he need our help?

I could hardly think through my dizzying disbelief.

Not nearly as disoriented, Fen responded with perfect calm. "We'll be there as soon as we can." He placed the phone back in his pocket and met my dumbstruck stare. "Looks like our celebration will have to wait."

Thank you so much for reading *Blood & Breath*!
The *Of Myth & Man* series contains a total of four books, of which *Blood & Breath* is book 3.

In the final installment, *Siege & Seduction*, Morgan Le Fay teams up with a sworn enemy to help her achieve a life-long desire, uncovering truths about the villainess that will change everything. Siege & Seduction ties together the four previous books in a romantic adventure full of jaw-dropping twists and heart-stopping heroics you won't want to miss!

Make sure to join my Facebook reader group and keep in touch!
Jill's Ravenous Readers!

A NOTE FROM JILL

For those of you who persevered through the harrowing darkness of Cat's tale to see her safely through to the other side, thank you. Parts of her journey might have been hard to read, but they were essential to her development into the strong young woman she was meant to be.

Each of the characters in the Of Myth & Man world had to come into their own before they could possibly unite against the most wicked villain of all. With one one couple remaining, our team is almost complete.

Everything you've read up until now will come together in an epic finale. Secrets will be revealed. Hearts will be mended. Blood will be shed. The fourth and final book is my absolute favorite, and I know you're going to love it!

ABOUT THE AUTHOR

Jill Ramsower is a life-long Texan—born in Houston, raised in Austin, and currently residing in West Texas. She attended Baylor University and subsequently Baylor Law School to obtain her BA and JD degrees. She spent the next fourteen years practicing law and raising her three children until one fateful day, she strayed from the well-trod path she had been walking and sat down to write a book. An addict with a pen, she set to writing like a woman possessed and discovered that telling stories is her passion in life.

SOCIAL MEDIA & WEBSITE

Release Day Alerts, Sneak Peak, and Newsletter
To be the first to know about upcoming releases, please join Jill's Newsletter. (No spam or frequent pointless emails.)
Jill's Newsletter

Official Website: www.jillramsower.com
Jill's Facebook Page: www.
facebook.com/jillramsowerauthor
Reader Group: Jill's Ravenous Readers
Follow Jill on Instagram: @jillramsowerauthor
Follow Jill on Twitter: @JRamsower

GLOSSARY OF TERMS

Below are a number of the important terms and characters from *Blood & Breath* and the *Of Myth & Man* series thus far. I have included pronunciations as I would say the word, not pronunciations as the dictionary would offer because I have no idea how that works.

Arthur—Powerful Fae General who broke away from Queen Guin and formed the Wild Hunt.

Battle of Tirath—Battle where the Seelie forces were outnumbered and lost many lives during The Great War.

Beltane—The day halfway between the spring equinox and the summer solstice (early May). One of the naturally occurring days when the veil between worlds is the thinnest and the availability of magic is greatest. The Druids celebrated the day with bonfires and used ashes to ensure the protection of their crops and livestock.

Bergresar—Ancient, evil Shadow Fae.

Blood Magic—An ancient, dark magic that requires the use of sacrificial blood. Used too many times, blood magic eventually creates a bloodlust in the user so intense he or she is reduced to a state of mindlessness in the search of blood. This condition is considered a flagrant violation of the laws of nature by most Fae, and thus the use of blood magic is often punishable by death.

Brownie—Small green-skinned Fae that lives peacefully in homes, often known to clean and sometimes steal items for itself.

Cormac Doyle—Soldier who abandoned his post during a special mission in The Great War against the Unseelie.

Draug (*drog*)—Shadow Fae creature that can dissolve into shadow and is drawn to finding jewels and other treasure.

Druid (*drew-id*)—Descendants of the people who were taught the use of rune magic by the Fae.

Elders—Druid leadership council made up of 11 district members, one of which is elected as the chief elder who presides over council meetings.

Erlking (*earl-king*)—The elected leader of the Wild Hunt.

Faery—A world with latent magic that can be accessed from Earth via portals.

Fae—The inhabitants of Faery, also known as Faeries.

Fenodree (*Fen-oh-dree*)—The Fae man exiled to live in the Shadow Lands because he broke Seelie law by marrying a human woman.

Gally Trot—(aka Knight) The name given to Merlin's k-nine companion by the Fae.

Glamour—The use of magic to change one's appearance.

Guinevere—Queen of the Seelie Fae.

Hellfire—Unnatural green fire that burns through anything it encounters. One of the only know beings to wield the substance is the Nuckalavee.

Hell Hound—Unseelie creatures usually found in pairs. They are roughly the size and look of a large Earthen dog but have red glowing eyes and violent temperaments.

Hilde (*hild*)—Fenodree's human wife who was killed by Queen Guin.

Lambton Worm—Dragon-like aggressive Unseelie Fae who lives primarily in water but can survive on land as well.

Leannan-Sidhe (*Lee-an-an shee*)—Vampire-like Unseelie that uses glamour to lure Fae or human prey. They feed their magic through the draining of their victim's blood.

Mab—Extremely powerful Queen of the Unseelie killed by her twin brother Merlin.

Merlin—Eccentric Fae sorcerer.

Nukalavee—Shadow Fae that is so ancient and malevolent that it is believed even the mention of its name brings bad luck. It is known for its unique ability to create Hell Fire, and can manipulate dreams among its numerous dark powers.

Oberon— (aka Alberich) The leader of the Wild Hunt and foster father to Lochlan.

Phooka (*poo-kah*)—Small Unseelie about the size of a young child usually found near large bodies of water.

Portal—Magical doorway between worlds.

Red Cap—Vicious Unseelie known for cannibalism and wearing caps soaked in the blood of their victims.

Rune—Magical symbol used in spells.

Seelie (*See-lee*)—The Fae who live peaceably under the Seelie Queen's rule; most of the Seelie possess light magic.

Shadow Fae—The inhabitants of the Shadow Lands. Not technically Fae, but became known as such after their world became joined with Faery.

Shadow Lands—A dark and dangerous place believed to have been joined with Faery in an ancient cataclysm of worlds. The landscape steeped in perpetual darkness appears barren, and its inhabitants are a vicious face of beings who possess dark magic.

Sight—The ability to see through a Fae glamour.

Sluagh—(aka The Unforgiving Dead) A host of malevolent souls of deceased evil Fae.

Sword of Light—(aka Excalibur) A sword crafted by an ancient species able to imbue iron with magic. The sword is also known as "The Answerer" for its ability to force any at its blade to tell the truth.

The Great War—Early in Guinevere's reign, the war between Seelie and Unseelie.

Trace—The ability to transport instantly from one place to another.

Twilight Realm—A temporal plane between worlds that can only be accessed with a combination of light and shadow magic.

Unseelie (*Un-see-lee*)—The Fae who refused to be governed by the Seelie Queen and are thus forced to live in the Wilds of Faery. They tend to be vicious and solitary creatures.

Wild Hunt—The group of Fae men who separated from the Seelie kingdom when the Erlking Arthur had a falling out with the Seelie Queen Guinevere. They are self-governed warriors with no lands of their own and who choose to roam in search of prey to hunt.

Wilds—The uncivilized parts of Faery outside of the Seelie kingdom inhabited by the animalistic Unseelie.

Wollyhog (*wa-lee-hog*)—Small warthog type creature in the Shadow Lands.